P9-AOO-398

THIS DARK ENDEAVOUR

THIS DARK ENDEAVOUR

The Apprenticeship of Victor Frankenstein

HARPERCOLLINS PUBLISHERS LTD

Published by HarperCollins Publishers Ltd

First Canadian edition

HarperCollins books may be purchased for educational,
business, or sales promotional use through
our Special Markets Department.

HarperCollins Publishers Ltd
2 Bloor Street East, 20th Floor
Toronto, Ontario, Canada
M4W 1A8

www.harpercollins.ca

Library and Archives Canada Cataloguing in Publication
information is available upon request

ISBN 978-1-55468-339-0

Printed in Canada

DWF 9 8 7 6 5 4 3 2

for Philippa

Chapter 1

MONSTER

We found the monster on a rocky ledge high above the lake. For three dark days my brother and I had tracked it through the maze of caves to its lair on the mountain's summit. And now we beheld it, curled atop its treasure, its pale fur and scales ablaze with moonlight.

It knew we were here. Doubtless it had smelled us coming, its flared nostrils drinking in our sweat and fear. Its crested head lifted slightly, almost lazily. Coins and jewels clinked and shifted as its body began to uncoil.

"Kill it!" I roared. My sword was in my hand, and my brother was at my side, his own blade flashing.

The speed with which the beast struck was incomprehensible. I tried to throw myself clear, but its muscular neck crashed against me, and I felt my arm break and dangle uselessly at my side. But my sword hand was my left, and with a bellow of pain I slashed at the monster's chest, my blade deflecting off its mighty ribs.

I was aware of my brother striking at the beast's lower regions, all the while trying to avoid its lashing barbed tail. The monster came at me again, jaws agape. I battered its head, trying to stab its mouth or eyes, but it was quick as a cobra. It knocked me sprawling to the stone, perilously close to the precipice's edge. The monster reared back, ready to strike, and then shrieked in pain, for my brother had severed one of its hind legs.

But still the monster faced only me—as if I were its sole adversary.

I pushed myself up with my good hand. Before the monster could strike, I hurled myself at it. This time my sword plunged deep into its chest, so deep I could scarcely wrench it out. A ribbon of dark fluid unfurled in the moonlight, and the monster reared to its full height, terrible to behold, and then crumpled.

Its head shattered on the ground, and there, amid the bloodied fur and cracked crest, was the face of a beautiful girl.

My brother came to my side, and together we gazed at her, marvelling.

"We've broken the curse," he said to me. "We have saved the town. And we have released her."

The girl's eyes opened, and she looked from my brother to me. I knew she didn't have long to live, and a question burned inside me. I knelt.

"Why?" I asked her. "Why was it only me you attacked?"

"Because it is you," she whispered, "who is the real monster."

And with that, she died, leaving me shaken. I staggered back. My brother could not have heard her words—they were spoken so softly—and when he asked me what she'd said, I only shook my head.

"Your arm," he said with concern, steadying me.

"It will heal."

I turned my gaze to the pile of treasure.

"We have more than can ever be spent," my brother mu. mured.

I looked at him. "The treasure is mine alone."

He stared back in astonishment, this brother of mine who looked so much like me, we might have been the same person. And indeed we were, for we were identical twins.

"What do you mean?" he said.

I lifted my sword, the tip against his throat, and forced him, step by step, toward the edge of the precipice.

"Why should we not share this," he demanded, "as we've shared everything else equally?"

I laughed then, at the lie of it. "No twins are ever completely equal," I said. "Though we're of one body, we are *not* equal, brother, for you were born the sooner by two minutes. Even in our mother's womb you stole from me. The family birthright is yours. And such a treasure that is, to make this one look like a pauper's pittance. But I want it, all of it. And I shall have it."

At that moment the monster stirred, and in alarm I turned— only to see its final death contraction. But in that same instant my brother drew his sword.

"You will not cheat me!" he shouted.

Back and forth across the ledge we fought. We were both strong, with broad shoulders, and taut muscles that thrived on exertion. My brother had always been the better swordsman, and with my broken arm I was even more disadvantaged. But my cold serpent's resolve was strong, and before long I had smacked the sword from his hand and forced him to his knees. Even as he stared at me with my own face, and pleaded with me in my own voice, I plunged the sword into his heart and stole his life.

I gave a sigh of utter relief and looked up at the moon, felt the cool May air caress my face.

"Now I shall have all the riches in the world," I said. "And I am, at last, *alone*."

For a moment there was only the shushing of the breeze over the glacial lake—and then applause burst forth.

Standing on the broad balcony, I turned to face the audience, which had been watching us from their rows of chairs just inside the ballroom. There was Mother and Father, and their friends, their delighted faces bathed in candlelight.

My brother Konrad sprang to his feet, and together we ran back to the crumpled monster and helped our cousin emerge from her costume. Her luxuriant amber hair spilled free, and her olive complexion glowed in the torchlight. The applause grew louder still. The three of us joined hands and took a bow.

"Henry!" I called. "Join us!" We waved him out. Reluctantly our best friend, a tall blond wisp of a fellow, emerged from his lurking spot near the French doors. "Ladies and gentlemen," I announced to the audience. "Henry Clerval, our illustrious playwright!"

"Bravo!" cried my father, and his praise was echoed round the room.

"Elizabeth Lavenza as the monster, ladies and gentlemen," said Konrad with a flourish. Our cousin made a very pretty curtsy. "My name is Konrad. And this"—he looked at me with a mischievous grin—"is the hero of our tale, my evil twin, Victor!"

And now everyone was rising to their feet, to give us a standing ovation.

The applause was intoxicating. Impulsively I jumped up

onto the stone balustrade to take another bow, and reached out my hand for Konrad to join me.

"Victor!" I heard my mother call. "Come down from there at once!"

I ignored her. The balustrade was broad and strong, and, after all, it was hardly the first time I had stood on it—but I had always done so secretly, for the drop was considerable: fifty feet to the shore of Lake Geneva.

Konrad took my hand, but instead of yielding to my pull he exerted his own and tried to bring me down. "You're worrying Mother," he whispered.

As if Konrad hadn't played on the balustrade himself!

"Oh, come on," I said. "Just one bow!"

Our hands were still joined, and I felt his grip tighten, intent on bringing me back to the balcony. And I was suddenly angry at him for being so sensible, for not sharing my joy at the applause—for making me feel like a childish prima donna.

I jerked my hand free, but too fast and too forcefully.

I felt my balance shift. Already weighed down by my heavy cape, I had to take a step backward. Except there was nowhere to step, and suddenly I was falling and my arms were wind-milling. I tried to throw myself forward, but it was all too late, much too late.

Half turning I saw the black mountains, and the blacker lake, and directly below me the rocky shore—and my death, rushing up to meet me.

Down I fell toward the jagged shallows.

But I never reached it, for I landed hard upon the narrow roof of a bow window on the chateau's lower floor. Pain shrieked from my left foot as I collapsed and then rolled—and my body began to slide over the edge, legs first. My hands scrabbled, but there was nothing to grasp and I was powerless to stop myself. My hips went over, then chest and head—but the roof had a lip of stone, and it was there my frenzied hands finally found purchase.

I dangled. With my feet I kicked at the window, but its leaded panes were very strong. Even if I could've cracked the glass, I doubted I could swing myself inside from such a position.

More important, I knew I could not hold on for very long.

With all my might I tried to pull myself back up. My head crested the roof, and I managed to hook my chin over the lip of stone. My flexed arms trembled with fatigue, and I could do no more.

From directly above me came a great clamour, and I glimpsed a throng of people. peering over the balustrade, their faces ghastly in the torchlight. I saw Elizabeth and Henry, my mother and father—but it was Konrad on whom my gaze locked.

Around one of the balustrade's posts, he had tied his cloak so that it hung like a rope. I heard my mother's shrieks of protest and my father's angry shouts as Konrad swung himself over the balustrade. He grabbed hold of the cloak, and half climbed, half slid, down to its very end.

Even as the strength ebbed from my arms and hands, I watched, enthralled. Konrad's legs still dangled some six feet from my little roof, and his landing spot was not generous. He glanced down, and let go. He hit the roof standing, teetered off balance—to the gasps of all the onlookers—but then crouched, low and steady.

"Konrad," I wheezed. I knew I only had seconds left before

my muscles failed and my fingers unlocked. He reached out for me.

"No!" I grunted. "I'll pull you off!"

"Do you wish to die?" he shouted, making to grab my wrists.

"Sit down!" I told him. "Back against the wall. Brace your feet against the ledge!"

He did as I instructed, then reached for my hands with both of his. I did not know how this could work, for we weighed the same and gravity was against us.

And yet . . . and yet . . . with our hands grasping the other's wrists, his legs pushing against the stone ledge, he pulled with all his strength—and then something more still—and lifted me up and over the roof's edge. I collapsed on top of my brother, shaking and crying and laughing all at once.

"You fool," he gasped as we hugged each other tight. "You great fool. You almost died."

Chapter 2

THE DARK LIBRARY

"It's a terrible thing," I said, "to be crippled in the prime of one's life."

"You've *sprained* your ankle," said Konrad wryly. "Elizabeth, why on earth do you keep pushing him around in that wheelchair?"

"Oh," said Elizabeth, laughing, "I find it amusing. For now."

"Dr. Lesage said it mustn't bear any weight for a week," I protested.

Afternoon sunlight streamed through the windows of the west sitting room, one of the many large and elegantly furnished chambers in the chateau. It was a Sunday, four days since my brush with death. Father had gone into Geneva to tend to some urgent business, and my mother had accompanied him to visit an ailing aunt in town. My two younger brothers, Ernest, who was nine, and William, who had scarcely learned to walk, were with Justine, their nanny, in the courtyard, planting a small vegetable garden for their amusement.

"Honestly," said Konrad, shaking his head, "it's like a nursemaid with a pram."

I turned to Elizabeth. "I think our Konrad wants a turn in the chair. He's feeling left out."

I glanced back at my brother, hoping for a satisfying reaction. His face was virtually identical to my own, and even our parents sometimes had trouble telling us apart from a distance, for we shared the same brooding demeanour: dark and abundant hair that had a habit of falling across our eyes, high cheekbones, heavy eyebrows, a square jaw. Mother often lamented what she called the "ruthless turn" of our lips. A Frankenstein trait—it did not come from the Beaufort side of the family, she was quite certain.

"Victor," my brother said, "I'm starting to doubt that your ankle's even sprained. You're play-acting. *Again.* Come on, up you get!"

"I'm not strong enough!" I objected. "Elizabeth, you were there when the doctor examined me. Tell him!"

Elizabeth raised an eyebrow. "I seem to recall he said it might be sprained. *Slightly.*"

"You should be ready to hobble about, then!" Konrad proclaimed, trying to haul me from the chair. "You don't want to get sickly!"

"Mother will be vexed!" I said, fighting back. "This could leave me permanently lame—"

"You two," said Elizabeth with a sigh, and then began giggling, for it must have been a comic sight, the two of us wrestling while the wheelchair rolled and skidded about.

At last the chair tipped over, spilling me onto the floor.

"You madman!" I cried, getting to my feet. "Is this how you treat an invalid?"

"A little diva is what you are," said Konrad. "Look at you, standing!"

I hunched, wincing for effect, but Konrad started laughing, and I did too. It was hard to watch oneself laughing without doing the same.

"It's still *sore*," I said, testing the foot gingerly.

He passed me the crutches Dr. Lesage had brought. "Try these," he said, "and let Elizabeth have a rest."

Elizabeth had righted the wheelchair and arranged herself gracefully on the cushioned seat. "You little wretch," she said to me, her hazel eyes narrowing. "It's *very* comfortable. I can see why you didn't want to get out!"

Elizabeth was a distant cousin of ours, from Father's side of the family. When she was only five, her mother died, and her father remarried and promptly abandoned her to an Italian convent. When Father got word of this some two years later, he travelled at once to the convent and brought her home to us.

When she first arrived she was like a feral cat. She hid. Konrad and I, seven years old, were forever trying to find her. To us it was a wonderful game of hide-and-seek. But it was no amusement to her; she just wanted to be left alone. If we found her, she became angry. She hissed and snarled and hit. Sometimes she bit.

Mother and Father told us she needed time. Elizabeth, they said, had not wanted to leave the convent. The nuns had been very kind to her, and their affection had been the closest thing she'd known to a mother's love. She hadn't wanted to be torn away from them to live with strangers. Konrad and I were told to let her be, but of course we did nothing of the sort.

We continued to pursue her for the next two months. Then,

one day, when we found her latest hiding place, she actually smiled. I almost yelped in surprise.

"Close your eyes," she ordered us. "Count to a hundred and find me again."

And then it truly was a game, and from that moment the three of us were inseparable. Her laughter filled the house, and her sullenness and silence disappeared.

Her temper, however, did not.

Elizabeth was fiery. She did not lose her temper quickly, but when she did, all her old wildcat fury returned. Growing up together, she and I often came to blows over some disagreement—she even bit me once, when I suggested girls' brains were smaller than boys'. Konrad never seemed to infuriate her like I could, but she and I fought tooth and claw.

Now that we were sixteen, all that was far behind us.

"Well, then," said Konrad, grinning wickedly at Elizabeth, "you shall finally have your turn in the chair."

At top speed he propelled her out of the sitting room and down the great hallway, me hurrying to keep up on my crutches, and then tossing them aside and running after them on my miraculously healed ankle.

Great portraits of our ancestors looked smugly down at me as I ran past. A full suit of armour, brandishing a sword still stained with blood, stood sentry in a niche.

Ahead, I saw Konrad and Elizabeth disappear into the library, and followed. Konrad was in the middle of the grand book-lined room, spinning Elizabeth round and round in a tight circle until she shrieked for him to stop.

"I'm too dizzy, Konrad!"

"Very well," he said. "Let's dance instead." And he took her hands and pulled her, none too gently, from the chair.

"I can't!" she protested, staggering like a drunk as Konrad waltzed her clumsily across the room.

I watched them, and there was within me a brief flicker of a feeling I did not recognize. It *looked* like me dancing with Elizabeth, but it was not.

She caught my eye, laughing. "Victor, make him stop! I must look ridiculous!"

Having grown up with us, she was used to such rough play. I was not worried for her. If she so wanted, she could have freed herself from Konrad's clutches.

"All right, My Lady," said Konrad, "I release you." And he gave her a final spin and let go.

Laughing still, Elizabeth lurched to one side, tried to regain her balance, and then fell against the shelves, her hand dislodging an entire row of books before she collapsed to the floor.

I looked at my twin with mock severity. "Konrad, look what you've done, you scoundrel!"

"No. Look what *I've* done!" Elizabeth exclaimed.

The bookshelf behind her had swung inward on invisible hinges, revealing a narrow opening.

"Incredible!" I exclaimed. "A secret passage we haven't discovered yet!"

Chateau Frankenstein had been built by our ancestors more than three hundred years ago, outside the village of Bellerive, not four miles from Geneva. The chateau was constructed as both home and fortress, and its thick walls and high turrets rose from a promontory overlooking the lake, surrounded on three sides by water.

Though we also had a handsome house within Geneva itself, we usually stayed there only in the winter months, and at the first signs of spring, we moved back to the chateau. Over the years, Konrad, Elizabeth, and I had spent countless hours and days exploring its many levels, its sumptuous chambers and ballrooms, boathouse, stables, and ramparts. There were damp subterranean dungeons, portcullises that clanged down to block entranceways—and, of course, secret passages.

We had naively thought we'd discovered all of these. But here we were, the three of us, staring with delight at this gap in the library wall.

"Fetch a candlestick," Konrad told me.

"*You* fetch a candlestick," I retorted. "I can practically see in the dark." And I pushed the thick bookshelf so that it swung farther inward—enough for a person to squeeze through if he turned sideways. The darkness beyond was total, but I resolutely moved toward it, hands outstretched.

"Don't be daft," said Elizabeth, grabbing my arm. "There might be stairs—or nothing at all. You've fallen to your death once already this week."

Konrad was pushing past us now, a candlestick in his hand, leading the way. With a grimace I followed Elizabeth, and hadn't taken two steps before Konrad brought us up short.

"Stop! There's no railing—and a good drop."

The three of us stood, pressed together, upon a small ledge that overlooked a broad square shaft. The candlelight did not reveal the bottom.

"Perhaps it's an old chimney," Elizabeth suggested.

"If it's a chimney, why are there stairs?" I said, for jutting from the brick walls were small wooden steps.

"I wonder if Father knows about this," said Konrad. "We should tell him."

"We should go down first," I said. "See where it leads."

We all looked at the thin steps, little more than plank ends.

"They might be rotted through," my brother said sensibly.

"Give me the candle, then," I said impatiently. "I'll test them as I go."

"It's not safe, Victor, especially for Elizabeth in her skirt and heeled shoes—"

In two swift movements Elizabeth had slipped off both shoes. I saw her eyes flash eagerly in the candlelight.

"They don't look so rotted," she said.

"All right," said Konrad. "But stick close to the wall—and tread carefully!"

I badly wanted to go first, but Konrad held the candle and led the way. Elizabeth went next, lifting her skirts. I came last. My eyes were fixed on the steps, one hand brushing the wall, as much for reassurance as balance. Three . . . four . . . five steps . . . and then a ninety-degree turn along the next wall. I paused and looked back up at the narrow bar of light from the library door. I was glad we'd left it ajar.

From below rose an evil, musty smell, like rotted lake weed. After a few more steps Konrad called out:

"There's a door here!"

In the halo of candlelight I saw, set into the side of the shaft, a large wooden door. Its rough surface was gouged with scratches. Where the handle ought to have been was a hole. Painted across the top were the words

ENTER ONLY WITH A FRIEND'S WELCOME

"Not very friendly to have no handle," Elizabeth remarked.

Konrad gave the door a couple of good shoves. "Locked tight," he said.

The stairs continued down, and my brother held the candle at arm's length, trying to light the depths.

I squinted. "I think I see the bottom!"

It was indeed the bottom, and we reached it in another twenty steps. In the middle of the damp dirt floor was a well.

We walked around it and peered inside. I couldn't tell if what I saw was oily water or just more blackness.

"Why would they hide a well in here?" Elizabeth asked.

"Maybe it's a siege well," I said, pleased with myself.

Konrad lifted an eyebrow. "A siege well?"

"In case the chateau were besieged, and all other supplies of water were cut off."

"Makes good sense," said Elizabeth. "And maybe that door we passed leads to a secret escape tunnel!"

"Is that . . . a bone?" Konrad asked, holding his candle closer to the ground.

I felt myself shiver. We all bent down. The object was half buried in the earth, very small and white and slender, with a knobby end.

"Maybe a finger bone?" I said.

"Animal or human?" Elizabeth asked.

"We could dig it up," said Konrad.

"Perhaps later," said Elizabeth. "No doubt it's just a bit of another Frankenstein relative."

We all giggled, and the noise echoed about unpleasantly.

"Shall we go back up?" Konrad said.

I wondered if he was scared. I was, but would not show it.

"That door . . ." I said. "I wonder where it goes."

"It may simply be bricked up on the other side," said Konrad.

"May I?" I said, and took the candle from his hand. I led the way back up the splintered stairs and stopped outside the door. I held the flame to the small hole but still could not see what was beyond. Passing the candle down to Elizabeth, I swallowed, and stretched my hand toward the dark hole.

"What are you doing, Victor?" Konrad asked.

"There might be a catch inside," I said, and chuckled to conceal my nervousness. "No doubt something will grab my hand."

I folded my hand small, slipped it into the hole—and immediately something seized me.

The fingers were cold and very, very strong, and they gripped so tightly that I bellowed in both pain and terror.

"Victor, is this a joke?" Elizabeth demanded angrily.

I was pulling with all my might, trying to wrench my hand free. "It's got me!" I roared. "It's got my hand!"

"*What's* got your hand?" shouted Konrad from below.

In my hysteria all I could think was, *If it has a hand, it has a head, and if it has a mouth, it has teeth.*

I pounded at the door with my other fist. "Let me go, you fiend!"

The more I pulled, the tighter it held me. But even in my panic I suddenly realized that this grip did not feel like flesh. It was too hard and inflexible.

"It's not a real hand!" I cried. "It's some kind of machine!"

"Victor, you idiot, what have you done now?" Konrad said.

"It won't release me!"

"I'm going for help," said Elizabeth, carefully moving around me and up the narrow steps. But just before she reached the door, there was a dull thud, and the glow from the library disappeared.

"What happened?" Konrad called out.

"It closed itself!" Elizabeth called back. "There's a handle but it won't turn!" She began to pound on the thick door and call for help. Her voice echoed about the shaft like a bat's flurry of panic.

All this time I was still struggling to pull my hand free.

"Be calm," said Konrad at my side. "Elizabeth, can you return the candle to us, please?"

"I'll be trapped down here forever!" I wailed, thinking of the bone we'd seen in the dirt. I now understood the deep scratches in the door, no doubt gouged by desperate fingernails. "You'll have to saw my hand off!"

Exhausted, I stopped fighting the mechanical hand, and instantly it stopped tightening—but it did not release me.

"'Enter only with a friend's welcome,'" Elizabeth said, reading the message painted on the door. "It's some kind of riddle. "A friend's welcome . . ."

"Crushing someone's hand to pulp!" I said.

"No," she said. "When you welcome a friend, you say hello, you ask how they've been, you . . . *shake their hand!* Victor, maybe it wants you to shake hands!"

"I've been shaking hands with it for ten minutes!"

But had I? I'd been pulling and thrashing wildly about. I forced myself to take a deep, calming breath. As smoothly as I could, I tried to lift my hand. Amazingly, I was permitted to do so. Then I pushed gently down—and then politely pumped up and down once more. Instantly the mechanical fingers sprang apart, my hand was released, and the door creaked open a few inches.

I cradled my molested hand, flexing my fingers to make sure none were broken. "Thank you," I said to Elizabeth. "That was a very good idea."

"You troublemaker," she said angrily. "Your adventure's got us locked in—*Victor*, what are you doing now?"

"Don't you want to have a look inside?" I said, poking the door open a little more.

"You must be mad," said Konrad, "after what that door just did to you."

"It may be our only way out," I said. I was aware that I'd done a good deal of wailing and shrieking. At least I hadn't wept. But I wanted to save face—and I was genuinely curious to know what was inside.

"Come on," I said to Elizabeth, plucking the candle from her grasp.

I pushed the door wide, stood to one side, and waited. Nothing flew out. Cautiously I stepped in, and peered behind the door.

"Look at this!" I exclaimed.

An elaborate machine, all gears and pulleys, was bolted to the back of the door. Against the hole was an amazing mechanical hand with jointed wooden fingers.

"What an ingenious lock," said Konrad in amazement.

"And look here," I said, pointing up. "I bet those ropes go to the library door. Didn't it close and lock after the machine grabbed my hand? I'd wager we can unlock it from here. A brilliant trap to guard the room."

"But why," Elizabeth began slowly, "does it need to be guarded?"

As one, we all turned. The skin of my neck turned to gooseflesh, for I honestly did not know what to expect. A gruesome torture chamber? Human remains?

I held the candle high. We were in a surprisingly large chamber. Nearby was a torch jutting from a wall sconce, and I quickly lit it. The room brightened, an orange glow flickering over tables scattered with oddly shaped glassware and metal instruments—and row upon row of shelves groaning with thick tomes.

"It's just a library," I said, relieved.

"We must be the first to discover it," Elizabeth said in wonder.

I stroked my finger through the thick dust on the closest table, looked at the cobwebs sagging from the corners of the low ceiling. "Maybe so," I murmured.

"Curious instruments," said Konrad, peering at the glassware and scales and sharply angled tools arranged atop the table.

"It looks a bit like an apothecary shop," I said, noting the large sooty hearth. "Maybe one of our ancestors made primitive medicines."

"That would explain the well," Elizabeth said. "They'd need water."

"But why do it in a secret chamber?" I wondered aloud. I walked over to one of the shelves and squinted at the books' cracked spines. "The titles are all Latin and Greek and . . . languages I've never seen."

I heard Elizabeth laugh, and turned.

"Here is a spell to rid your garden of slugs," she said, paging through a black tome. "And another to make someone fall in love with you." Her eyes lingered a bit longer on this one. "And here is one to make your enemy sicken and die . . ." Her voice trailed off. "There is a very upsetting picture of a body covered in running sores."

We laughed, or tried to laugh, but we were all, I think, in awe of this strange place and the books it held.

"And here," said Konrad, paging through another volume, "are instructions on how to speak to the dead."

I looked at my brother. I often had the uncanny feeling that I was waiting for his show of emotions so I could better know my own. Right now I saw fear—but not my own powerful fascination with this place.

He swallowed. "We should leave."

"Yes," said Elizabeth, replacing her book.

"I want to stay a little longer," I said. I was not pretending. Books usually held little interest for me, but these had a dark lustre, and I wanted to run my fingers over their ancient pages, gaze upon their strange contents.

I caught sight of a book titled *Occulta Philosophia* and thirstily drew it from the shelf.

"Occult Philosophy," said Konrad, looking over my shoulder.

I turned the first few vellum pages to find the author's name.

"Heinrich Cornelius Agrippa," I read aloud. "Any idea who this old fellow was?"

"A medieval German magician," said a voice, and Elizabeth gave a shriek, for the answer had come from behind us.

We all whirled to behold, standing in the doorway . . . Father.

"You've discovered the Biblioteka Obscura, I see," he said, torchlight and shadow dancing disconcertingly over his craggy face.

He was a powerfully built man, leonine with his thick silver hair and steady hunter's gaze. I would not have wanted to stand before him in his courtroom.

"It was an accident," Elizabeth said. "I fell against the books, you see, and the door opened before us."

Father's mood was rarely as severe as his fierce demeanour, and he grinned now. "And naturally you had to descend the stairs."

"Naturally," I said.

"And would I be right in assuming, Victor, that you were the one to shake hands with the door?"

I heard Konrad chuckle.

"Yes," I admitted, "and it very nearly crushed my hand!"

"No," said my father, "it was not designed to crush the hand, just to hold on to it. Forever."

I looked at him, shocked. "Truly?"

"When I discovered this secret passage as a young man, no one had descended the stairs for more than two hundred years. And the last person to do so was still here. What remained of him, anyway. The bones of his forearm dangled from the door. The rest of his ruined body had fallen into the shaft."

"We wondered if we'd seen . . . a finger bone down there," Elizabeth said.

"No doubt I missed a bit," said Father.

"Who was it?" Konrad asked.

Father shook his head. "Judging by his clothing, a servant—unlucky enough to have discovered the secret passage."

"But who built all this?" I asked.

"Ah," said Father. "That would be your ancestor Wilhelm Frankenstein. By all accounts he was a brilliant man, and a very wealthy one. Some three hundred years ago, when he constructed the chateau, he created the Biblioteka Obscura."

"Biblioteka Obscura," Elizabeth said, and then translated the Latin. "Dark Library. Why was it kept in darkness?"

"He was an alchemist. And during his lifetime its practice was often outlawed. He was obsessed with the transmutation of matter, especially turning base metals into gold."

I had heard of such a thing. Imagine the riches, the power!

"Did he succeed?" I demanded.

Father chuckled. "No, Victor. It cannot be done."

I persisted. "But maybe that explains why he was so wealthy."

There was something almost rueful in Father's smile. "It makes a fine story, but it is nonsense." He waved his hand at the shelves. "You must understand that these books were written centuries ago. They are primitive attempts to explain the world. There are *some* shards of learning in them, but compared to our modern knowledge they are like childish dreams."

"Didn't the alchemists also make medicines?" Elizabeth asked.

"Yes, or at least tried to," Father said. "Some believed they could master all elements, and create elixirs that would make people live forever. And some, including our fine ancestor, turned their attentions to matters even more fantastical."

"Like what?" Konrad asked.

"Conversing with spirits. Raising ghosts."

A chill swept through my body. "Wilhelm Frankenstein practised witchcraft?"

"They burned witches back then," Elizabeth murmured.

"There is no such thing as witchcraft," Father said firmly. "But the Church of Rome condemned virtually each and every one of these books. I think you can see why the library was kept in darkness."

"He was never caught, was he?" I asked.

Father shook his head. "But one day, in his forty-third year, without telling anyone where he was going, he mounted a horse and rode away from the chateau. He left behind his wife and children, and was never seen again."

"That is . . . quite chilling," said Elizabeth, looking from Konrad to me.

"Our family history is colourful, is it not?" said Father humorously.

My gaze returned once more to the bookshelves, glowing in the torchlight. "May we look at them some more?"

"No."

I was startled, for his voice had lost its affectionate joviality and become hard.

"But, Father," I objected, "you yourself have said that the pursuit of knowledge is a grand thing."

"This is not knowledge," he said. "It is a *corruption* of knowledge. And these books are not to be read."

"Then, why do you keep them?" I asked defiantly. "Why not just burn them?"

For a moment his brow furrowed angrily, then softened. "I keep them, dear, arrogant Victor, because they are artifacts of an ignorant, wicked past—and it is a good thing not to forget our past mistakes. To keep us humble. To keep us vigilant. You see, my boy?"

"Yes, Father," I said, but was not sure I did. It seemed impossible to me that all this ink could contain nothing but lies.

"Now, come away from this dark place," he told the three of us. "It's best if you do not speak of it to anyone—especially your little brothers. The stairs are perilous enough, and you already know the hazards of the door." He looked at us gravely. "And make me a promise that I will not find you here again."

"I promise," the three of us said, almost in unison. Though I was not so sure I could resist the strange allure of these books.

"Excellent. And, Victor," he added with a wry grin, "wonderful to see you on your feet again. Now, if I'm not mistaken, it is nearly time for us to prepare dinner for the servants."

"Surely that's enough now," I muttered, tossing another peeled potato into the heaping bowl.

"A few more, I think," Konrad said, still diligently peeling. He glanced over at Ernest, who was sitting beside us at the long table, his brow furrowed with concentration as he worked away at a potato. He in no way resembled Konrad and me. He took after our mother, with fair hair and large, blue eyes.

"Remember, push the knife away from yourself," Konrad said gently. "You don't want to cut your hand. Good. That's it."

Ernest beamed at Konrad's praise; the boy practically hero-worshipped him.

I added yet another potato to the bowl and looked about the crowded kitchen. Mother and Elizabeth were preparing the ham, and chatting happily with some of the maids. Mother was much adored by all the servants. She was younger than Father by nearly twenty years, and very beautiful, with thick blond hair, a high forehead, and frank, gentle eyes. I couldn't remember her ever speaking sharply to any of our staff.

At the far end of the table, Father chopped parsnips and carrots for the roasting pan, and talked to Schultz, his butler of twenty-five years, who was currently sipping our finest sherry while my father worked.

Our home was a most peculiar one.

The city of Geneva was a republic. We had no king or queen or prince to rule over us. We were governed by the General Council, which our male citizens elected. We had servants, as all wealthy families did, but they were the best paid in Geneva, and were given ample free time. Otherwise, as Father said, they would have been little better than slaves. Just because they did not have our advantages of wealth and education, Father said, that did not make them lesser.

Both Mother and Father were considered exceedingly liberal by many people.

Liberal meant open-minded.

Liberal meant making dinner every Sunday night for our own servants.

"It's terrible, sir, this situation in France," Schultz was saying to my father.

"The terror these mobs are spreading is despicable," Father agreed.

"Do you still think the Revolution so good a thing now, sir?" Schultz asked in his frank way, and I could see all the other servants in the kitchen pause and look over, curious and nervous both, waiting for their master's reply.

In France, the King and Queen had been beheaded, and landowners were now dragged from their beds in the middle of the night, arrested, and executed—all in the name of the Revolution. I too watched Father, wondering how far his liberality would extend.

"I am still hopeful," he said calmly, "that the French will

establish a peaceful republic like ours, which recognizes that all men were created equal."

"And all women, too," said Mother, then added tartly: "Equal to *men,* that is."

"Ah!" Father said with a good-natured grin. "And that, too, may come in time, my dear."

"It would come sooner," Mother said, "if the education of girls were not designed to turn them into meek, weak-minded creatures who waste their true potential."

"Not in this house," said Elizabeth.

Father smiled at her. "Thank you, my dear."

Mother came and affectionately kissed the top of his greying head. "No, this house is indeed the exception to the rule."

Father was one of the four magistrates of our republic. His expertise was the law—but there was no subject under the sun that didn't win his interest. Indeed, so great was his respect for learning that he had resigned many of his public duties and business dealings so that he could devote himself to our education. The chateau was his schoolhouse, his own children his pupils—and that included Elizabeth.

Every day Elizabeth took her place between Konrad and me in the library to receive our lessons in Greek, Latin, literature, science, and politics from Father and Mother and whatever tutors they thought fit to teach us.

And there was one other student in our eccentric classroom: Henry Clerval.

Henry was exceedingly clever, and my father had won the permission of Henry's father to allow our friend to be tutored in our home. He was an only child, and his mother had died some years ago. As his merchant father was often away on business for weeks, or even months, at a time, Henry spent many of his days—and nights, too—at our home, and we considered him practically one of the family.

I only wished he were here right now to help me peel potatoes.

No other family I knew did this. I admired my parent's high-minded ideals—but was this bizarre Sunday ritual really necessary? Sometimes I wondered if our servants felt entirely comfortable with it. Some of them, the older ones especially, seemed a bit ill at ease, even faintly grumpy, at seeing us take over their kitchen. And often they'd start lending a hand when they saw us bumbling about or doing something wrong.

For my part, I did not look forward to Sunday nights. I would much rather have had my meal made for me, and served upstairs. But Konrad had never confessed such unworthy feelings, so I would not reveal mine.

A pudgy, starfish-shaped hand suddenly reached up onto the kitchen table and dragged off a handful of peelings. I looked down to see little William cramming them gleefully into his mouth.

"William, stop!" Konrad said, snatching away the remaining scraps. "You can't eat those!"

Instantly, William began to wail. "*Tay-toe! Toe!*"

I put down my knife and knelt to comfort our littlest brother. "Willy, you've got to wait till they're cooked. They're yummier that way. Much, much yummier."

William gave a brave sniff. "Yummier."

"That's right," I said, giving him a hug. His plump arms squeezed tight around my neck. I was tremendously fond of Willy. He'd just learned how to take his first steps and was a complete terror. He was loud, often annoying, and loved being the centre of attention like me, so I had a soft spot for him. And amazingly he seemed to prefer me to Konrad. I wondered how long that would last.

"He's teething," Mother said from across the room. "He probably just wants something to chew."

I saw a clean wooden spoon on the table and passed it to William. With touching gratitude he grabbed it and promptly shoved it deep into his mouth. A look of utter bliss crossed his face.

"Works a treat," I said.

"How's your foot, young sir?" one of our new stable hands asked me.

"I am recovered, thank you," I replied.

"That play of yours was something," he said.

"You enjoyed my villainy, did you?" I asked, pleased—and hoping for more praise. Many of the servants had watched the play from the back rows.

He nodded. "Oh yes."

"That swordplay at the end took a long time to master. No doubt you saw that spectacular roundhouse swing I did at the end."

"Please don't encourage him," said Elizabeth, with a roll of her eyes, "or he'll want to re-enact the entire scene for us again."

"I liked the pretend parts," the stable hand said, "but the way young master Konrad rescued you at the end, that was real heroics."

"Ah, yes," I said, looking back at my potato, "it certainly was."

"How did you do it, sir?" the stable hand asked my brother

in utter admiration. "I couldn't have done it for gold, not with my fear of heights."

"Oh, it wasn't so high, Marc," Konrad told him with a chuckle. He knew the fellow's name—of course. Konrad always knew all the servants by name. "And how are you finding Bellerive?"

"The countryside's very fine," said Marc.

"When you have a chance, you should take one of the horses up into the foothills, and admire the view of Geneva and the Jura Mountains."

"I will, sir, thank you."

One of the reasons I disliked these dinners was that Konrad was so much better at them than I. When we all finally sat down at table, masters and servants united into one very large and unusual family, my twin brother effortlessly struck up conversations with everyone. He asked Maria, our housekeeper, how her nephew's broken arm was healing. He asked Philippe, the groom, how Prancer, our pregnant mare, was faring. And before long, the servants were telling their own stories, which I truly did love to hear, for their lives were so unlike my own. Kurt, our footman, had once been a soldier and fought a bloody battle and lost several toes; Celeste, my mother's maid, had served an evil duchess in France who would beat her with her slipper if the cake tasted stale.

Afterward, as we helped the servants clean the dishes and pots and pans, I marvelled at the work they did for us each and every day.

And I was very glad we did this but once a week.

* * *

Floating on the lake, gazing up at the clear night sky: perfection.

It was Tuesday after dinner. Henry, Elizabeth, Konrad, and I were drifting on the lake in a rowboat, lying back on cushions. It was one of our favourite pastimes. We'd grown up so near the water that it was like a second home to us. Konrad and I had learned to sail not long after we'd learned to walk. So assured were our skills that our parents never worried when we spent time on Lake Geneva.

Tonight, we had reason to celebrate, for Henry was to stay with us an entire month. His father had just embarked on a lengthy business trip, and our parents had happily invited Henry to stay with us for the duration.

"I wonder why Wilhelm Frankenstein suddenly left like that," he said, after we'd finished our tale of the Dark Library. "It has the makings of a wonderful play."

When Henry was excited he reminded me even more of some strange pale bird. His blond head flicked quickly from person to person, his eyes very bright, his fingers sometimes fluttering for emphasis like he might take flight at any moment.

"Maybe he was bewitched," Elizabeth said. "Driven mad by all he'd learned!"

"Intriguing," said Henry with an approving nod.

"More likely he met with some misfortune on the road," Konrad said.

"Brigands who murdered him and bundled his body off the mountain," suggested Henry eagerly. "I like brigands. They can make for an excellent plot."

"Or perhaps," I said, "he truly discovered the secret of eternal life and went off to begin afresh."

"Oh, that is good," said Henry. "I like that very much as well." He patted his pocket for a pen and bit of paper and sighed when he found neither.

For a moment we were all silent, enjoying the gentle rocking of the boat and the scented air.

"Look, another shooting star!" Konrad pointed out.

"God's creation is very vast," Elizabeth murmured, staring at the night sky.

"Father doesn't believe in God," I said. "He says it is an out-moded—"

"I know very well what he says," Elizabeth interrupted. "An outmoded system of belief that has controlled and abused people, and that will wizen away under the glare of science. How original you are, Victor, to mimic your father."

"You're wiser than him, of course," I said.

"You two, please," sighed Konrad.

Elizabeth glared at me. "I'm not saying I'm wiser. I am saying he is wrong."

"Oh-ho!" I said, looking forward to a quarrel.

"Can't we talk about Wilhelm Frankenstein some more?" Henry said. "I really do think his story has the makings of—"

But Elizabeth wasn't about to be thrown off the scent. "Victor, I doubt you're truly an atheist, and if you are, it's only because your father taught you to be."

"And you are a Catholic because your mother taught *you* to be. And some nuns too!"

"Nonsense," she said. "I have considered it carefully, and find no other possible explanation for"—she waved her hand at the night sky, and the lake, and us—"all of this!"

"There is no proof of God," I said, quoting Father.

"There is *knowing,* and there is *believing,*" said Elizabeth. "They are two different things. Knowing requires *facts.* Believing requires *faith.* If there were *proof* of God's existence, it wouldn't be a *faith,* would it."

This puzzled me for a moment. "I simply don't see the point," I said. "Faith seems worthless to me, then. One might have faith in any fancy. Singing flowers or—"

"Worthless?" cried Elizabeth. "My faith has given me sustenance for many years!"

"Victor, enough," said Konrad. "You'll hurt her feelings."

"Oh, Elizabeth can take care of herself," I said. "She's no delicate blossom."

"Certainly not," she retorted. "But in future I will only argue with my intellectual equals."

"I'm considering pushing you into the lake," I said, beginning to stand.

"I'd like to see you try," said Elizabeth, with a flare of the wildcat in her face.

"Please, *please,* don't dare him," said Henry, gripping the sides of the rocking boat in alarm. "Victor always does dares. Remember what happened last time?"

"We nearly capsized," Konrad recalled, as a bit of water splashed over the side.

"Getting wet upsets me," said Henry. "Victor, do sit down."

I narrowed my eyes at Elizabeth; she narrowed hers back.

"I've read," said Henry quickly, "that if you stare long enough at the heavens, your future will become clear. Have you tried it, Victor?"

It was such an obvious ploy that I couldn't help laughing. I slouched back comfortably against the cushions.

"And what is it you see for yourself, Henry?" I asked my diplomatic friend.

"Well," he said, "the view is clear for me. I will become a merchant and in time take over my father's business."

Elizabeth pushed herself up on her elbows, indignant. "That's dismally practical of you, Henry."

"Nothing wrong with being practical," Konrad remarked.

"But, Henry, what of your interest in literature?" Elizabeth demanded.

"You can't eat it, that's the problem," he said. "I've tried, it's very dry, not at all nutritious. And a man does have to earn a living."

"But look at the applause your play won!" she reminded him.

"I felt like an imposter taking credit," said Henry. "The idea was *yours*."

This was true. But Elizabeth had thought the audience might be horrified to know that a young lady had invented such a violent and bloodthirsty tale.

"Well," said Elizabeth, pleased, "a story comes easily enough to me, but the writing was all yours, Henry. You have the soul of a poet."

"Ah, well," said Henry. "A merchant does not need to rhyme. What do *your* stars tell you?"

"I will write a novel," Elizabeth said with decision.

"What will it be about?" I asked, surprised.

"I don't know the subject yet," she said with a laugh. "Only that it will be something wonderful. Like a bolt of lightning!"

"You'll need a pen name," Konrad said, for the idea of a woman writing a novel was scandalous.

"Perhaps I will shock the world with my own," she said. "'Elizabeth Lavenza' has such a literary flair, don't you think? It would be a shame to waste it."

"And what of marriage?" Konrad asked.

"It would take a remarkable man to make me marry," she said. "Men are mercury. Always changing. Look at my father. He remarried and just sent me away. I was packed up like a bit of furniture. And he visited me only once in two years."

"Scoundrel," I said.

"Not all men are so bad, surely," said my brother.

She laughed. "No doubt. I will have a fabulous husband and many beautiful, talented children. Now, I have embarrassed myself enough. Victor, what do you see in your future?"

I thought a moment, and then said, "When I see the stars, I think of the planets that must orbit them, and I would like to travel among them. And if we could do so, would not we be gods?"

"A modest goal, then," said my twin. "Victor just wants to be a god."

Laughing, I elbowed him in the ribs. "I'm imbued with high hopes and lofty ambitions. And if I can't travel between planets—"

"Always good to have a backup plan," Henry interjected.

"—then I will *create* something, some great work that will be useful and marvellous to all humanity."

"You mean a machine of some kind?" asked Konrad.

"Yes, perhaps," I said, thinking more seriously now. "An engine that will transform the world—or a new source of energy. It seems scientific discoveries are being made every day now. In any event, I will be remembered forever."

"Statues and monuments will bear your name, no doubt!" Konrad said with a grin.

"Very well, let us hear your *little* dreams!" I said.

Konrad stared at the sky. "I will follow Father's example," he said thoughtfully. "I would like to help govern Geneva, to make it even greater than it is now. But I'd like to see the world too. Perhaps cross the ocean and see the new America, or the British colonies to the north. They say there are still vast landscapes there, untouched by Europeans."

"Then you would abandon us all," Elizabeth asked, "and marry some exotic native princess?"

Konrad chuckled. "No. I will make my journeys with a soul-mate."

"You'd just want me to carry all your supplies," I joked. "You'd best find another travel companion."

But I loved the idea of having a grand adventure with Konrad.

It had always been a favourite game of ours, since we were very young, to lie side by side on the library floor with the great atlas before us, picking the countries we would visit together.

I still yearned for such a trip, just the two of us. West to the New World: to some remote, wild place—where no one would compare us.

Chapter 3

THE ALPHABET OF THE MAGI

"*En garde!*" I panted, lifting my foil. Konrad and I were near the end of our match, and we were tied. Whoever scored next would be the winner. In the chateau's armoury, Signor Rainaldi, our fencing master, watched over us, as well as Henry and Elizabeth, both suited up on the sidelines, awaiting their own match.

I took the offensive and made an unimaginative lunge, which Konrad parried easily. I was weary and my movements were getting sluggish.

"You can do better than that, little brother," said Konrad.

I could not see his face behind his mask, but doubted it was as slick with sweat as mine.

Almost from the first moment Konrad held a rapier, he'd seemed born to it. But not me. So I had practised and practised, asking Signor Rainaldi for extra drills so I could keep up. It paid off, for Konrad and I were now closely matched, though he still beat me more often than not. Fencing with my twin posed another unique challenge, for we knew each other's instincts so well, it was near impossible to surprise each other.

I parried his attack, and planned my next move.

"Pacing, pacing!" cried our master. "I have seen old men with more verve!"

"I do not want to tire my brother," Konrad replied.

I feinted once, and then feebly struck Konrad's foil at the midpoint.

"Rather a waste, don't you think?" Konrad goaded me.

"Indeed," I said. But it was what I wanted. *Let him mock me.* I had my plan now.

Konrad returned to the *en garde* position, and we circled warily. I watched him, waiting for his attack, waiting for the flex of his knee as he lunged. When it came, I was ready.

I performed a *passata sotto,* a difficult manoeuvre I had been practising secretly for weeks now. I dropped my right hand to the floor and lowered my body beneath Konrad's thrusting blade. At the same time, I lunged with my own foil. His blade hit empty air. Mine struck his belly.

"A hit, a very palpable hit!" cried our master. "The match is Victor's. A *passata sotto.* Well done, young sir."

My eyes went to Elizabeth, who was clapping with Henry. I pulled up my mask, grinning. It wasn't often I bested Konrad, and the victory was sweet indeed.

"A very fancy move," said Konrad. "Congratulations."

He removed his mask, and I was taken aback by his pallor.

"Are you well, young sir?" our fencing master asked, frowning.

Elizabeth walked toward us. "You two have fought too hard," she said. "Konrad, sit down a moment."

He waved her away, shivering. "I am fine. I am fine."

Elizabeth put her hand to his head. "You're scalding."

"Merely from our exertions," I said, and gave a lighthearted laugh. "It was quite a match. Shall we fetch the wheelchair for you?"

"He is feverish, Victor," she said to me sharply.

As I looked more carefully at my brother, I knew he was truly ill. His skin had a parched look to it, and beneath his eyes were smudges of darkness.

"I am not feverish," said Konrad—and then he fainted.

Elizabeth and I caught him clumsily before he hit the floor. He was not long unconscious, and by the time he awoke, Henry had fetched Mother and Father and they were at his side.

"To bed with you, Konrad," Father said. "We will have Maria bring you some broth."

I helped my father raise him to his feet and walk him unsteadily from the armoury, with Elizabeth and Mother keeping pace with us. I kept hoping Konrad would meet my eye, give a playful wink to set my mind at ease, but he seemed groggy and withdrawn.

"Was it too many nights on the balcony, practising our play?" Elizabeth said anxiously, as though she herself were to blame.

"More likely too long on the lake without a cloak," said Mother.

"He will be up for dinner," I said, trying to sound confident. "Just a chill, no doubt."

Dr. Lesage arrived later in the afternoon to examine Konrad. To everyone's huge relief, he said it wasn't plague. He advised

I looked over at Henry, and then Elizabeth, and caught her quick, nervous glance at Mother. Suddenly my stomach clenched and turned over, and I had to rush from the table to the nearest water closet, where I retched, again and again, tears welling from my eyes. I could not remember feeling sicker.

What had happened to Konrad had happened to me.

An eternal night spent tossing and turning, shivering and sweating. When awake, I lay in the grips of terror; and when I slept, it was only in cruel snatches, and my dreams were foul. In one, Konrad and I were play-acting, joyfully at first, but then with more and more fury, and when I slew him with the sword, it was a real sword, and real blood poured from his chest, and I laughed and laughed—and started awake, drenched and panting.

Throughout the night, I was dimly aware of Mother and Father and the servants checking on me.

Finally I must have slept properly, for when I next opened my eyes, it was dawn, and Dr. Lesage stood over me, taking my pulse.

"Let us have a good look at you, young Master Frankenstein," said the doctor, gently helping me sit up.

Limply I submitted to his grave proddings. He seemed to take a great deal of time, which made me all the more agitated.

"It is the same ailment as Konrad's," I rasped.

"I will speak with your mother," the doctor said, and with that he left.

The next five minutes might have been hours. I was filled

with dread. I stared out the window and saw the sunshine and the mountains, and it was as though it had nothing to do with me. It was a different world, one from which I was cut off forever. I was certain of the news I was about to hear.

It was not Mother who came in finally, or Father, but Elizabeth. Anger radiated from her face.

"There is *nothing* wrong with you!" she said.

"What?" I exclaimed.

She sat down on the edge of my bed and burst into tears. "You are fine," she said. "Dr. Lesage said you are absolutely *fine.*"

The power of the mind must be a miraculous thing, for at that very moment I felt my fever and sickness lessen. I sat up and patted her shoulder, but she batted my hand away.

"I wasn't *play*-acting," I objected. "I truly felt . . . I felt terrible, as though all my strength had left me."

"You had us all so worried," she said. "And it was merely in your head."

"I didn't know!" I retorted, but I felt foolish and ashamed. And strangely jealous, too, for I suddenly realized she was not crying for me, but for Konrad.

"The doctor said it's not unexpected," she said, wiping at her eyes.

"What's not?"

"He has seen such a thing before, with twins. He knew of one who, when his brother had his arm crushed in a machine accident, screamed, and could not use his arm for weeks for the pain."

"I must see Konrad," I said. "How is he?"

I stood up and suddenly remembered I was in my nightshirt. Though Elizabeth and I had grown up together, I now felt self-conscious to be around her in so little state of dress. I noticed a flush to her cheek as she turned her face away.

"The fever is not so high."

"That is good news."

"Better if the fever were gone altogether."

"Has Dr. Lesage any better idea what it is?" I asked. She shook her head. "All he knows is that it isn't any typical infection. It is not contagious. It is some ailment within him that he must fight alone."

"Let's go see him right now," I said.

"Ah, Victor," said Konrad, "I hear you had another near scrape with death."

"A false illness," I admitted sheepishly.

He put his hot hand on mine. "Do try to keep out of trouble, little brother," he told me.

"Of course," I said. "It would be better, though, if you stopped lazing about, so you can keep an eye on me."

"Oh, I'll be up shortly. I feel a bit stronger today."

Elizabeth beamed at me. The windows of his room were thrown wide, and the scent of cut grass from the fields wafted in, along with the sound of the lapping lake, and it felt like the spring itself was enough to heal any ills.

"You've had Mother in a terrible state," I said.

Konrad rolled his eyes. "Everyone's making a fuss for nothing. Remember Charlie Fancher? He was laid up with ague for two weeks before it left him. I'll be up and about soon."

"Good," I said, "because Henry and Elizabeth have been plotting another play, and this time you are to be the hero."

"Excellent," he said.

But later when he tried to get up, he did not have the strength to stand for more than a minute without shaking. His face had a gaunt look.

He was as weak as a newborn.

Over the next several days I tried to stay hopeful and tell myself Konrad was on the mend.

The fever didn't return with its earlier ferocity, but it refused to leave him altogether. After a morning lull it would come on again in the late afternoon—like some infernal gale that paused only to renew its strength.

Now that we knew he wasn't contagious, Elizabeth spent a good deal of her time helping Mother and the servants tend to him, reading to him to distract him from his aches. When he felt well enough, Henry and I would drop by to talk with him, or sometimes even play a game of chess. These were rarely finished, as he complained of headaches, or simply felt too unwell to concentrate.

I felt oddly incomplete moving about the chateau without my twin. Not that we had always been side by side, but I felt his absence more intensely now. Once, when we were six, and Mother was unwell during her pregnancy with Ernest, Father sent us each to stay with different relations for a fortnight.

It was one of the loneliest and most miserable times of my life.

But this was worse.

Why wasn't Konrad getting better?

"You must take me to Mass, Victor," Elizabeth said Sunday morning during breakfast in the dining room.

I looked up from my boiled egg, my mouth still full of bread, uncomprehending for a moment because I was so used to Konrad escorting her to the cathedral in Geneva or the small village church in Bellerive.

"Yes, of course," I replied.

"Philippe will ready the trap for you," Father said.

Though my parents had no faith themselves, they had no desire to deprive Elizabeth of hers, and I was certain no Sunday had ever passed without her attending a Roman Catholic service.

It was a relief to be away from the chateau, to be in the warm spring air, holding the reins, driving the trap along the lake road. We travelled in silence, but our worries of Konrad kept pace with us.

When we arrived at the small church, Elizabeth said, "You can come inside if you like."

"I will wait here, I think."

"You could light a candle for Konrad."

"You know I don't believe in such things."

She nodded and looked at the other parishioners entering the church with their families. For the first time it occurred to me that it must have been lonely for her, attending Mass alone all these years.

"Did Konrad go inside with you?"

"Not at first."

I helped her down, and watched as she walked into the church. I thought of how she would light a candle and pray—and I envied her.

"What are you doing?" Ernest asked, coming into the library.

It was Monday afternoon, and I'd spent nearly the entire day with books spread all around me, taking notes furiously.

"I'm trying to learn about the human body and its ailments," I said.

My nine-year-old brother came forward, looking gravely at the book's illustrations.

"Konrad will get better, won't he, Victor?" he asked.

To my shame, I realized how little I'd thought of Ernest and how his older brother's illness might be affecting him. Little William was far too young to understand—and it was a great comfort to me sometimes just to hold his little body, and try to lose myself in his warmth and laughter and oblivious good cheer—but at nine, Ernest, like all of us, was having to endure the gloomy weather change that had beset our house.

I put down my pen and smiled as Father did when trying to reassure us. "Of course he will get better. I have no doubt whatsoever. He is strong, like all of us Frankensteins!"

He pointed seriously at the book. "Is the cure in there?"

I laughed. "I don't know. Perhaps."

He became interested in the diagram of a man's spleen. "What does that do?"

"They used to think it ruled our temperaments."

"You'll find the cure, Victor," he said. "You're almost as clever as Konrad."

"*Almost* as clever?" I snapped. "And how would *you* know that, little boy?"

His eyes widened in astonishment and hurt, and I instantly regretted my outburst. How could I fault him, after all, when it was abundantly obvious? Konrad had always been the better student, and my father took no pains to conceal it. Still, Ernest's words smarted. Even to a nine-year-old it was clear that Konrad was the brighter star in our family's constellation.

Had I been just a year younger than Konrad—or even a *non-identical* twin—it would have been easier to bear. But he and I were supposed to be the same in every respect. So what excuse had I to be the weaker?

Elizabeth appeared in the doorway. "Ernest, Justine is looking for you in the garden."

I gave Ernest an apologetic smile and clapped him on the shoulder, but his parting look to me was wary.

"Still here?" Elizabeth said, coming in.

"You have your prayers," I said. "I cannot pray, but I must do something, or go mad."

Restlessly I looked back at my book, a huge tome written mostly in Latin. My Latin was poor, and every sentence was a struggle, but I refused to give up. I had been a lacklustre student, but I would remedy that with hard work.

Elizabeth gently closed the cover. "You cannot expect to cure him on your own."

"Why not?" I demanded. "Someone has to."

My eyes strayed to the bookshelf that concealed the secret passage to the Dark Library.

"You have been here all day," she said. "You can't simply abandon Henry."

I sighed. "I am sorry if Henry feels abandoned, but there are so many books here to understand . . ."

"Go riding," she suggested. "You will get gloomy if you spend any more time here. Take Henry up into the meadows for an hour or two."

I looked forlornly at my desk. "Just a short break," I said.

So Henry and I changed into our riding gear and took our horses out for several hours. And I did enjoy the sunlight and air on my face, even as I felt guilty leaving Konrad in his sickbed.

As I neared home again, I dared to hope. When I saw Mother and Father, they would be smiling, and saying that Konrad's fever had broken for good and he was on the mend and all would be well.

But it was not so. He was the same.

The very next day, a second physician accompanied Dr. Lesage to see Konrad. He was a handsome, fashionable-looking gentleman called Dr. Bartonne, who exuded confidence like an overpowering cologne. I disliked him on sight.

He strode into the room, took one look at my brother, and said he had a disturbance of the blood. Therefore he needed to be bled.

The physician placed slimy leeches all over my brother's pale body and let them suck his blood until Konrad swooned. The fellow was greatly satisfied, and announced that he had purged Konrad of the poisons that had caused his fever, and that when my brother woke in the morning he would feel weak but improved.

It is true that he was cooler that night—who would not be cooler after having most of his blood sucked away? Nonetheless we all had great hope that this would speed Konrad on his recovery.

Come morning, however, the fever returned. Dr. Bartonne was summoned yet again. After he left, I went to seek out Mother to ask what he'd said.

Walking along the upper hallway, I overheard her talking to Maria in the west sitting room. I stopped before I reached the doorway, for I could tell from Maria's hushed tones that they were talking about something terribly serious.

" . . . might be of some help," Maria was saying, "for many say there is great power in it."

"You love him, as we all do, Maria," Mother replied. "But you know that Alphonse cannot bear talk of alchemy. He thinks it primitive nonsense, and I am inclined to agree with him. Please do not speak of this to him."

"Very well, ma'am," said Maria.

"I know you mean well, Maria. Do not think me angry."

"No, ma'am. It's just—I overheard what the doctor said about . . . not knowing how to treat him, and how, if he continues to weaken . . ."

My blood congealed in my veins as I strained to listen. What had the doctor said? But there were no more words spoken, only sniffing, and little sobs, and I sensed the two of them were embracing and comforting each other. Then came my mother's voice, a little shaky.

"You are a dear, dear member of our family, Maria," she said.

"I could not love him more were he my own son."

"We are doing all we can. Alphonse has heard of another doctor, a Dr. Murnau, who's a specialist in rare diseases at the university in Ingolstadt. We've sent a messenger to make inquiries."

"I will keep praying, then, ma'am," said Maria, "if that does not offend you."

"Of course not, Maria, certainly not. I must confess, I have found myself praying too of late. I doubt anyone hears but me, though."

"With respect, ma'am, someone is listening. You mustn't despair so."

I turned and silently walked away down the corridor, for I did not want them to know I'd been eavesdropping.

I desperately wished I knew what Maria had said earlier, about alchemy.

Did she know of some treatment that might help Konrad?

That night as I slept, my mind took me to Father's library, and there I sat, surrounded by medical books, struggling with Latin and Greek, striving to cure Konrad.

I turned a page and there, embedded in the thick paper, was a seed. With great excitement I plucked it out and cradled it in my cupped hands, for I knew I had to plant it immediately or it would perish. But the door to the great hallway was locked, and though I rattled it and shouted, no one came to open it.

My panic grew, for the seed was already starting to decay. There was a stirring of air, though no windows were open, and I looked across the library to see the secret door ajar.

I'd promised Father, but what else could I do? The seed must be planted and I knew there was a well, and water, and earth down there.

The seed gripped in my hand, I hurried through the door to find no splintered planks, but a swirling marble staircase. At the bottom, bathed in impossible sunlight, was the well, surrounded by fragrant and fertile soil.

I dug a small hole with my hands and planted the seed. Almost at once a green tendril shot up, thickening and sending out slender branches—and from the branches dangled little white bones.

I was frightened by this and stepped backward, but I could see that growing among the bones was also fruit—red and luscious. And from the highest branch—for the tree was already taller than me—blossomed a book.

I started to climb up, but the tree kept growing, taking the book higher still.

I climbed faster, and with increasing desperation and rage, knowing that I must have that book.

But I could not reach it.

"We must return to the Dark Library," I said fiercely.

It was the morning after my dream and we were hiking in the hills behind Bellerive—Elizabeth, Henry, and me. The day could not have been more beautiful. An unblemished blue sky spanned the white-capped mountain ranges encircling the lake. Everywhere things were growing: wildflowers sprang from the fields, trees bloomed, new leaves unfolded from branches. Life everywhere—and Konrad trapped at home in his sickbed.

"For what purpose, Victor?" Elizabeth asked.

"So we can heal Konrad," I said.

"Isn't that best left to the doctors?" said Henry.

"Damn the doctors!" I said. "They're little more than barbers with pills. I wouldn't trust them to groom my dog! Konrad's getting weaker by the day. We must take action."

"Action?" said Henry. "What manner of action?"

"For someone whose imagination is so ripe, you can be a bit dim sometimes, Henry," I said. "We must seek our own cure."

Henry looked shocked, as did Elizabeth, who said, "Victor, we made your father a promise—"

"—that he would never *find* us in the library again. Yes. Those were his exact words. I don't intend to break that promise. He will not *find* us in it."

"That is not what he meant, and you know it!"

I waved my hand impatiently. "There is learning in there that has not been tried."

Henry nervously rubbed at his blond hair. "Your father said it was all rubbish."

I snorted. "Think, you two. Those books were kept hidden because they scared people. Why? There must be something to them, some kind of power. Silly, harmless things do not scare people."

"But what if they are harm*ful?*" Elizabeth said.

"What options do we have left to us?" I demanded. "Shall we watch Dr. Bartonne apply leeches once more? Or dead doves? Or perhaps we can ask dear Dr. Lesage to scratch at his wig and mix the dust with another vial of Frau Eisner's Invigorating Tinctures."

"Your father—" Elizabeth began, but I cut her off.

"My father is a brilliant man, but he cannot know everything. You yourself said he can be wrong."

I felt as though a door had been cut into the air before me, and I had passed through it, never to turn back. All my life I had assumed that Father knew everything. I had *wanted* him to know everything. It made me feel safe. But he'd been confident the doctors would heal Konrad—and they had not.

"We must try other means," I said. "Extreme times call for extreme measures. We must be willing to take risks if we want to save Konrad's life."

"You truly think it a matter of life and death?" said Elizabeth, and I felt a stab of guilt, for I could see she had not thought of it in such terms before—or avoided doing so by sheer will. She looked scared.

"All I know is that the doctors are baffled. They are *worried*."

Henry looked away uneasily toward the Jura Mountains, but Elizabeth met my gaze with grave determination.

"The Church condemned those books," she said.

"The Church condemned Galileo for saying the sun did not revolve around the Earth. They can be wrong too."

"The place frightens me," she said.

Henry swallowed and looked uneasily from Elizabeth to me. "Are you so sure these forbidden books hold an answer?"

"All I know is this: If I don't at least try, I will go mad. I can't bear it a day longer. And I need the both of you," I said. "Your knowledge of Latin and Greek is better than mine."

I could see Elizabeth hesitate, and then something changed in her eyes.

"When?" she said.

"Tonight."

"Good," she said. "Let us meet at an hour past midnight."

Not long after the church bells of Bellerive had tolled the hour of one, the three of us met in the hallway and made our way toward the library. Henry kept glancing about with nervous birdlike movements, peering beyond the flickering light of our candles, as though expecting something to swoop down on him. When he stayed at the chateau, he often complained of strange rustlings at night. And despite our constant assurances, he still believed the place to be haunted.

"I sense something," he whispered. "I'm telling you, there's some presence up there."

"We should tell him the truth," Elizabeth said to me with a sidelong wink.

"Truth about what?" squeaked Henry.

I sighed. "Cousin Theodore."

Henry's eyes snapped to me. "You never told me about Cousin Theodore."

I shrugged. "He died young, and this was his favourite place to play."

"So you've *seen* him?" demanded Henry.

"Well, *part* of him," I replied. "He was, well . . ."

"It was a dreadful accident," said Elizabeth solemnly, and then giggled.

"You scoundrels," said Henry, narrowing his eyes. "You

know my imagination's excitable, but go ahead, torment me. What could be more amusing, after all?"

"I'm sorry, Henry," said Elizabeth, squeezing his arm affectionately.

We all fell silent as we neared and passed Konrad's room, for we did not want to disturb him, or wake Mother, who we knew was sleeping at his bedside tonight.

There was scarcely a moment of the day when my brother's illness did not inhabit my thoughts. Passing his bedroom, I imagined him sleeping in his bed, his body fighting and fighting. A great sorrow welled up in me. I was glad of the shadows, for my eyes were moist.

We were all of us in our nightclothes, swathed in robes, for nights on the lake were sometimes cold when a northern wind brought with it a glacial chill.

"Have you ever realized," said Henry nervously to me, gazing at the flickering portraits in the grand hallway, "what a grim bunch your ancestors were? Look at that fellow there! Have you ever seen such a grimace?"

"That's the Frankenstein smile," whispered Elizabeth.

"And who's this fellow here?" Henry asked, pointing.

Looking up at the oldest of all the portraits, I felt a sudden chill. "That," I said, "is Wilhelm Frankenstein."

"The alchemist?" Henry whispered.

I nodded, studying the oil painting. Strange that you could pass a certain thing every day of your life and never once look properly at it. In the candlelight the portrait glowed warmly. Wilhelm still looked like a young man, and stared just past us with a small, slightly disdainful smile on his lips. He had a secret and would not share it. He wore a black doublet with a white ruffled collar, and a black cap in the Spanish style. He stood, one slim hand upon his hip, the other holding a book upon a table, one finger keeping his place within the pages.

"We should go," Elizabeth said, tugging at my arm.

"Yes," I murmured, pulling my eyes away.

As we entered the moonlit library, my heart gave a terrified lurch. Father sat in a leather armchair by the window, glaring at us. But no—I exhaled. It was only shadows, shaped no doubt by my guilt, for I knew I was defying him.

Elizabeth found the shelf and once more triggered the secret latch. There was a dull *thunk*—louder than I remembered—and the bookcase swung inward.

"Remarkable," breathed Henry.

"Just wait," I told him as we all slipped inside.

His reaction was satisfying indeed. "Good Lord," he said. "You didn't mention the steps were quite so flimsy."

"They're perfectly safe," I assured him, leading the way.

At the door, as I prepared to put my hand through the hole, I felt some of my confidence abandon me.

"Do you want me to do it this time?" Elizabeth asked.

That spurred me on. "No, no," I said, and thrust in my arm. At once the eerie hand seized me. I battled against instinctive revulsion and this time did not fight but merely pumped the hand up and down.

Our greeting done, the door opened itself.

"And in we go," I said with a smile.

Truly the Dark Library was well named, for it seemed to suck at our candle flames, making them pucker and smoke.

I felt something new, something I had not noticed during our first visit in the middle of the day. Mingled with the mildew and mustiness, there was fear, excitement—and an unshakable sense of hungry expectation.

"Let's get to work," I said, bringing my light to the shelves of cracked leather tomes. "We are looking for anything on the subject of healing."

"What a place," Henry murmured.

We cleared space on one of the dusty tables. After gathering books, we perched on stools, spreading the volumes all around us, passing them to and fro if we needed help translating or reading a script so spidery that it was all but invisible in the half-light of our candles.

"Here is something," said Henry, and I eagerly looked up. "It is in *Occulta Philosophia.*"

"That's the book I pulled out on our first visit!" I said to Elizabeth. "The one by Agrippa."

"What have you found?" she asked Henry.

His eyes skimmed over the page and he began to read, slowly translating from the Latin. "'From the grand scholarship of ages past, and my own modern learnings, I have created a formulation . . . that has great power to remedy all human suffering. And not only to remedy, but to prolong life . . . so that he who imbibes it will avoid all deaths but those of a violent nature, and will enjoy a multitude of years such as Methuselah.'"

"Methuselah?" I said, frowning. "I do not know the fellow."

Elizabeth sighed. "Have you never read the Bible, Victor?"

"I can't keep all the names straight."

"Methuselah," Elizabeth said, "lived a very, very long time."

"How long?"

"Nine hundred and sixty-nine years," Henry answered, still looking at the tome before him.

"Read on," I said impatiently.

"'And so,'" Henry continued,. "'after many years of failed attempts have I at last this Elixir of Life perfected, and herewith have transcribed it, in the manner of Paracelsus, for all the ages.'"

I lunged across the table and snatched the book from Henry. "Elixir of Life! This is just the thing we seek. Where is the recipe?"

I had the book before me now, my eyes trying to find the right place. I saw the Latin text, found the words "*Vita Elixir*," but afterward came such a language that I had never set eyes upon.

"What is this?" I demanded, jabbing at the vellum page.

Henry stood and leaned over the tome. "If you hadn't snatched it away, I might have had a better look. As it is, I do not know."

"Elizabeth?" I said. "Can you make sense of this?"

She moved her stool closer. "It is not Aramaic," she said. "Nor Sanskrit."

It was a strange-looking thing, to be sure, all curves and angles and sudden flourishes. It went on for ten pages.

"Gibberish," I muttered, and flipped ahead, trying to find some kind of glossary or key to its translation.

"You are too hasty, Victor," said Elizabeth. "As always."

She sounded just like Konrad then, and I shot her a resentful scowl.

"Go back," she said. "Is there not a clue in what came before?"

"What do you mean?"

Carefully she turned back the pages. "Here. He wrote, 'I have transcribed it in the manner of Paracelsus.' What is Paracelsus?"

"Or who?" I said.

I was almost sure I'd seen that word on the spine of a book. I stood and hurried back to the shelves, my eyes scouring the bindings.

If not for the sharp shadow cast by my candle, I would have missed it, for the gold of the tooled letters had flaked away altogether, leaving only a series of indentations.

Paracelsus.

And then, farther down on the spine, again almost without colour, the title in German, *The Archidoxes of Magic.*

"Paracelsus," I said, dragging the volume from the shelf and giving it a triumphant shake above my head. Immediately I wished I hadn't, for a shower of sooty fragments rained down upon me.

"Carefully, Victor!" Elizabeth said, rushing over and taking the book in her own hands. Sheepishly, I let her have it.

She carried it back to the table, and now I could see that this book had obviously been burned. A big triangular section of the cover was charred and crumbling.

"You think Agrippa's strange letters were invented by Paracelsus?" I asked Elizabeth.

"Let us hope," she said.

"Why would it be burned?" Henry asked.

"Father said it was all thought witchcraft," I said. "No doubt it was gathered up by the Church or the townspeople and thrown into a bonfire."

"But Wilhelm Frankenstein rescued it," said Elizabeth.

"You Frankensteins are so enlightened," said Henry with a nervous chuckle, and we all glanced about, as though that long-dead ancestor might still be here in the Dark Library with us, watching.

Very gently Elizabeth opened the cover. The frontispiece was a portrait of a man, but his features were hard to make out, for the page was half burned. Only a skeletal trace of his stout face remained. Either he was wearing a strange, angled hat, or his skull was of a most bizarre and deformed shape. His eyes, strangely, were still clear. They were shrewd and confiding, and seemed to be looking out at us intensely.

I watched Elizabeth, and could see that the image had the same disturbing effect on her, for her lips trembled a bit.

"It's like a man who's been terribly burned, and only a ghost of his former self survives," she whispered.

"It is Paracelsus, though, no question," said Henry, pointing to the bottom of the portrait, where, like words painted upon a wooden sign, it read:

Famoso Doctor Paracelsvs

The doctor's body had not been so damaged by the fire. With a shudder I saw that one of Paracelsus's hands rested over the edge of his own portrait, his fingers curled overtop of the little sign bearing his name. It was just part of the painting, of course, but it made it seem like he could simply step out of the picture.

If he so wanted.

I swallowed back my unease.

"He was a German physician," said Elizabeth, reading the tiny print beneath the portrait. "Also an astrologer and alchemist."

I began, with great care, turning pages. It was an agonizing, heartbreaking business, for many of them had been fused together by the flames, and just the action of turning them tore them free and sent silky bits of ash floating up.

On many pages it was really only the lower half, near the binding, that was even legible.

"We are destroying the book even as we examine it," said Henry miserably.

Again and again I carefully turned pages.

Until I found it.

"Is that it?" I said excitedly. At the very bottom of the page was one of the strange characters we'd seen in Agrippa's *Occulta Philosophia.*

"Yes," said Elizabeth, nodding back at me. "It's very distinctive."

"We will have our translation, then!" I exclaimed. "Surely if Dr. Paracelsus invented this language, he must have laid out its translation in the common alphabet."

But when I tried to turn the page, I could not. It had been completely fused by fire into a thick papery clump.

"Stop, stop!" said Elizabeth. "You'll tear it!"

It was all I could do to keep myself from hurling the book across the chamber.

As if sensing my rage, Elizabeth took hold of my hand and pointed at the open book. "Look there," she said.

Above the strange character was written something in Greek. I squinted but could not make sense of it.

"The Alphabet of the Magi," Elizabeth translated.

"But its key is lost to us," I moaned. "The book is unreadable!"

"We know the alphabet's name at least," Elizabeth said.

I nodded and took a breath. "And now we must find someone who can translate it for us. We must find ourselves an alchemist."

I slept but a few hours and, after breakfast, went downstairs to the servants' quarters. I waited in the hallway outside the kitchen until Maria turned the corner and saw me. Her face lit up.

"Konrad?" she said, with such joy that I felt guilty to disappoint her—and then disgruntled, too, for Konrad had always been her favourite when we were little.

"It is Victor, Maria," I said, coming more into the light.

"Victor, forgive me. You gave me a start. For a moment I thought it was your brother, up and about . . ." She stopped herself. "Is everything all right upstairs? Does your mother need me?"

"No, no, all is well," I said. "I am sorry to bother you, Maria, but there is something I wanted to ask you." I waited as Sasha, one of the kitchen staff, passed by in the hall, giving us a curious look. In a lowered voice I said, "Of a rather confidential nature."

"Yes, of course," she said. "Come into my office."

As housekeeper she had a comfortable suite of rooms, some of which looked out toward the lake. She led me into her small office, where all the business accounts of the household were carefully maintained. She was a meticulous woman, and I'd often heard my mother say that we would all be utterly helpless without her.

"What is it you wanted to speak to me about, Victor?" she asked, closing the door. She should have called me young master, but she had raised me from a yowling whelp, and it would have felt odd to be called master by her.

"I am very worried about Konrad," I began cautiously.

She nodded, and I was not surprised to see her eyes moisten.

"I worry that the doctors do not know how to cure him," I said, watching her, "and I wonder if perhaps there are healers with different skills who might be more successful."

She said nothing, but her eyes would not meet mine.

"Do you know of any such people, Maria?"

She took a breath. "I do not."

I sat back, discouraged, and tried to think of another subtle line of questioning, but couldn't.

"But I heard you talking to Mother," I blurted out, "about some fellow you know of, an alchemist."

"You little villain! Eavesdropping!" she said, and I suddenly felt five years old again and caught out at some mischief.

"Who was it you were talking about?" I persisted.

"I promised your mother I would not speak of it."

"To Father," I said. "She asked you not to speak of it to *Father.* But you can tell *me*, Maria."

She glared at me, then looked away. "You must promise me you will not speak of this to your parents," she said. "And I do this only because I am so worried about your brother."

"Of course," I said.

"I put little faith in these doctors. Some cannot even cut hair straight, much less deliver a baby without killing the mother." She sighed. "There was an incident a good many years ago; you and Konrad were just newborns. One of the city's generals had a daughter, no more than six, who sickened suddenly. The general spared no expense. He summoned the finest physicians of

Europe. All of them said the girl was beyond hope and would die before the winter was through. But the girl's mother could not bear the thought, and sought out an apothecary right here in Geneva. Some said he was a gifted healer. Some said he was an alchemist. Some said he trafficked with the devil. But the mother did not care about any of that. She went to him and he prepared a medicine, and he saved that little girl."

Maria's voice trembled. I took my handkerchief and passed it to her, and counted five seconds while she dabbed her eyes, but I was too impatient to wait any longer.

"His name," I said urgently. "What was the fellow's name?"

"Julius Polidori."

I had never heard of him, which was odd. Geneva, though an important city, was no vast metropolis like Paris or London, and my father's position made him aware of anyone of prominence.

"And is he still in the city?" I asked Maria.

"I don't know, Victor. But I think maybe you should find out."

I smiled at her. "I will. I most surely will."

Chapter 4

THE ALCHEMIST

The next morning as Konrad slumbered, Henry, Elizabeth, and I traveled to Geneva with Father in the carriage. Father had business to attend to at the Palais de Justice, and the three of us had convinced him that we should spend the day studying the history of our great republic by exploring its oldest buildings and monuments: St. Peter's, the Magdalen Church, the town hall. It was to be part of our schooling. Father, of course, was delighted at our keenness, and happy, too, to see us temporarily removed from the chateau and all its gloom.

As we approached Geneva along the south lake road, I admired the high ramparts that surrounded the city in the shape of a protective star. There were only five gated entrances, locked every night at ten o'clock, and the portcullises were not raised until five in the morning. The guards were under the strictest instructions never to deviate from this schedule, even if ordered by the magistrates themselves. Our city had seen many wars and sieges, and these current times, my father often said, were uncertain ones.

We stabled the horses and carriage at our city house, for we kept a small staff there even in the summer when we were mostly at the chateau. Father bade us farewell and we agreed to meet at two in the afternoon for the drive home.

"To the town hall, then," I said after Father had disappeared from view.

We had discussed our strategy the night before, and agreed this seemed the most sensible place to begin our search. The land registry office would have records of all the city's property owners.

But when we asked the fussy town hall clerk to check, he found no entry for a Polidori.

"All this tells us is that he doesn't own property," I said outside in the square.

"He may well take rented rooms," said Elizabeth.

"As a great many do," added Henry.

Our next step was to ask at the various apothecary shops. If this fellow was as famous as Maria had said, others would have heard of him. But several young apprentices just shook their heads and claimed no knowledge of him.

An older fellow looked at us gravely over the top of his spectacles and said, "I have not heard that foul name mentioned in many years. I know nothing of his whereabouts, nor care to know."

Our search had started near the centre of the city, but slowly we were moving away from the elegant flowered fountains and airy public squares. The cobbled streets narrowed. There were fewer gentlemen about, and more sailors and labourers and women dressed in coarser fashion. I didn't like the looks a couple of wharf hands gave us as we passed in the lanes.

I was beginning to despair, for we had asked now at some half dozen establishments, and no one had been able to tell us anything helpful about Julius Polidori.

"We are idiots," said Henry suddenly.

I turned to see him looking into a greasy window where a row of typesetters sat hunched over tables, their blackened fingers plucking individual letters from trays.

"The *Geneva Gazette*," said Henry. "This story of Maria's—surely it would have been written up."

"It must have been," said Elizabeth eagerly. "The child of a general! Of course it would have been the talk of the town. Victor, did Maria give you an exact date?"

"She said it was the year of my birth, that it was winter."

"Now we must hope that the newspaper keeps a proper archive," said Henry.

I was not hopeful when we entered the offices, for the place was in a chaos of activity and noise and ink. At first it seemed no one would have a second to spare for us, but Elizabeth picked out the kindliest-looking young gentleman she could find. She walked to him and very prettily told him we had been set a historical assignment by our tutor, and would it be possible to look at some past issues of the newspaper.

It was quite remarkable, how helpful the fellow was. He gave us all candles and escorted us down to a cellar, but then my heart truly sank, for I saw tower after tower of newspaper, stacked to the very ceiling.

"It is like a city of paper," I murmured to Elizabeth.

"Will it be difficult to find the period we seek?" she asked the young fellow.

"Not at all, miss, not at all." He promptly led us to a particular tower, thrust his hand into it, and, like a magician, pulled out a wad of old newspapers.

"I believe these will suit you," he said, beaming at Elizabeth.

Elizabeth beamed back. "Thank you so much, sir. You've been so kind."

"If you need any further assistance, I shall be upstairs," he said. He gave his name, bowed, and disappeared.

"He could not have been more helpful had he been on puppet strings," Henry said in amazement.

Elizabeth blushed modestly.

We each took several papers and in the light of our candles searched through them.

It seemed hardly any time at all before Elizabeth exclaimed, "I have it here! Here is the story . . ." She read aloud hurriedly, jumping ahead until she came to what we sought. "'Julius Polidori, of Wollstonekraft Alley . . .'"

"It is not five minutes' walk from here," I said with a grin.

The alley stank of urine—and worse. The few shops had a defeated look about them, tattered awnings and dirty windows with dusty displays that probably hadn't been changed for years.

"This must be the place, here," said Henry. The windows were shuttered, but over the door hung a wooden sign. Flaking paint showed an apothecary's mortar and pestle.

"It does not look promising," said Elizabeth drily.

In the door was a small, grimy window, but it was too dark

inside to make out much more than the shadows of shelves. The place looked all but abandoned, but when I turned the knob, the door swung open and a small bell clanged.

I entered with Henry and Elizabeth. "Good morning!" I called out.

Mingled with the fragrance of a hundred different herbs was dust and a powerful smell of cat. At one time the shop must have been more prosperous, for the shelves were of rich dark wood. On our left was an entire wall of drawers, each fancily labelled.

"Hello?" I called out again.

Henry drew open one drawer, and then another. "Empty," he said. He looked all about him, wide eyed, perhaps recording every detail for some horrifying poem or play he would later concoct.

Directly before us was a long counter, behind which were shelves filled with elaborate mixing vessels. It did not look like anything had been mixed here in quite some time. In the middle of the shelves was a glass-paned door. I saw a flicker of light, and then a shadow growing larger.

Quite suddenly the door swung open and a man in a wheelchair propelled himself into the shop. His legs were wizened, the fabric of his breeches loose and flapping. He seemed no more than fifty, and though his upper body was powerfully built, his face had a gaunt and defeated look to it. His wig rested crookedly, and was many years out of fashion. But it was his eyes that most gave him the look of defeat. They contained not a spark of light or hope.

He seemed surprised when he saw us. No doubt he didn't get many customers as well dressed as us in his shop—if he got any customers at all.

"How may I help you?"

"You are Mr. Julius Polidori?" Elizabeth asked politely.

"I am, miss."

The three of us glanced quickly at one another, for this fellow seemed so far from the picture conjured by Maria's story. A healer. A man of power who cured a little girl when all the wise men of Europe could not.

This man before us positively reeked of failure.

I felt an instinctive disdain rising in me. What kind of healer could this be? This broken person in a chair with a crooked wig? His shop was a ruin. No doubt his clothing had not been laundered recently. He was laughable. I was tempted to turn and leave that very moment.

"Might there be some medicine you're needing?" he asked.

"I think perhaps—" I began with a sniff, but Elizabeth cut me off.

"Indeed there is," she said, and gave me a warning look, for she knew how quickly my temper could flare. In that way, we were not so different. To Polidori she said, "But it is of an . . . unusual nature."

He looked at us steadily, saying nothing.

I was still far from convinced any good could come of this, but we were here now. I drew closer to the counter. "You are the same apothecary who cured the general's girl, some years ago?"

He drew in a breath and released it with a rueful nod. "I am."

"We have heard that you are a man of wide-ranging knowledge," Elizabeth said. "A healer with remarkable powers."

He actually laughed then, bitterly. "Is this some joke? Have you nothing better to do with your days?"

"No, sir," said Henry. "I mean, no, this is not a joke and we are here on a matter of the greatest urgency."

"We're searching for the Elixir of Life," Elizabeth said quietly.

Polidori stared at us with his dull eyes. "Good day to you, young sirs, and young lady," he said curtly, and with a deft movement, swivelled his chair back toward the doorway.

"Please, sir, wait," I said, striding forward, taking from my satchel a volume from the Dark Library and putting it on the counter. "I have here a work by Heinrich Cornelius Agrippa . . ."

Polidori paused. He chuckled sadly and then turned around, barely glancing at the book.

"*Occulta Philosophia.* Am I correct?"

I nodded, startled.

"Young sir, put it back into your satchel. Add two large stones, say goodbye, and throw it into the deepest part of the harbour."

Henry looked over at me, confused. "Is that a spell of some sort?"

"That is advice, and the best I have to give," said Polidori. "That book will only bring you grief."

"Sir," I said, "The physician Agrippa—"

"*Magician!*" Polidori scoffed.

I persisted. "He writes of something called the Elixir—"

"Yes, yes, I know," he said impatiently. "The Elixir of Life. He was hardly the first to dream up such a thing. There are many, many recipes for fantastical potions meant to cure all ills, perhaps even guarantee immortality. Such things are delusions, sir. They do not exist."

"I am confused," said Elizabeth. "I thought you yourself—"

"Yes," he said. "There was a time when I too was seduced by

such fancies and sought them with great passion. I even created an elixir of my own."

"And you succeeded with that little girl," I said.

Again he laughed. "She was cured," he said. "But not by me. It was *chance,* or God's divine power, a miracle! But it was not me."

"Why do you say that, sir?" Henry asked.

Polidori frowned. "You know my name, yet you don't know my full story? You have not come merely to torment me?"

I shook my head, wondering why Maria had withheld something. The honesty in our surprised faces must have convinced Polidori, and the suspicion faded from his eyes. He sighed.

"After that girl recovered, my business flourished. People beat my door off its hinges, wanting the same medicine." He waved a hand around his shop. "For a short while I was a wealthy man, welcomed into the finest homes in the city. But that elixir I gave the girl, the *very same thing,* was not reliable. Sometimes it made a patient well. Sometimes it had no effect at all. Sometimes it seemed to make a patient worse. Still, people craved it, even though I grew more and more reluctant to prepare it. Some months later there was a ship owner, Hans Marek, a man of some wealth and power in the city, whose wife was very ill. He came to me and demanded the elixir. I told him I was no longer making it. He offered me a great sum in gold, and foolishly I accepted. Marek took my elixir home, and his wife died shortly after taking it. He was so enraged, he wanted me hanged for witchcraft." Polidori chuckled. "You see, when a medicine works, it is blessed science, and when it fails, it is witchcraft. I was brought before a magistrate, a fine and enlightened gentleman who dismissed the charges as barbaric and primitive. But he forbade me from making the elixir ever again, or practising alchemy."

"This magistrate," Henry asked. "What was his name?"

The same question had been on my lips as well, and I waited anxiously for the answer.

"His name was Alphonse Frankenstein," said the apothecary.

I felt a great pride in my father's fairness, but when I saw that Elizabeth was about to reveal our connection, I quickly touched her hand. I did not think it wise for Polidori to know our identities, not yet anyway.

"I owe Frankenstein my life," Polidori was saying, "what is left of it. But his ruling offered no satisfaction to Hans Marek. Several nights later I was dragged from my bed by a drunken mob, taken up to the city ramparts, and pushed."

Elizabeth gasped.

"Clearly I survived the fall," he said. "A small miracle in itself. But I was paralyzed from the waist down." He patted at his legs. "I have virtually no business now, but I have been frugal with my savings and so am able to carry on, as you see. Now, you have listened to a long and weighty tale, and if it has any moral, it is this: Rid yourself of that book before it brings you ill luck. Good day to you."

Once more he began to turn his wheelchair away.

"It is my brother—" I began, but my voice broke.

Polidori sighed. "I am very sorry to hear it," he said sadly. "It is always the way. I have seen it many, many times. When a loved one falls desperately ill, and all else fails, any risk is worth the taking."

"Yes," said Elizabeth.

Polidori shook his gaunt head. "The last time I took pity on such a patient, it cost the patient her life, and me nearly mine."

"We have money," I said.

But Polidori raised his hand wearily. "I cannot. I will not. And if I may give you a further piece of advice, give up your search altogether. Agrippa's recipe has never been replicated. Why? Because it is written in a strange and complex—"

"The Alphabet of the Magi," I said. "We know."

"Very good," he said. "But did you also know that it has no translation? It is unreadable."

"What about Paracelsus?" Elizabeth demanded. "*The Archidoxes of Magic.*"

Polidori looked startled, impressed even. "Every edition is gone, burned," he said with a trace of wistfulness. "Extinct! And even if it weren't—"

From my satchel I took the volume of Paracelsus and placed it carefully before him on the counter.

In silence he stared at it with a curious expression I couldn't quite fathom. Then it came to me. It was the way a cat beholds its prey just before the pounce. His grey eyes lifted slowly to mine.

"Where did you find this?" he asked softly.

"That is my secret." I was afraid if he knew too much about us, he might guess my parentage and refuse to help us further. "Will you assist us?"

"Your parents, young sir, do they know of this visit?" he asked.

"No."

Polidori glanced out to the street, as if afraid someone might be watching. He looked at all three of us, as if reluctant once more, but then his gaze fell back on the Paracelsus.

"Come," he said. "Bring these books of yours into my parlour. Let us have a look at them."

He led us into the dim room behind the counter. It too was lined with shelves, but these held books instead of vials and tins. The faded Oriental carpet was rutted with wheelchair tracks. Two armchairs and a threadbare sofa were arranged around a small hearth. There was a table that had not been entirely cleared of its last meal. He lived humbly indeed.

We were not five paces into the room when something leapt at Polidori from the shadows. Elizabeth and I both gave cries of surprise, and Henry shrieked outright.

Polidori swivelled around in his chair to face us, and we all stared at the extraordinary creature curled up on his lap.

"That," said Henry, his voice more highly pitched than usual, "is a very large cat!"

It was a magnificent creature to be sure. Its body was lithe and long and short tailed. Its tawny coat was marked with dark spots. Beneath its neck was a ruff of white and black striped fur that looked rather like a bow tie. And from the tips of the creature's tall triangular ears rose tufts of stiff black hair.

I looked at Elizabeth, and she returned my curious gaze.

"It isn't by any chance," she began uncertainly, "a—"

"A lynx, yes," said Polidori with a smile, clearly enjoying our surprise.

"Ah," said Henry a bit weakly.

Many wild animals inhabited the forests around our lake:

bears and wolves, chamois, and lynx who could live almost at the height of the highest Alps.

"I did not know they could be trained as . . . pets," I confessed.

Polidori raised an eyebrow, as if questioning my use of words. "He is quite tame. He came to me as a mere kitten and is as amiable as any house cat. Aren't you, Krake?"

Polidori's fingers vigorously kneaded the fur between Krake's ears, and the lynx gave a luxuriant yawn, revealing wickedly sharp teeth. He hopped off his master's lap and padded toward me. He gave me a sniff, and then rubbed against my legs with such force that he nearly knocked me off balance.

"He likes you, Victor," said Henry.

"And I like Krake," I said with forced joviality, hesitantly patting the creature on the head. He looked up at me with a green-eyed gaze that was just a touch unsettling, it was so intent. Then, to my relief, the lynx jumped back up onto Polidori's lap.

Polidori invited us to sit down, then extended his hand. "May I?"

I passed him the volume of Paracelsus, and he took it gently. Silently he inspected the spine and binding before even opening the cover. For a long time he gazed at the portrait of the author, and then proceeded more deeply into the book's burned pages, his careful fingers breaking off scarcely a fragment of ash.

When he came to the page that bore the beginnings of the Alphabet of the Magi, he stopped. I realized I'd been holding my breath, and exhaled noisily. Krake turned and looked at me severely.

"It is unreadable," I said.

"We had hoped," said Elizabeth quietly, "that you might know of some other book that holds a translation."

Polidori shook his head. "There is none, I can assure you. But this . . ." He prodded delicately at the fused pages. "I think there may be some hope for this."

"You do?" said Henry, his voice echoing the delight and surprise I felt.

"Perhaps," he said. "I have some experience in restoring texts that have been . . . damaged, shall we say. Let us go to my workshop."

I expected him to lead us back to the storefront, but he wheeled his chair in the opposite direction, through another doorway and along a short corridor. I glimpsed a tiny kitchen and, down a second short passage, a bedchamber, and a small water closet that released a faint but unpleasant whiff of sewage.

At the end of the corridor was a narrow doorway, scarcely wide enough to admit Polidori's wheelchair. He went through first, and right away swivelled his chair around to face us. By the light of his candle I could see he was inside a room that was really nothing but a large cupboard.

"I think we will all fit," he said. "Come inside."

"This is your workshop?" I asked, confused.

"This is the *way* to the workshop," he said. "It is a kind of dumbwaiter. I call it an elevator. I had it constructed after my accident."

"How ingenious," said Elizabeth, stepping into the compartment.

"Is it . . . structurally sound?" Henry asked uncertainly.

"I have used it for more than a decade."

"And it will bear all our weight?"

"Yes, young sir, it will."

I entered the elevator, followed by Henry, and the three of us crowded around the wheelchair. The floor groaned ominously beneath my feet.

"Krake, I fear you will have to wait upstairs," Polidori told his lynx.

Without hesitation the cat leapt from his lap and sat down beyond the portal, licking his paws meditatively.

Twin doors hung at the entrance, one on either side, and Polidori pulled these snugly shut, enclosing us in the conveyance.

"From the hallway, it looks like a dead end," he said. He passed me his candle. "If you would hold this, please." With both hands he grasped one of the ropes that dangled from the ceiling of the elevator.

"A simple system of pulleys," said Polidori, and as he tugged, the elevator gave a downward jerk.

Polidori's strength must have been considerable to lower the weight of all four of us. As we descended, a dank smell wafted up to us. I glanced at Elizabeth and saw her eyes, dancing and lively in the candlelight.

"This descends to the cellar, does it?" Henry inquired, looking quite pale.

"A cellar beneath the cellar," Polidori said. "I had it dug specially after my accident. This elevator is the only way to reach it."

We dropped slowly past the timbers of the floor, and then a stone foundation, then brick, and rougher stone still, until the wall finally gave way.

A cellar opened before us, and soon the elevator came to a halt.

Polidori rolled himself out. With his flame he lit more candles. The cellar seemed as big as all his upstairs rooms combined. I noticed that, unlike in his storefront, all the shelves had been built at a level that allowed Polidori to reach them from his wheelchair. I caught sight of worktables and more flasks and jars and apparatus than I had ever before seen.

Polidori must have guessed my thoughts, for he said, "Any work I do, I prefer to do down here, rather than upstairs. After being accused of witchcraft and threatened with hanging, one becomes more cautious. Now, let us go over here."

He led us to a long narrow table on which rested several trays that might have been made of tin or zinc.

"Young sir," he said to me, pointing, "could you please fetch those three green jars. And you, sir," he said to Henry, "gather the candles and bring them to the table."

His voice and manner had become suddenly more authoritative, and we hurried to do as he bid us. Over each candle he placed a special lantern of red glass. The cellar was suddenly bathed in a lurid red glow.

Carefully he opened the green jars one at a time, pouring a measure into a flask and then into one of the metal trays before him. When he was done, there was a shallow film of liquid at the bottom of the tray, red in the lantern light.

It might easily have been blood.

"We will need this later," Polidori said, pushing the tray to the back of the table. From a drawer he took a thick cloth wallet and opened it beside the volume of Paracelsus. Arranged within the wallet was a startling array of instruments that, at first glance, looked like those of a surgeon. There were all manner of tweezers and forceps, and minute scalpels. I glanced at Henry and saw him shiver.

"You would all like to assist, I assume," Polidori stated. To Henry he said, "You shall be timekeeper. There is a clock there, and you must watch seconds when I ask later." To Elizabeth and me he said, "I trust you will be able to help me in the surgery."

"Surgery?" said Elizabeth in surprise.

"Of course," said Polidori. "This is as precise as any medical procedure."

He proceeded to name all the instruments for us, and then took a diffuser filled with some liquid and misted the book with it. He then turned to me.. "If you might hold the specimen steady, please, we will begin. The Gutenburg scalpel, there."

Promptly Elizabeth handed it to him, and he set to work.

Several months ago, Father had taken us to the dissecting room of the celebrated physician Dr. Bullman. In the sloped theatre, filled to the ceiling with eager anatomy students, we'd watched as Bullman had opened up the corpse of a newly hanged convict. We saw its heart and lungs, the spleen and stomach. Henry had had to leave. But Konrad and I—and Elizabeth, too—had stayed to the very end. It was dreadful and fascinating both, to see the body's innermost secrets laid open.

I felt exactly the same enthrallment as Polidori's hands hovered over the tome, and then cut. Perhaps it was the noxious smell of the chemicals in the tray, or the mustiness of the room, but I thought the book flinched and exhaled.

Polidori's goal was to separate the burned, fused pages, and it was a delicate task. He used a bewildering array of instruments to tease apart the sickly parchments. Sometimes it went well. Sometimes a tiny piece tore loose, and Polidori muttered an oath.

The heat in the room grew more intense, as if a great furnace burned nearby. Sweat slithered into my eyes, and I blinked to clear my vision. My gaze never wavered from Polidori's steady hands and the tips of his instruments. And for a moment the book seemed not a book at all but a living body, and instead of paper, I glimpsed pulsing viscera and blood and organs. I blinked again, not trusting my vision. But—and this was most strange and repulsive—the book seemed to emanate the smell of a slaughterhouse, of entrails and offal.

Wondering if it was just the wanderings of my mind, I looked to Elizabeth, and saw her nose wrinkle. She steadied herself with a hand, but her gaze did not flinch as she watched this strange surgery upon Paracelsus's tome.

"I have done as much as I can," Polidori said finally, and with one sure stroke he slit from the book's binding the pages he'd been working on. With padded tweezers he grasped them and held them above the tray of liquid.

"Young sir," he said to Henry. "Set the clock for sixty seconds. Be precise, now!"

Henry reached for the ornate timepiece and turned back the slender hand, holding it in place.

"Release it . . . now!" cried Polidori, and he immersed the charred pieces of paper into the bloody liquid, swishing them gently back and forth. At first they stuck together, but within moments they floated apart.

"They are free!" Elizabeth cried in excitement.

Polidori arranged the charred pages side by side in the tray. "Time is critical now."

"What does this liquid do?" I asked.

"Brings back what was lost. A second too long, though, and we will lose it all forever."

We stared, riveted, at the tray. Twenty seconds, thirty . . . Nothing was happening. In the red light the blackened paper hovered in the liquid, as unreadable as ever. Forty seconds . . .

"Look!" breathed Elizabeth.

Something was happening. Within the darkness of the pages appeared faint scratchings—completely illegible, but something.

"It comes . . ." said Polidori in a hoarse voice. "It comes . . ."

"Fifty seconds," said Henry.

On all the pages the scratchings grew thicker, released shoots like strange seedlings growing with freakish speed. I recognized the bizarre characters from the Alphabet of the Magi, and then some familiar letters beneath them: the translations!

"Fifty-five seconds," said Henry.

"We must have more time!" said Elizabeth, for parts of the pages were still unreadable.

"We dare not," snapped Polidori, readying his tweezers. "Look!"

The edges of the pages were beginning to curl and dissolve, as if in acid. And the parts of the text that had once been plain to see were starting to blur dangerously.

The clock chimed, and instantly Polidori drew the pages out and placed them flat on a special drying rack.

"This will have to do," he said.

"Is there enough, though?" I asked, squinting in the lurid half-light.

"It is a good start," he said. "A beginning. Return in two days, and I will tell you what I have found."

I took my purse from my pocket and tried to offer him money, but he shook his head.

"Let us wait for that, young sir. This may all come to naught. Let us wait."

"That is very kind of you, sir," said Elizabeth. "Thank you."

For the first time Polidori smiled, as though genuinely surprised at these gentle words. He looked at me.

"I hope your brother improves," he said, "and makes all this toil needless."

We left Polidori's shop, each of us silent. I felt I'd witnessed something incredible, something dangerous, even. The streets beyond the alley appeared strange to my eyes. All the people and horses and carriages and bustle had nothing to do with me. My eyes were still focused on the pages of Paracelsus's tome, the ancient words swimming into view after long centuries of oblivion.

"It's like we've brought something back to life," Elizabeth murmured.

I looked at her, startled. "Yes. That is just how I feel. There was something about that volume . . . it seemed no mere book."

"It lived," said Elizabeth simply.

"Indeed it did!" I exclaimed. "I felt it move in my hands, like a patient writhing."

"Was there not the smell of blood?" she said.

"Is it possible it was our fevered emotions tricking us?" said Henry. "That we all imagined such phantasmagorical things because we wanted to see them?"

"You are very sensible, Henry," said Elizabeth tartly, "for someone whose pen makes such flights of passion."

"Yet they are inventions only," Henry persisted. "Not reality. If we truly believe that book moved, we are believing in . . . magic." He lowered his voice. "Witchery."

"There is no such thing," I said. "Just things we do not yet understand. Father would say the same."

"Your father would condemn what we've done," said Henry.

I swallowed. "He will not know."

"Are we fools?" said Henry nervously. "Deceiving your father is one thing, but even if Polidori can translate the recipe, is the elixir something that should be made?"

"If it is Konrad's only chance at life, yes," I said. "And damn the consequences!"

"Polidori himself said there were no end of magical elixirs—and their effect could be dangerous," Henry persisted.

I said nothing.

"I trust him," said Elizabeth. "Polidori. He will advise us well."

We were all surprised when we heard St. Peter's bells toll two o'clock, for we'd lost all track of time inside the laboratory. Down the cobbled streets of the city we ran, toward our house, to meet Father.

After dinner I went to visit Konrad, but he was already asleep, our unfinished game of chess still on the bedside table. With a sigh, I sat down and looked at the board. Yesterday he'd actually dozed off, it had taken me so long to figure out my move.

I examined the position of his pieces carefully, and almost at once understood his stratagem. It was very good. He would have me in three moves if I wasn't careful.

I made the move for him, then turned the board around to take my own turn.

Hunched over in the chair, I played against myself—and I knew Konrad so well it was very much like playing him properly—but suddenly the sadness of it struck me hard, and I realized how desperately I missed him, and how badly I wanted him to get out of that bed for good.

"We had a rather exciting day," I whispered to his sleeping face.

I'd been longing to tell him since we got home from Geneva, but I knew it was best kept secret. Now, though, I could at least utter the words.

"I've got a great plan to gather the ingredients for the Elixir of Life, and once we're done, you'll be able to drink it."

He shifted in his sleep, turned his head away, as though doubting me.

"I promise," I said, kissing him on the forehead. "If no one else can make you better, I will."

That night I woke suddenly with the dreadful sensation that someone was in my room.

Cautiously I peered through my bed curtains to see my chamber bathed in moonlight. Elizabeth stood before the window in her nightgown, gazing out over the lake.

"Elizabeth," I said softly. "What's the matter? Is it Konrad?"

At once I worried she'd come to bring me some terrible news, but she did not turn. She had not heard me at all.

In the moonlight her face was ghostly pale, her brow furrowed. She seemed to be holding something in her arms, and kept looking down at it anxiously.

"Elizabeth?"

No response. She was awake, yet asleep.

It was not the first time. When Elizabeth first came to our house as a small child, she sleepwalked. My parents would find her in the hallways, looking about her in confusion, or staring intently at some invisible view. Father said her mind was temporarily disordered by the great changes in her life, and even in sleep it would not let her rest, and would make her walk the house in the early hours of morning, trying to puzzle things out. In time it would pass, he said.

Once, in those first few months, I awoke with a start, to find her body pressed against mine. Her thin arms encircled me tightly. She was shaking. I dared not wake her, for Father had said you must never wake someone who was sleepwalking. So I just lay very still. Gradually she stopped trembling, her breathing calmed, and we both fell asleep. In the morning she was most indignant to find herself in someone else's bed, and woke me with a punch in the shoulder, before flouncing out of my room.

But that was many years ago, when we were little more than seven.

We were sixteen now, and I was almost afraid to approach her, for she seemed to emanate an eerie power. She was herself, and not herself, and it was like having a stranger in the room. I felt I ought to guide her gently back to her own bedchamber, if possible. Father had said the best thing to do with someone sleepwalking was to talk to them very calmly and matter-of-factly.

"Elizabeth," I said. "This way."

When she turned to me, her face was stricken with anxiety. In her arms she cradled an old doll. I shivered, for her gaze seemed to look right through me, to someone just behind me.

"The baby's not dead," she said fiercely.

"No," I said.

"She's just cold."

"Yes," I said.

"She needs warming." So urgent and penetrating was her gaze that for a moment I looked back at the doll, just to make sure it wasn't real. "That's all. Just a little warmth and she'll be fine."

"You are warming her right now," I said soothingly. There was something so childlike and beseeching in her look that I felt my heart ache. "She will be wonderfully warm and happy soon."

She looked down at the doll, kneading it with her hands. "Yes," she said.

"You see," I said. "The baby's fine. I'm sure she just needs a good sleep. I'll show you the way."

I started walking toward my door, and checked to make sure she was following. I quickly lit a candle and made my way down the hallway to her bedchamber. The door was ajar. We went inside. I pointed at her bed, the sheets in a tangle.

"Here we are," I said. "You and baby can rest here."

"The bed will be warm," she said.

"Of course."

I tried to smooth the sheets for her, but she lay down on them before I could finish, still clutching the baby. It was a good thing it wasn't a real baby, for Elizabeth was lying on top of its head and torso. Her eyes were already closed and she was properly asleep. I found a blanket in her armoire and gently laid it over her. I watched her for a moment, then left the bedchamber.

At breakfast, Elizabeth said not a word about her sleepwalking. She remembered nothing, and I was not about to remind her.

Chapter 5

DR. MURNAU

The famous Dr. Murnau from Ingolstadt arrived at the chateau the following day.

I'd expected someone dignified and grey-haired who would emanate knowledge and quiet confidence. But this fellow was surprisingly young; he couldn't have been more than thirty—and he looked like he needed a doctor himself. I don't think I'd ever seen anyone so thin and pale. His fingers were positively skeletal. Behind his dusty spectacles, his watery eyes appeared permanently startled.

He was to stay with us at least a week, and Father had given him one of the turret rooms with an adjoining parlour to use as his surgery and laboratory. As his carriage was unloaded after breakfast, I counted no fewer than six trunks, no doubt filled with all sorts of chemicals and apparatus.

Father said Dr. Murnau had lectured at the finest universities and was widely thought the best, and most progressive, healer in Europe. If anyone could devise a cure for Konrad, it would be him.

He spent a full hour examining my brother, and the whole

time Elizabeth and I paced the hallway outside—when we didn't have our ears pressed to the door.

When the doctor finally emerged, he actually gave a little jump of surprise when he saw us.

"So. What is your diagnosis, Doctor?" I asked.

"Oh, I'm afraid I don't have one yet," he said in a nasal voice.

I blinked in confusion and disappointment, for he had seemed so wise. The other doctors had needed no more than twenty minutes to make their decisions.

"I'll have to conduct many other examinations," he said with a nervous smile. "After lunch I'll bleed him. Now if you'll excuse—"

"He's already been bled," I said, thinking of the useless Dr. Bartonne.

"Yes, so I understand," replied Dr. Murnau.

"It did no good," Elizabeth added. "Only weakened him further."

Dr. Murnau nodded so vigorously that his glasses slipped down his nose a bit and he pushed them back with a bony finger. "Don't worry. Listen, I know there are many doctors who put great store in bleeding, but I'm not one of them. It's completely useless. You might as well—I don't know—chant druidic incantations." He gave a strange little titter of laughter. "But when I said I'd bleed your brother, I only meant I'm going to take some of his blood—to study."

"Study?" Elizabeth said with a frown.

"Exactly." He licked his lips. "Just a small quantity, mind you. Now, there's some reading I really must do."

And with an awkward bow he left us alone in the hallway.

"What do you make of him?" I asked Elizabeth.

"Apart from the fact he's clearly insane?" she said.

"What can he learn from Konrad's blood?" I said. "Except that he needs it in his body to live!"

"There is something ghoulish about it."

"He's like a vampyre," I said.

When I'd first heard about Dr. Murnau, I'd felt hopeful—and more than a bit foolish. This man had spent years of his life studying, practising his discipline. And here was I, with books of alchemy, seeking out a legendary elixir of life.

But now that I knew of his outlandish plans—to study blood!—they seemed even more fantastical than any tome of ancient spells.

The next day we would return to Mr. Polidori, to see what success he'd had translating the Alphabet of the Magi.

"I have made progress," Polidori said, ushering us into his musty parlour.

"That is excellent news!" said Elizabeth.

Once more the three of us had come into the city with Father, and secretly made our way to Wollstonekraft Alley. Polidori had greeted us eagerly.

"So you were able to translate the alphabet?" I asked.

"It is a devious thing," he replied, leading us to a table covered with books and parchments. "Not all the alphabet could be recovered. And it is no simple matter of substituting a letter of our own alphabet for each arcane symbol. No, no. It is an ever-changing cipher, you see, and every twenty-six letters, the meaning of the symbols alters completely."

"Good Lord," exclaimed Henry, "then how can you discern the meaning of the next characters?"

The alchemist wagged a finger. "The clues, you see, are implanted in the previous transcription, and from there you must riddle out the rest. As you might imagine, this is time-consuming. And even when one has a small triumph, what is produced is an archaic form of Latin that necessitates a further translation—"

"But you have made progress," I prompted.

"Oh, indeed. I have translated the preface."

"Just the preface?" I said, and felt myself sag in disappointment. Why would he waste time with the preface? I never read prefaces. Skip the preface and move on to the meat of the thing!

Curled near the hearth, Krake the lynx gave a low purr and stared at me, as though chiding me for my impatience.

"In the preface," said Polidori, "there is important information. Agrippa tells us there are three ingredients."

"Three is not so many," said Elizabeth, sounding encouraged.

"And," said Polidori, smiling at us, "just last night I discovered the first of them."

"You have the first ingredient!" I cried in delight. "That truly is excellent news. Well done, sir! Do you have it here?"

"Unfortunately I do not, young master."

"Do you need us to purchase it elsewhere?" Elizabeth asked helpfully.

"There is no apothecary that will sell this," said Polidori. "Come, and I will show you."

On the table a great volume lay open. "Here it is. Look," he said, pointing to a coloured engraving.

"It is a fungus, or lichen, of some sort," I said.

"Very good," said Polidori. "A lichen. *Usnea lunaria.*"

"It is beautiful," said Elizabeth.

The engraving had been rendered with painstaking detail. The lichen was a brownish-grey, its complicated filaments delicate as lacework. I stared at the image a long time, trying to memorize its shape, colour, and texture.

"It has healing properties, then?" Henry said.

"It is a toxin," Polidori replied simply.

"A toxin?" Elizabeth said in alarm. "You mean a poison?"

"Yes, but a poison to destroy other poisons," Polidori said. And then he must have seen the uncertain look on my face, for he added, "Healing is a complicated business. To heal, sometimes we must harm the body, but hope that the overall effect is beneficial."

"It is true," Henry said to me. "I remember your father saying arsenic was sometimes administered as a curative."

"The dose is critical," Polidori said. "And Agrippa is very specific about it. Let me worry about that. Right now our first task is to procure the lichen."

"Where does it grow?" Elizabeth asked.

"It is a tree lichen," said Polidori. "I once collected it myself, but"—he waved a hand at his withered legs—"that is no longer possible."

"Where do we find it?" I asked.

"We are most fortunate. It can be found not half a day's ride from here. Throughout the year it migrates across the trunks of the tree to follow the moon. Not surprisingly, it grows at the summit of only the tallest trees."

"The tallest trees are in the Sturmwald," I said.

I knew the forest well, since it rose from the steep hills behind our chateau in Bellerive. The trees that tended to thrive there were strong, for in winter they were racked by terrible winds. Some had reached great heights, and were said to have been growing since before the time of Christ.

"I have here a map," said Polidori, producing a piece of paper so many times folded that it was almost in tatters. "I kept it, you see, in case I ever had need of the lichen again. You will see here some landmarks to help you on your way. On the actual tree where I found the lichen, I cut a blaze in the bark, but there is no guarantee it will still be seen. It was many years ago, before I lost the use of my legs."

I glanced again at his legs, and thought how I would hate to have that freedom taken from me.

"Thank you," I said, placing his map carefully inside my pocket.

"It will not be easy," he said. "Though the lichen needs the moon to live, it can only be seen on the darkest nights."

I shook my head, not understanding.

"It must be the exact same colour as the bark on which it grows," said Elizabeth, looking at the engraving.

"Exactly so," said Polidori. "Even in the moon's full glare you will not be able to discern it. But in the darkness you will see it."

"How can this be?" Henry asked.

"It exudes a very pale glow," said Polidori. "But you must make sure there is no moonlight whatsoever. That is how you will find it."

"How much must we gather?" Elizabeth asked sensibly.

Polidori passed her a glass vial padded in leather. "This should be ample."

I looked at Elizabeth and Henry in turn. "Well, it seems simple enough," I said jokingly. "We must navigate the Sturmwald in total darkness, find and climb the tallest tree, and then, at the summit, discover the lichen."

"Have you *seen* the trees of the Sturmwald?" Henry said to me. "Many don't even have branches until they are fifty feet high!"

"You will certainly need rope," the apothecary said.

"How can one climb a tree in total darkness while holding a lantern?" Henry demanded. "Two free hands are needed!"

"Dr. Polidori has done it, and we can do it too," said Elizabeth, her eyes flashing angrily at Henry.

"But your friend is right," said Polidori. "Climbing a tree at night is a tricky business. A torch would set the tree alight, and a lantern is too cumbersome. I have something that may be of even greater use."

He passed me a thick padded wallet.

"What is this?" I asked.

"The ingredients for a simple compound. I would mix it for you myself, but its potency is brief and must be used within hours of being prepared. I have written instructions inside. And it will make your nighttime journey much easier."

I saw Elizabeth and Henry look at me uneasily.

"Does this involve the devil's works in any way?" Henry asked.

Polidori laughed. "Good sir, neither the devil nor the angels have any part in my work."

"What exactly does the mixture do?" Elizabeth asked.

"It gives you," Polidori said, "the vision of the wolf."

* * *

When we returned home from the city, I was passing Dr. Murnau's rooms and saw the door to his laboratory ajar.

I stuck my head in and could see no sign of the doctor. But on a long trestle table was a great array of apparatus, and among them an open box filled with metal needles, glinting in the light. There was a whole row of them, of varying lengths. As if drawn, I stepped closer. The needles were hollow, their points more wickedly tapered than a serpent's fang.

My eyes travelled over the table to a rack that held six slim stoppered vials of ruby red blood. In shallow round glass dishes still more red fluid rested. Konrad's blood. It was everywhere.

I felt a chill. When I'd said to Elizabeth that the doctor was like a vampyre, it had been half in jest, but now I was not so sure. Why would one collect a person's blood?

"Would you like to look?" a voice said, and I jerked round with a start, to see Dr. Murnau emerging from his bedchamber, dressed for dinner.

"I am sorry for intruding, sir," I said, but his gaunt face showed no signs of anger.

"You seem a curious lad," he said. "Come here. Let me show you."

Near the window was set up an impressive microscope, the mirror angled to catch the light and illuminate the specimen. On the tray was a glass slide, with a bright red smear in the centre.

"This is Konrad's blood," I said.

"Please." With his bony finger he gestured for me to look through the eyepiece.

I lowered my face and closed one eye to peer in—

And was astounded. There was a living world before me. Rounded objects moved and collided. As I watched, some pinched in half and became two. Others clung to one another until one withered and died.

"This is all in his blood?" I said, terrified.

"Your blood wouldn't look dissimilar."

"What are they all doing?"

"Ah." He raised his eyebrows. "I'll share my thoughts with all of you tonight."

I said nothing, staring into the microscope. We were all hosts, it seemed, to countless millions of organisms, each with its own complicated intelligence.

"Fascinating, isn't it?" he said.

I nodded, still staring. The world was filled with mystery, and I wanted to discover all its secrets.

"Is his blood normal?" I asked.

"No."

I looked up at him quickly. "Can you make it so?"

"That is a matter of further investigation," he said. "And a matter for your father and me to discuss."

"Of course," I said, standing.

"In future, Victor, I'd rather you didn't enter my laboratory unless I'm here. My equipment's delicate. I'll see you at dinner," he said, and I realized I had been dismissed.

I returned to my room to dress.

"I believe that your son has a self-generated abnormality of the blood," said Dr. Murnau.

It was after dinner. William and Ernest had been taken to the nursery by Justine, and the rest of the family had retired to the west sitting room. I glanced over at Elizabeth and Henry, then Mother and Father, and could tell they were all just as eager as me to hear what the strange doctor would say next.

"Blood is an incredible substance," he explained as he accepted a glass of port from Father. "It's no simple fluid. Think of it as a liquid metropolis. Thriving with activity!"

"What kind of activity?" Mother asked.

"The blood's filled with what I call cells, Madame Frankenstein. Tiny, enclosed compartments—invisible to the naked eye—inside of which all sorts of important work is being done. The cells are like living machines that go about their work completely without our knowledge or will."

None of my tutors had ever been this excited about their subject. There was definitely something hypnotic about the way this bizarre, cadaverous doctor spoke—I was hanging on his every word, desperate to understand more about the microscopic world I'd glimpsed earlier in his laboratory.

"There are so many of these cells," he continued, "that a man could spend a lifetime observing them and still not understand them all. What I do know is this. Almost all of these cells do some vital work to keep the body healthy. Some carry nutrients. Some fight disease. Some send messages that spur other cells into action." He paused to push his glasses back up his nose. "Sometimes, though, the body, through some freak of nature, produces cells designed to destroy itself."

"Destroy itself?" murmured Elizabeth.

It was a frightening idea, to think that our own bodies could turn against us.

"In Konrad's blood," Dr. Murnau went on, "I've identified many rogue cells making mischief, and I believe these have been the cause of his wasting fever."

Making mischief. He made it sound no more serious than a children's game.

"Is there a cure?" Mother asked, her fingers tight around her goblet.

Dr. Murnau cleared his throat. "The disease is rare, but I've had some early success developing a treatment."

I noticed he did not say "cure"—but I remained silent.

"With the samples I've taken," the doctor said, "I'm hoping to produce a compound that will attack these rogue cells."

"Have you any idea how long this will take?" Father asked.

"I'll need two or three more days to prepare. As for the treatment itself, it will take place over a week, as I inject the medicine into his veins."

"Into his veins?" I asked, remembering all those needles with a shudder.

"Oh yes. It's the most direct route," said Dr. Murnau, licking his lips.

My parents looked at each other. Father took Mother's hand and nodded.

"Very well, Doctor," said Mother. "Please proceed with all possible speed."

I wondered how great my parents' confidence was in Murnau. Were they filled with hope? Or did they think his treatment no more reliable than a recipe from an alchemist's book?

* * *

Three days later, Konrad's treatment began.

Beside his bed was a metal stand. Hanging from it, upside down, was a sealed glass flask. It was filled with some manner of clear fluid—the special medicine Dr. Murnau had concocted. From the flask's rubber stopper snaked a long tube that joined a hollow-tipped needle snugly tied to my brother's forearm. The tip of the needle pricked his flesh and entered one of his veins. The liquid, through some ingenious device, dripped slowly, entering his blood gradually, minute by minute, hour by hour.

Dr. Murnau had given my brother a potent sleeping draft.

For two days, Konrad lay in bed, still and pale as death.

Tomorrow night, during the new moon, we would make our trip to the Sturmwald.

Chapter 6

STURMWALD

Inside the boathouse, where the mighty foundation of Chateau Frankenstein rose slick and black from the lake, there was a thick door reinforced with bands of iron. It was always kept locked, though long ago Konrad and Elizabeth and I had found the key, hidden within a chink in the wall.

It was late afternoon when I took the key and opened the door. The dank smell of the dungeons wafted up to me. Hundreds of years before, the captured enemies of the Frankenstein family would have been dragged here, manacled. I stepped inside, lit my lantern, and closed the door behind me.

Ten steep steps brought me down to a narrow corridor, on either side of which were six cells. The doors hung open now. I went from cell to cell, sticking my lantern inside. So near the beauty of the lake, the mountain air—yet you would hardly know it here, with only a small barred window set high into the thick stone. My lantern light picked out some writing on the wall. A name: *Guy de Montparnasse*. And not far from it, another, even fainter name. Casting my light about the cell, I saw five names—all prisoners from different times. I imagined them scratching the stone—with what? A tin spoon? A broken fingernail? A rotted tooth? Leaving some sign of themselves, like a cry to the outside world. A plea for remembrance. For a moment I felt breathless, but I forced myself to the next cell, and the next, until I found the one I sought.

My memory was correct. At the very end of the corridor was a larger cell. Perhaps for the most important prisoners. It had a crude wooden table and several chairs, and some shelves on the walls.

This would do.

On the table I set down my lantern, the wallet Polidori had given me, and a small bundle of measuring apparatus I had smuggled out of the kitchen. I needed a place where I could work in total secrecy, in case there was a spill, or a telltale odour that would alert my parents to my work.

Carefully I took out the vials of ingredients and set them in a row, then the mortar and pestle, and the set of minuscule measuring spoons. As promised, Polidori had written instructions for me.

My laboratory. I felt a curious eagerness and excitement. Never had I excelled at schoolwork. I was impatient, I was sloppy. But I had been charged with creating something and was determined to do it well.

Polidori had not lied. It was a simple concoction, and his instructions were clear. Yet I was extremely nervous. The success of our enterprise might rest on this. I measured everything twice and even thrice before adding it to the flask. And with every completed step, I felt a growing sense of satisfaction, and pride.

As I poured in the final ingredient, I started at the sound of footsteps.

"It's only me," whispered Elizabeth, and I saw the spill of her lantern light outside in the corridor before she appeared in the doorway. "Do you remember, when I was ten, you and Konrad dared me to stay here half an hour without light?"

"And you did it," I said, laughing.

"Of course," she said, entering the cell and looking at the table. "Is it done?"

"It is," I said, stoppering the flask and shaking it vigorously.

"You are very clever, Victor," she said.

"Anyone might have done it," I said, nevertheless pleased by her praise.

"What is it, exactly? This vision of the wolf."

"It is not as devilish as it sounds. Polidori explains it in his note. You remember when Father told us about the workings of the eye?"

"It is like a lens," said Elizabeth. "When it needs light, the pupil opens wider to admit it."

"Yes," I said. "But the human eye isn't accustomed to working well in the dark, not like many animals' are. So this compound lets your eyes dilate more than usual to make use of whatever starlight is available."

"It makes perfect sense," she said. "Have you tested it?"

I shook my head. "There's not enough. And we must use it sparingly, and only when necessary, for it lasts only an hour or so. And then we must not use it again for at least a month."

"Why's that?"

"Polidori says it can damage the tissues of the eye."

"It doesn't sound entirely safe," she remarked.

"He says it is, as long as we heed his instructions. How are the other preparations?"

"We are ready," she said, and gave me her report.

She and Henry had found a good measure of lightweight rope and knotted it at regular intervals so we might climb it. They had assembled lanterns and matches, water flasks and cloaks, for it promised to be cold tonight—and hidden it all at the entrance to the Sturmwald.

"There is one thing you have forgotten," she said.

"What?" I asked.

"If I am to navigate the woods in total darkness and climb a tree, I need proper clothes. Clothes they do not make for women. I will need some trousers."

"Trousers?" I said, amazed.

"You sound surprised."

"I just assumed it would be Henry and me climbing the tree."

"Oh." She nodded humbly. "Yes, I suppose that makes most sense. I can just wait at the bottom and do needlepoint by the light of the lantern—"

"Elizabeth—" I said, hearing the fire kindling in her voice.

"—or just daydream about the latest Paris fashions."

"Polidori said the tree is extremely high."

"Rather like the one I rescued you from a few years ago?"

"I'm not sure I know what you're talking about," I lied, fighting hard not to smile.

"Yes you do! The great elm in the east pasture? I can see by your face you remember!"

I remembered it exactly. Like me, Elizabeth was a keen climber of trees, and we had both gone very high. But when I looked down, I was paralyzed with fear. Elizabeth reassured me, and bullied me safely down to the ground.

"Oh, that!" I said with a dismissive wave. "I was only eleven."

"So was I. You needed me then, and you need me now. You won't get Henry up the tree anyway."

"Why not?"

"Henry? Come, Victor, he's no adventurer."

"He's very practical," I said.

Elizabeth sniffed. "A pair of your trousers should do nicely. Some breeches and a tunic of some sort."

"Yes, yes, of course," I said. "I'll bring some to your room."

"Thank you." She looked about the cell. "I am amazed you could concentrate in this place."

"I was absorbed in my work."

"Dr. Murnau seems very learned," she said. "I wonder sometimes—"

"If we are being foolish in our quest?" I said.

She nodded. "His knowledge seems so modern, and ours is ancient and—"

"Do you worry it is sinful?" I asked.

She took a breath. "No," she said firmly. "God is the Creator, and anything on this earth is here by His permission. I cannot think He minds if we use His creations—only how. For good or ill. What we seek is for good, so I will not worry about it."

I wondered if she believed herself or merely wanted to.

"I felt the power of that book." I said. "I cannot deny it."

"Let us leave this place," she said, "and get a little rest before tonight."

Fitful starlight was our only guide as we left the chateau on foot. It was near midnight. Clouds streamed across the sky, driven by an icy northerly. We skirted the village of Bellerive and climbed up through Alpine meadows toward the Sturmwald, a swath of deep blackness against the horizon.

Resting for a moment, we looked back and saw the lake and the city glimmering below us. Far away a church bell tolled one in the morning. We hurried, and before long reached the forest's edge and found the place where Elizabeth and Henry had hidden our gear.

"There will be a storm," Henry said with a shiver. Overhead, branches swayed with the wind.

I lit a lantern. It was most strange to see Elizabeth in my clothes. I was used to her in flowing dresses. My breeches, cinched tight around her waist, made me aware of her hips for the first time. And I was aware too of the tightness of the tunic across her chest. Far from making her seem more boyish, my clothes made her young womanhood all the more obvious. She had knotted her long auburn hair into a single braid.

"I do not enjoy the breeches," she said to me. "They are tight on my thighs. But it is quite wonderful to feel so light, after so many layers." She giggled as she gave a graceful pirouette. "No wonder you men manage the affairs of the world. It is far less tiring in lighter clothes!" She poked me in the chest. "I know your secret now."

"Ha," I said awkwardly. "Here." I handed her a furred cloak, and passed another to Henry before putting on my own.

"The stars will soon be gone," said Henry, peering out at the cloudy sky above the lake.

We each carried a rucksack and shouldered a coil of knotted rope. We lit two more lanterns.

I looked once more at Polidori's map. "This way," I said, venturing into the Sturmwald on a narrow path.

Among the tall trees, what little starlight remained was all but blocked. Though we each held a lantern, we could see no more than a few feet before us. We staggered on uphill. Sheathed in my belt was a dagger taken from our armoury. Having it made me feel safer.

The sound of wind was building, and all around us in the undergrowth I heard animal noises. A distant pair of eyes flashed in the glare of our lanterns, and then was gone. They were not small eyes.

"Victor," Henry said tightly, "there is an animal."

"I saw it too," said Elizabeth, and added hopefully, "perhaps a deer."

"It's long gone," I said. "Nothing will come near the light."

I said no more, but I sensed that the three of us were not alone. Some other presence kept pace with us, travelling on padded feet, its eyes capable of parting the night as easily as a curtain.

The trees grew taller. The wind moaned. The path narrowed, then seemed to disappear altogether. I paused to look again at the map.

"We should have reached a clearing by now," I muttered.

"We're lost, then," said Henry.

"These lanterns are useless," I said. "I feel trapped in their glare."

I also felt vulnerable. Everything could see me, and I could see nothing. I envied the animals their dark vision. From my pocket I took the vial I had mixed earlier.

"Is that Polidori's potion?" said Henry uneasily.

"The vision of the wolf," I said, setting down my lantern. I pulled out the stopper, tilted my head, and tapped the vial. A thick drop welled out and hit my cheek. I tried again, and this time the liquid hit me squarely in the eye. I fought the urge to blink it away, and moved to my other eye. The next drop hit home.

"Is it working?" Elizabeth asked.

"It stings," I said, and then suddenly the stinging became a searing pain. Instinctively I clenched my eyes shut. My fists flew up to scrub at them. What if I'd made the potion improperly? What if I were blinded? Fear broke free in me.

"Get me the water flask, Henry!" I cried.

"Here, here!" I heard him shout.

"I cannot see!" I bellowed.

"Give me the flask!" I heard Elizabeth tell him, and I felt her firm hand on my arm. "Stay still, Victor! Tip your head back. I will douse your eyes. Open them wide!"

I opened them wide—and abruptly the stinging stopped.

"Wait!" I said, and roughly pulled away from her. I blinked and stared about me.

The forest seemed eerily illuminated, the trunks painted silver, the earth beneath my feet glowing. Between the trees, amid the undergrowth, I caught sight of tiny animals, shrews and moles, going about their nighttime hunting. Swarms of newly hatched mosquitoes scudded like clouds above the grass. From the base of a tree, a mouse tentatively lifted its head from its nest—and higher up, an owl's head swivelled, listening, predatory.

"Victor," Elizabeth was saying, "Victor, are you all right?"

I realized I had not spoken a word for several seconds, had been looking all about me, drinking in the night with my eyes.

"Vision of the wolf," I murmured. "It works. *It works!*"

I turned toward Elizabeth, and her lantern's light sent a piercing pain through my eyes.

"It is too bright for me," I said, whirling away.

"Give me some," said Elizabeth, setting down her lantern.

"It's very painful at first," I warned her.

"I want the vision too!"

"Very well. Come close." I tipped her head back—and her lovely pale throat seemed to flash in the night. I tapped a drop into each of her hazel eyes.

"Ah!" she cried out, her hands flying to her face, just as mine had. "Water! Please, Victor, please!"

"No," I said, and held her firmly as she struggled against me, whimpering. Then she opened her eyes and grew still. She drew away from me.

"I see you as though it were merely twilight," she said.

"Yes."

For a moment we just stared at each other with our wolf eyes. She looked different somehow. Perhaps it was the fur of her collar around her throat, but she was like some lithe animal.

"Henry," I said, shielding my face from his lantern, "will you take some?"

"I will not," he replied, and I could almost smell his fear as he beheld us warily, as though we were somehow changed.

"Put out the lanterns, then," Elizabeth told him. Was her voice lower, almost hoarse, or was I imagining?

"I think it wise to keep mine lit," Henry said. "It will keep any animals at bay."

"Very well," I muttered, though I had no fear of other animals now. "Walk behind, so we are not blinded."

"There is the clearing," said Elizabeth, pointing.

Before, we might have walked right past it, but now it was obvious. I hurried through the trees and undergrowth and emerged before a vast heap of bleached bones.

I tilted my head to one side, trying to make sense of it. The hair lifted on the back of my neck. Elizabeth crouched beside me, breathing quietly. A moment later Henry's lantern light blazed off the bones, and he gave a cry. It was hard to tell what animals the bones came from, since most were so splintered and broken.

"What kind of creature could have done this?" Henry gasped.

My eyes saw some larger bones. Instinctively I sniffed. A rabbit? A wild dog? I could not tell.

"They are mostly very small," said Elizabeth decisively.

I gave a low growl as one of the bones twitched—and had a terrible image of the entire pile assembling itself into some monstrous spectre that would consume us. But almost at once I could see several small animals moving among the bones, feeding on the last of their meat and marrow.

Elizabeth chuckled softly, looking up into the glowering sky.

"Birds," she said. "*They* have made this heap. Don't you remember your father telling us about the Lammergeier? How it drops its prey onto rocks to break the bones so it can more easily get at the marrow?"

"I must have missed that lesson," said Henry. "What is a Lammergeier?"

"Bearded vulture," I murmured. "The locals call them tree griffins. They're quite large."

"Ah, excellent," said Henry. "This adventure grows more enjoyable by the second."

"Which way now?" Elizabeth asked me. A heat came off her that I found strangely distracting.

I pulled out my map. "From here there is a trail that should take us right to the tree."

She was already walking with a hunched intensity. I followed.

"Wait for me, please," said Henry. "This doesn't look like a path!"

"It's just overgrown," I said gruffly. With my wolf's eyes I could see it like a silvery river running deeper into the forest.

I loped behind Elizabeth, scarcely aware of the steep climb.

"You're going too quickly," I heard Henry say. "I'll lose you in the darkness!"

Reluctantly I slowed down. The smells of the forest were keener somehow, and I caught myself swinging my head from side to side, tasting the air, peering among the trees. My earlier feeling of being followed was more intense and—

There. A distant pair of eyes met my own as we kept pace through the Sturmwald. Perhaps it was a wolf. I was not afraid. Somehow I felt we were kin right now, aprowl in the night.

Elizabeth found the tree. On the immense trunk the X mark was still faintly visible. I looked up. The first branches were very high, maybe over fifty feet. We set down our gear at the base. I took the light rope, which I had weighted at one end as a hurling line.

Standing back from the trunk, I heaved it toward the branches. The line paid out perfectly from its coil, but then fell back. Again I threw, with all my might. I squinted, trying to follow its ascent, but not even my wolf eyes could penetrate the high gloom of the tree.

My line was still paying out.

"I think you've done it!" said Elizabeth.

"There is the weighted end!" Henry cried.

Exactly as I'd hoped, it had looped over a branch and was pulling the rope up even as it fell earthward. It hit the ground at our feet.

We tied the light line to a stouter climbing rope, and fed it up and over the branch and back to earth.

"It's a good sixty feet," said Henry as we tied the rope's end securely around the trunk. I gave it a good tug and then jumped up onto it. It held firm.

"Henry, will you climb?" I asked him.

"I would, normally, yes, if it weren't for my intense fear of heights."

"I never knew you had a fear of heights."

Queasily he looked up into the tree. "Oh, yes."

"It will inspire you! Think of the poetry you will write!"

"Ah. That is what imagination is for," he said. "So I do not have to have unpleasant experiences."

I glanced at Elizabeth. She smiled at me in a most self-satisfied way.

"Henry," I said. "I am disappointed."

"Victor, do not force him," said Elizabeth. "It's just as well to have someone on the ground in case something happens to us in the tree."

"I'll watch over you. From here," said Henry.

"Excellent plan," I said. "There may be bone-crunching predators to fend off. I'll go first."

I removed my cloak. Despite the wind, I was too hot, as though my own body were clad in fur. I began my climb, the knots in the rope giving good purchase for my hands and feet. I felt an unusual energy in my limbs, and before I knew it, I was at the branch—and a good thick one it was—and hauling myself onto it. I shuffled over toward the trunk to wait for Elizabeth.

Watching her climb, I was filled with admiration. She showed no sign of hesitation or fear and was scarcely out of breath as I helped her up onto the branch. As she panted softly, I felt a most powerful and savage pounding through my veins, and wondered if she too felt the same strange keening. I wanted to grab her by the hand and disappear into the forest. I was a wolf and she was my she-wolf, and the night belonged to us.

I tore my eyes from her and began to climb for the summit. Among the big limbs grew smaller ones that got in our way, and stabbed at my flesh. My hands were soon sticky with sap, my hair matted with needles and insects.

"How much higher?" Elizabeth asked, just below me.

"I feel the breeze," I said. "We must be close."

Then I spied, not far above my head, a thick wall of sticks and dried grasses built out from the trunk. I pointed it out to Elizabeth.

"A nest," she whispered.

It was a marvel of engineering: a huge cone shape, three feet deep, and at least six across at its top. I'd once seen a grand eagle's nest on a sheer rock face of the Salève Mountain. This nest was bigger—and it blocked our way to the tree's summit.

"Perhaps it's abandoned," I said, thinking we might climb right through it. But my answer came on a gust of wind: the rancid odour of fresh bird droppings and regurgitated meat, making me nearly gag.

From the ground Henry suddenly bellowed, "How are you? Have you reached the top?"

"Shush!" I called back to him.

Inside the nest something rustled.

"We can climb around. There, look," Elizabeth said.

"Tricky," I said. It would take us closer than I liked to the nest, and the branches were shorter and skinnier there. The wind had picked up, and it seemed to me the sky's blackness had intensified, if that was possible. I saw the faraway lights of Geneva, and then they were blotted out as great sooty strands of cloud blew toward us.

"A storm's coming," Elizabeth said.

I nodded. "We've got to be quick."

Hastily we climbed around the nest, giving it as wide a berth as possible. We were some distance from the trunk, and I missed its security. Out here on the skinnier branches there was much less to grip if we slipped.

Below: a drop of a hundred feet.

A smattering of icy rain hit my face.

"Are you all right?" I whispered to Elizabeth. "Do you wish to go down?"

"Absolutely not," she said. "Hurry now!"

We were level with the nest, and as we climbed past it, an

unearthly squawk made me freeze. I looked down and saw a head emerging over the rim.

What I saw was not an eagle.

I thought: *Griffin.*

A large, angry eye flashed, and a long, fierce beak opened. Bristling from the creature's lower jaw was some kind of dark crest. Its neck and shoulders were thick and gave the impression of immense strength. There was no colour at night, and a wolf did not see in colour anyway, not like humans. But I had the impression of bright, flaming orange fur cloaked with black feathers.

"The Lammergeier," I said.

Its wings opened and seemed to take forever to reach their full span. Eight feet, ten—I could not be sure. In the strengthening wind they billowed like feathered sails, then furled once more against the beast's body. A blow from those wings could knock us from the tree.

With false confidence I said, "It cannot see in the dark, surely."

Beyond the lake, over the mountains, the clouds were illuminated from within by a brilliant stutter of lightning, and in that split second Elizabeth and I were etched against the sky. The bearded vulture shrieked.

"I believe it has seen us now," I said.

"She will not leave her nest," whispered Elizabeth. "Her instinct will be to protect, not attack."

I was glad she'd been so attentive to my father's lectures; I remembered nothing of the sort.

Reluctantly, slowly, we made our way toward the tree's summit, not fifteen feet above the nest. I tried to ignore the vulture below, and scoured the bark for lichen.

"Here!" said Elizabeth.

On the southeast face was a small patch. Even with our wolves' vision, its glow was subtle. From my trousers I pulled the padded vial and a pair of tweezers and passed them to Elizabeth. Her nimble fingers went to work at once, scraping the lichen off the bark.

"Its grip is stubborn," she muttered.

"Do you want me to try," I asked, reaching for the tweezers.

"No!" she said fiercely.

More lightning, closer now, lit the sky. The rain came harder, and the treetop was rocking from the wind. We wrapped our legs about the trunk, holding on.

Another shriek pulled my gaze down. There was no longer just one head protruding from the nest, but two. And then—to my horror—three.

"Elizabeth," I said, as calmly as I could manage, though I fear my voice broke.

"Yes?"

"Do you have enough?"

"Not yet."

"Please hurry. There are three now."

She glanced down, gasped, and then started scraping madly at the bark. "I did read," she said, her voice shaky, "that the female will often choose two mates, and the three of them will share a nest and protect the young."

One of the vultures hopped up onto the rim of its nest, head flicking from side to side. I unsnapped the sheath of my dagger.

Not a hundred yards away a jagged shaft of lightning struck a tree, and it exploded into flame.

"We must go!" I shouted.

"The vial is not full!" she shouted back.

"It's good enough! Come on!"

She pushed the cork into the vial, and slipped it into a pocket of her breeches. I led the way down, keeping as far from the nest as possible. The vulture on the rim watched us intently, but did not move. We were exactly level with the nest. The branches were slick from the rain, and I was suddenly aware that I was squinting down to see them.

"Victor!" Elizabeth whispered in alarm. "My vision . . . !"

I looked toward her voice and was shocked that I could see her only as a shadow. I felt her hand touch my arm.

"It's wearing off," I said. "Quickly!"

But the vision left as swiftly as it had come. Suddenly I was virtually blind, a wolf no more.

I heard Elizabeth shuffle closer to me, then heard another sound. The billowing flap of a large bird's wings. A terrible stench wafted over us.

A great flash of lightning illuminated the night, and there, burned into the sky for a split second, was a bearded vulture, leering at us from the branch above.

Then pitch black again, and with the deafening sound of thunder came a stabbing pain in my hand. I swore, and tore my hand free from the vulture's beak—so quickly that I lost my balance. I flailed about and just managed to catch hold of another branch to stop me from tumbling out of the tree.

"Victor?" Elizabeth cried.

"Fine, I'm fine. Come lower!" I shouted.

Feeling my way I made it down to the next branch, and then the next, and started working back toward the trunk. I could hear Elizabeth's panting, and knew she was close by.

The storm was directly overhead now. Great javelins of lightning came one after another, and I saw things only in ghastly rain-streaked frozen images:

The vulture overhead, tensed to move lower.

Elizabeth's face, looking in horror at something beneath us.

A second vulture, hunched two branches down, beak parted in a silent shriek, for nothing could be heard above the demonic thunder. The entire tree shook, and I clung to the drenched limbs in terror.

"Victor!" Elizabeth was shouting in my ear. "There is one below us!"

"I know!" I shouted back.

"They are trying to force us off the tree!"

"Come here! Put your back against the trunk." I shifted to make space. I pulled my dagger from its sheath, then hooked my free arm tight around a branch and hoped for more lightning.

Let me see. Let me see them coming.

"Victor!" came Henry's frantic cry between thunder claps. "There's something slinking about down here!"

"Shut up and light another lantern!" I shouted back.

The storm was so close that the lightning and thunder came simultaneously, a great blinding stroke that hit the tree next to us, splintering wood and sending up a plume of smoke and flame.

Now I had my light!

And just in time—for my branch bounced and the vulture that had been below was suddenly right beside me. It flared its wings and lunged. I struck fast with my dagger, hitting it in the chest. The bird shrieked, but before I could scramble back, it swatted my arm with its wing and knocked the dagger from my grip. The weapon went spinning earthward.

From below came a hysterical cry from Henry. "Victor! Elizabeth! Something climbs the tree toward you!"

The vulture on my branch hopped closer. I bared my teeth and howled at it. And maybe there was a little of the wolf left in me, for the bird shrank back, hissing.

Elizabeth's scream made me turn. The other vulture was directly above her now, its sharp claws trying to impale her outstretched hand. Its eyes flashed, its beak opened, and in amazement I watched as Elizabeth, with her free hand, grabbed the creature and dragged it off the branch.

The vulture was so surprised that it had no time to unfurl its wings before Elizabeth sank her teeth into its throat. I didn't know who was more shocked, the vulture or me. The vulture made a most unholy sound and thrashed free. As it flailed to a higher branch, it struck me with its wing, and my foot slipped.

I fell, grabbing for anything—and the only thing nearby was the wing of the vulture on my other side. Its clawed feet sank deep into the bark, and it held tightly, and so unwittingly pulled me back from a deadly fall.

"Victor! Elizabeth!" Henry hollered again. "It comes! Look out!"

A sleek cat-like form hurtled toward me from the branches. I saw a mouthful of sharp teeth and threw up my arm to protect myself. But the jaws were not meant for me. The creature streaked past and sank its fangs into the vulture's throat, pinning it against the branch and holding it tight until the bird twitched no more.

The speckled cat finally released its grip, and the vulture's limp body slid off the branch, thudding down through the branches. The cat then turned, its maw spattered with blood, and I saw that it was Krake.

His green eyes met mine for a moment, and there was such bloodlust in them that I thought he would attack *me* next. But he did not. He glared up at the second vulture, still hovering uncertainly, and gave an ear-splitting yowl. The bird retreated at once, back toward its nest and mate.

Krake promptly stretched out on the branch and started licking himself clean.

"Krake!" gasped Elizabeth. "Good kitty!"

"Victor! Elizabeth!" Henry bellowed. "Are you all right? Tell me what's happening! I feel so *useless* down here!"

Elizabeth and I began to laugh, soaked to the skin in the rain.

"We are fine, Henry!" she called. "Krake came to our assistance!"

I looked at Elizabeth in amazement. "You bit the vulture! In the *throat*!"

She looked confused for a moment, then slowly nodded, and began laughing even harder. "It seemed—like the only—thing to do."

I could still see the savage expression on her face. It should have repelled me, but it only attracted me. I felt a powerful urge to crush her against me and drink in her heat and scent, which had been distracting me all night. My eyes settled on her mouth. I shook my head to dislodge the thought.

"What did it taste like?" I asked.

"I have no idea," she said, then wrinkled her nose and wiped her mouth, spitting. "Did I really bite it?"

I nodded. "Let's get out of this tree."

Carefully, for the tree was treacherously slippery and our limbs weak, we climbed down through the branches to the rope. Elizabeth went first, and then I, hand over hand, my body shaking. Henry was there to wrap my cloak about me as my feet touched earth. I sank down next to Elizabeth to catch my breath.

Henry seemed the most shaken of all of us. His cheeks were flushed and he paced about in the lantern light and fired questions at us.

"Sparks rained down on me from above; I feared the whole forest would ignite!" he exclaimed. "And then a wildcat was leaping for me and up the tree! I had no idea what to think! Honestly, Polidori might have told us he was sending Krake!"

The lynx landed on the earth beside us. I reached out and scratched the fur between his ears. He purred loudly. I wondered if it was Krake I'd seen, keeping pace with us through the forest. His green eyes settled on me calmly, and I knew his intelligence was not to be underestimated. Polidori had obviously trained him well, so well that he could follow us to the Sturmwald and watch over us, should we encounter danger.

"What matters is we got it," I said. "The first ingredient!"

"I just hope it's enough," said Elizabeth with a frown, pulling the vial from her pocket.

The lynx butted me gently with his head, then again more insistently. Tied around his neck was a small pouch. He looked at me expectantly. I unclasped the pouch, and inside was a handwritten note.

Dear Sir,

*I trust all went well in the Sturmwald, and that Krake
was of some assistance. I hope his presence did not
alarm you. To save you a trip to Geneva, you may
place the lichen in Krake's pouch and he will return it
to me immediately. My work on the translation continues. Come again in three days if you so please.*

Your humble servant,

Julius Polidori

I showed Elizabeth the letter.

"A strange messenger, but I'm sure most reliable," she said,
and placed the vial carefully within Krake's pouch.

Without delay, the lynx leapt into the forest, streaking back
toward Geneva and his master.

Chapter 7

MIRACULOUS TRANSFORMATIONS

I woke to the sounds of a chambermaid moving about my room. The curtains of my bed were still drawn, but I heard her opening my shutters and setting out my fresh wash-basin, and tea. I waited for the sound of her picking up my chamber pot and leaving.

But instead I heard her sit down with a contented sigh and start whistling. I frowned. What was she doing? Then I heard her pouring a cup of tea, and the clink of china as she sipped at it! We were a liberal household, but still, this was taking things a bit far!

"Are you going to lie there all day, you lazy carcass?" she asked.

Except that it wasn't a she. It was a he, and I knew the voice as well as my own.

I tore my curtains aside and stared.

Wearing a white nightshirt, my twin sat calmly in the dappled morning sunlight, sipping my tea.

"Konrad!" I exclaimed, and then felt dizzy and feared I was only dreaming. "Konrad?"

"Good heavens, Victor," he said. "You'd think you'd seen a ghost!"

He smiled, and suddenly the fearful spell was broken. I leapt off the bed and ran to him. He stood to meet me, and we threw our arms about each other.

"You are all better?" I cried.

"Much improved, anyway," he said.

Beneath his nightshirt I felt his bones. I pulled back to look at him. His face was still drawn, but his skin no longer had that papery look, and in his cheeks was a hint of colour.

"Your fever is gone," I said.

He nodded. "The good doctor's medicine seems to be working."

For a moment, just the smallest of moments, a curious thought swirled through my mind. *I* was meant to be the one to heal him, to put the Elixir of Life to his lips and watch as the colour and vigour rushed back into his body.

But then I was overcome with shame for such a petty thought, and was once more flooded with relief and sheer joy.

"Do Mother and Father know?" I asked.

"Not yet. I wanted to see you first."

"Let's go tell everyone!" I said. "Right away!"

It was indescribably wonderful to have Konrad at our table for meals, to see him dressed and walking about, to hear his laughter.

He was much thinner, and weak still, but he had a good appetite, and in no time at all, I was sure, he would be his old self again.

Every day for several hours he would need to return to his bed so that he could be pricked with Dr. Murnau's needle and have more medicine dripped into his veins. Dr. Murnau said he had to get a good deal of rest and not overexert himself.

For now it was like Christmas and everyone's birthday combined. Mother and Father seemed suddenly younger, Elizabeth's smile dimmed the sunshine, William and Ernest were giddy with excitement, and the servants fixed every single one of Konrad's favourite dishes.

In another two days Konrad's treatment was finished.

Dr. Murnau was greatly pleased with my brother's progress and made arrangements to return in three months to check on him again.

I helped the doctor pack up his laboratory. His glassware and apparatus reminded me of Mr. Polidori's, and I still wondered how different these two men were.

But I felt foolish. I'd had such grand thoughts of helping create a fantastical elixir of life. But Dr. Murnau had been methodical and scientific, and he had succeeded. As usual it seemed Father was right, and all these old books were nothing but nonsense.

"You have the fire of curiosity in you," Dr. Murnau said to me as I finished replacing the last of the flasks in their velvet casings. "Do you have an interest in the natural sciences?"

"I'm not sure," I said. "I believe I may."

"Ingolstadt has a very fine university," said the doctor. "We are always glad of keen students who can help advance our learning in chemistry and biology. Perhaps one day I will see you there."

"Perhaps," I said.

He offered me his hand. "Good luck to you, young Victor."

"Thank you, sir," I said.

The day was warm and beautiful, and Father had cancelled our morning lessons and ordered us to go out of doors and enjoy ourselves. Mother told us not to go far. We did not want to worry her—she had been through enough already—so we promised her we would stay within sight of the chateau at all times.

Moments after our boat had sailed clear of the dock, Konrad looked at Elizabeth and Henry and me, and said:

"You three have been having an adventure, I think."

We glanced at one another, and laughed.

"You lucky wretches!" Konrad said. "Tell me everything."

We enjoyed taking turns telling Konrad of our adventures: our secret visit to the Dark Library, the burned book of Agrippa, and Paracelsus's mysterious Alphabet of the Magi. We told him of Julius Polidori and his pet lynx, Krake.

"You're not inventing this!" Konrad broke in more than once, looking from Henry to Elizabeth, then to me, in bewilderment. "It seems the stuff of an overheated imagination!"

"It is all true!" I told him, laughing, and then described our nighttime escapade in the Sturmwald, the vision of the wolf, and our climb into the tallest tree during the tempest.

"You climbed the tree?" he asked Elizabeth in amazement.

"I did," she said.

Konrad looked at me and Henry severely. "Honestly, you two, what were you thinking? She might have come to harm."

Elizabeth's eyes sparked. "I'm quite capable of taking care of myself, Konrad, I can assure you."

"She bit a bearded vulture on the throat," I added.

Konrad's face flinched in revulsion. "You what?"

"You needn't have told him that bit," Elizabeth said, frowning at me.

"Well, it was very impressive," I said defensively. "*I* was very impressed."

Konrad looked astonished, so we hurried on and told him of our battle with the three Lammergeier, and how Krake had come to our rescue.

"No one could've invented this," said Konrad. "I believe it entirely!"

"It seems almost unreal now," said Elizabeth. She looked at me briefly, awkwardly, and I wondered if she was remembering how we'd gazed at each other hungrily with our wolves' eyes. My own feelings for her in the Sturmwald had been so powerful they made me blush now, and I looked away to check the trim of our mainsail.

"Anyway," Elizabeth said gaily, "it is over now. There's no point continuing, since the brilliant Dr. Murnau has put things to right."

I watched Konrad's face carefully as she said this, and suddenly my heart was like a fist, tightening in my chest.

"What is it?" I asked him quietly.

"Mother doesn't know," said Konrad, "and you must not tell her. Father doesn't think she could bear it."

"What?" said Elizabeth in alarm. "What must she bear?"

"It is not necessarily a cure," said Konrad.

"But look at you!" said Henry. "As fit as ever!"

"Dr. Murnau said it might come back." I saw my brother's eyes go to Elizabeth. "He has seen other cases where it has returned."

Henry gave a cheery chuckle. "Well, then, another dose of Dr. Murnau's famous elixir should be all you need, surely."

"He would not want to administer it again for quite some time," Konrad said. "Another dose too soon could be fatal."

"You assume the worst," Elizabeth said firmly, though she looked pale. "He said your illness might come back. *Might.*"

Konrad smiled, but it was the kind of smile a father gives children when trying to reassure them.

"Let's come about," I said, and pushed the tiller. The boom swung overhead and Konrad adjusted the foresail to our new course.

"Father should tell Mother," said Elizabeth, sounding annoyed. "It is wrong of him to keep it from her."

"You're not to say anything," said Konrad.

"Of course she can *bear* it. She's very strong. Just because she's a woman, he needn't treat her like a child."

"I agree," I said.

Konrad sighed. "He's doing her a kindness. He wants to spare her worry—most likely unnecessary worry."

I did not feel so kindly toward Dr. Murnau anymore. A doctor cured people. If a cure was not certain, was it any cure at all? For a while we said nothing, our boat skimming over the water. I watched Konrad and knew exactly what he was thinking.

"But I do believe," he said finally, "it might be a good idea to continue seeking out the Elixir of Life."

Elizabeth and Henry stared in astonishment. But I felt no surprise. I knew him as myself, and I would have made the same decision.

"Just in case," Konrad added.

"Absolutely," I agreed.

Henry looked decidedly queasy. "But we have only one of the three ingredients, and that was hard enough."

"Henry was quite sick with worry while we were up in the tree," I remarked wryly.

"You have no idea what it was like," he protested. "You two were up there with your crazy wolf eyes, and I had to keep my wits about me down on the ground and try to make sure you didn't get struck by lightning or eaten alive by a wildcat . . ."

"You did a good job stopping him, by the way," I quipped.

"It was hardest on you, really," Elizabeth agreed, and bit her lip so she wouldn't giggle.

"Oh, go ahead, have a good laugh," Henry said. "You should be grateful that at least one of us has some common sense."

"It won't be so bad, Henry," Konrad said, giving him a wink. "Now that I am well, I can help find the remaining ingredients."

The next day I came upon them in the music room.

The sound of the pianoforte had lured me there. I knew from

the song that it was Elizabeth at the keys. The door was ajar. Silent and unnoticed, I watched them. Konrad stood beside her, turning pages. As she played, he touched a stray strand of her curly hair and tucked it behind her ear, and let his hand linger on her cheek for three, four, five beats of my pounding heart. There was such tenderness on his face.

Elizabeth smiled, and the colour in her cheeks darkened to a blush. She stumbled over the notes, then lifted her hands from the keys and said something to Konrad in a low voice I could not hear.

I retreated a few steps, steeled myself, and then came whistling down the corridor before I entered the room. I pretended not to notice their surprised and embarrassed faces.

"Father is going into town tomorrow," I said. "We can go with him and see Polidori."

"Excellent," said Konrad. "I'm looking forward to meeting this fellow—and his lynx."

"You cannot come," I said.

Konrad chuckled. "Why not?"

"Polidori does not know who we are," I explained. "But if he sees the two of us, he may suspect. Most people in Geneva know Alphonse Frankenstein has twin sons. It is uncommon."

Konrad shrugged carelessly. "So what if he does?"

I shook my head in irritation. "Konrad, don't you remember? It was our father who tried him. Who ordered him never to practise alchemy again! If Polidori knows who we are, he will want nothing more to do with us."

"Even so," said my brother thoughtfully, "surely we have the advantage. He knows we can report him to Father if he refuses to help us."

"That is not a game I think we should play," I said.

"Victor is right," Elizabeth said, and I looked at her, pleased. "We cannot risk it, Konrad. We must keep our identities secret."

Konrad sniffed and looked so disappointed I almost felt sorry for him.

"It is for your own sake, you oaf," Elizabeth said, more tenderly than I liked.

"Yes, I can see that now," he said. "You are clear-headed, Victor. Thank you."

I said nothing. I could not accept his thanks with a pure heart, for I had another, selfish reason for keeping him from Polidori. The quest for the Elixir of Life had been my idea. I was in charge, and I wanted to keep it so. I wanted to be the one to shine. If Konrad walked into Polidori's laboratory, I feared we would be recognized, yes—but even more, I feared he would take command of our venture. With his natural charm and his keen, calm intelligence, it might happen in a heartbeat. And I would not stand for it.

"Good, then," I said. "We will proceed as before." I clapped Konrad heartily on the shoulder. "Don't worry. There will be plenty of adventure for you yet."

They love each other.

I'd never felt so foolish—or so betrayed. Konrad and I had never kept secrets, but he'd clutched this greedily to himself. For how long? I wondered. Why hadn't he told me?

And how was it I hadn't noticed, when I so often knew *exactly* what he was thinking?

It was as though, in one moment, he had become a stranger. And I a stranger to myself.

All my life I had wanted things: to be the smartest, and the swiftest and strongest. I'd dreamed of fame and wealth.

But looking upon Elizabeth's face, I suddenly knew there was something I wanted even more.

It took seeing them together for me to properly understand my own feelings. A lightning bolt could not have been more sudden. Watching Konrad touch her, it was like seeing myself touch her.

In the Sturmwald I had tried to ignore my feelings, told myself they were merely effects of the potion.

I am in love with Elizabeth.

Chapter 8

THE GNATHOSTOMATUS

"I wondered what had become of you," Polidori said the following morning, as he led us into his parlour. "Your brother, how does he fare?"

"He is much improved," I said.

I myself felt wretched. It had taken me forever to get to sleep, my mind twisting back again and again to Konrad and Elizabeth at the pianoforte. Konrad touching her. The heat in her cheeks. At dawn when I'd dragged myself out of bed, I felt positively battered.

"Well, that is excellent news about your brother," Polidori said. He turned in his wheelchair and smiled. "Do you wish to abandon this enterprise, then?"

His expression was calm, patient, but I noticed that Krake seemed to be watching me with great intensity.

"No," said Elizabeth. "We wish very much to continue."

"You are sure?" Polidori asked.

I nodded. "The doctor said the illness might return."

"I see. I am very sorry to hear it."

"You received the lichen, I trust," said Henry.

"Indeed. Before sunrise on the very morning."

"Is it enough?" Elizabeth asked worriedly.

"It is perfectly ample. As for the second ingredient, the translation has proved devilishly difficult. But last night I cracked it. Come."

Once more he led us down the malodorous corridor to the elevator. Krake was again made to wait beyond the threshold, a rather resentful look on his face.

"Krake is very clever," I said. "How did he manage to find us in the Sturmwald?"

Polidori began to lower us to the cellars. "Young master, did you not know that in many mythologies the lynx is known as Keeper of the Secrets of the Forest?"

My skin prickled. Some small, insistent part of me had wondered if Krake's surprising abilities could be explained by mere animal intelligence alone.

"Is that so?" I said. "Keeper of the Secrets of the Forest."

"Indeed. In medieval times there are accounts of how the lynx could dig a hole, urinate in it, cover it with dust—and in several days' time produce a gemstone. Garnet, actually. Some also thought the lynx capable of assisting in clairvoyance and divination."

The alchemist turned to me with a grin. "But all that is mere fancy, young sir."

"Ah," I said, relieved and disappointed both.

"Krake is merely very well trained. I confess that in his infancy I did feed him plants and oils that are well known to assist the mental faculties of humans. So he may be more intelligent than most of his species, but as for him finding you in the

Sturmwald, I knew you would be there on the new moon, so I let Krake out that night and told him to find you."

"Incredible," said Elizabeth. "He understands what you say!"

"Well, let's just say a lynx's sense of smell is very keen. He found you by scent."

"He saved us from some bearded vultures," Henry said.

Polidori looked over in surprise. "In the same tree as the lichen?"

"They had a nest," said Elizabeth. "Three of them."

He looked genuinely distressed. "Young lady and sirs, I am sorry your job was made so complicated. They are fearsome creatures."

"Oh, we managed it," said Henry breezily.

"I had little doubt you would," said Polidori. "Here we are."

After lighting candles about the laboratory, Polidori drew us to a desk strewn with books and quills and inkwells. This, I gathered, was where he was doing his translation. He took up a bit of parchment, squinting at it through his spectacles.

"What language is that?" I asked, peering over his shoulder.

Polidori lowered the paper with a small smile. "That is my own handwriting. But you are right. It is illegible, even to me sometimes. Now, here is the translation. There is a lengthy preamble—fear not, I won't read it—and then the thing itself that you must acquire." He looked up. "A Gnathostomatus."

"What in heaven's name is that?" Elizabeth asked.

"Gnathostomatus," I muttered, furiously dragging open the drawers of my mind, riffling through their contents, trying to remember my lessons. "It is from the Greek? Ha! *Gnathos* is 'jaw.' *Stoma,* 'mouth.' It is a group of animals—vertebrates with jaws, yes?"

I stole a look at Elizabeth, hoping to see admiration in her eyes, and was not disappointed.

Polidori nodded. "Very good. You have been taught well. Who is your teacher?"

My eyes shifted uncomfortably. "Oh, a wise old fellow hired by our parents."

"A *jawed* creature," Henry said uneasily. "It is rather vague."

"Indeed, but the text becomes more specific, you see. The creature you seek is the oldest of its lineage. It is an aquatic creature. The coelacanth. You have heard of it?"

I had indeed, and my heart contracted.

"Then our task is at an end," I murmured. "We're undone."

"Why?" Elizabeth said, turning to me in alarm. "Why do you say that, Victor?"

I gave a mirthless laugh. "Ah, this is one lecture you missed."

"The creature is extinct," said Henry, for he too had heard Father's lesson and gazed at the engraving of a fossilized specimen. It had swum with the terrible lizards, millions of years ago, but had not been seen alive for centuries.

"Surely there must be somewhere—" Elizabeth began hopefully.

"Search the world," I said. "It will not be found."

We had risked our lives in the heights of the Sturmwald to obtain the lunar lichen. How cruel that our hopes were to be dashed this easily.

"You despair too soon, young sir," said Polidori.

"How so?" I said. "Does it give an alternative ingredient?"

"It does not," said the alchemist. "But the coelacanth is *not* extinct. It is a Lazarus taxon."

This meant nothing to me, and I looked from Henry to

Elizabeth in bewilderment. To my surprise, Elizabeth was smiling.

"Victor," she said, "your Bible reading really is very poor. Lazarus was the man whom Christ raised from the dead."

"Yes," said Polidori, "'Lazarus taxon' is the name scholars have given to species that were once *thought* extinct. But then, lo and behold, one is found in the East Indies, or off the shores of Africa."

"Must we travel so far?" I said, discouraged, but already wondering how such a journey could be undertaken.

"Lake Geneva will suffice," said Polidori.

"Are you serious?" I demanded.

"Truly I am," he said. "I know a fisherman who has seen one."

"Do you trust this fellow?" Henry asked.

Polidori nodded. "And I will show you why." Quickly he wheeled his chair to a large armoire. He opened it and with both hands extracted a long glass case. Inside was a startlingly blue fish, some two feet in length, with a great many fins.

My heart leapt, and I heard Henry draw in his breath, for it was the very image of the etching Father had shown us.

"Why did you not tell us you already had one!" I exclaimed.

"Because it is of no use," Polidori told me, sharply enough that I felt rebuked. "It is dead two years. It has dried up." He tapped the parchment on his lap. "What is needed from this creature is the foul oil it exudes when alive. It renders the fish inedible. Fishermen have no use for them. But the oils from the fish's head contain nourishing and miraculous substances that are needed for the elixir."

"They live in our own lake!" cried Elizabeth, looking at me happily and grasping my hands.

"I am told they can grow to six feet in length," said Polidori. "Powerful creatures. This one of mine is small. A baby. And where there are babies, there are adults to make them."

"Let us go at once, then," said Elizabeth, "and charter a boat to trawl the waters!"

"It will not be so easy," said Polidori gravely. "When I spoke to the fisherman, he said this was the only one of its kind spotted in fifty years. They are not usually caught in nets. They live deep. They crave the cold. And the dark. You might fish for months and years without catching one."

"Then we'll go deeper," said Elizabeth with steely determination. "Where this fish lives, we will find it."

"Can we not just send Krake to get us one?" said Henry with a feeble laugh.

"There are diving bells that can take a man to great depths," I said, thinking aloud.

"That might not be necessary," said Polidori.

We all looked at him expectantly.

"These fish fear daylight so much, even the bottom of the lake is not dark enough for them. There are, I'm told, narrow fissures that lead to subterranean caves where they take refuge."

"But to find these caves underwater—" Henry began with a frown.

"Would be near impossible," I interrupted. "Unless there was another entrance from above ground."

"Just so," Polidori said. "The mountains that encircle our great lake are mazed with caves. They go deep."

"Has anyone you know made such a descent?" Elizabeth asked.

"Indeed," said Polidori. "But he's now dead."

"What happened to him?" asked Henry nervously.

"He made one too many trips into the depths," said Polidori. "He was an explorer, a mapmaker." He paused and looked at me. "But I believe his widow still lives just outside the city."

"Then we must pay her a visit," I said.

Polidori escorted us back upstairs, and as we were departing his shop, he called me back. "Young sir, a word, if I might."

Elizabeth and Henry waited for me outside in the alley.

"I'm not ignorant of the fact that these are difficult tasks," Polidori said kindly. "And I know my help is limited. But I do have something that might, shall we say, brighten an underground descent."

"Thank you very much," I said, curious to know what it was.

"You created the vision of the wolf successfully, yes?"

"I did."

"I had little doubt."

He seemed to be looking deep into me. I couldn't help feeling he was pleased by what he saw. "And I'm guessing that alongside Agrippa and Paracelsus, you might have some other books of a practical nature within your reach."

I looked at him, wondering if he were going to ask for them.

"If so," he said, "you might want to consult Eisenstein. If you care to try your skills once more."

Once more into the Dark Library in the witching hour.

I'd tried to sleep, but every time I closed my eyes I saw Elizabeth, and imagined it was me and not Konrad touching her. I'd stroke her cheek, and then bend to kiss her full mouth . . . and I couldn't bear it anymore, so I'd hurriedly got out of bed, needing to distract my mind—and glad I had some work to throw myself into.

In the library I spent nearly an hour peering at dusty volumes, until I found the right one, a slim green book with only the red initial *E* tooled in the spine.

Ludvidicus Eisenstein.

To my great relief the text was written in English. I began turning the gossamer-like pages, not exactly sure what I was looking for. My eyes skimmed the headings, surprised by how banal they were:

> The Testing of Ores
> The Properties of Dyes
> Ideal Temperatures at which to Fire Ceramics
> Preparing Saltpetre
> A Lover's Elixir

My eyes lingered on the page, dancing down the list of ingredients. But I forced myself onward, and shortly came to a page headed: "Preparation of the Flameless Fire."

I read on. This must be what Polidori had meant for me to find. An unquenchable source of light in the darkness. He had singled me out. He sensed I had a special aptitude, that I could create this substance on my own.

Imagine the look on Konrad's face when he beheld it.

Imagine Elizabeth's admiration.

I slipped the book under my robe, returned to my bedchamber, and slept deeply.

I am a thief.

In the afternoon Elizabeth left Konrad a secret note—and I stole it.

By sheer chance I was passing by the library, and through the leaded glass in the door I saw her drop a bit of folded paper into the Oriental vase. Just as she turned to look furtively about, I moved quickly past the window. I hurried down the hallway, rounded a corner and waited until I heard her shut the door behind her. Her footsteps faded.

I returned to the library. At the vase's bottom was the note.

It was not for me, but I scooped it out and slid it into my pocket.

I did not read it at once, for I felt stricken with guilt. But as I changed for dinner, curiosity and jealousy got the better of me. I unfolded the paper.

It said, *Will you meet me at midnight in the library?*

Later I lay sleeplessly in my bed. The church bells tolled eleven. I did not know what I should do.

I lie. I know exactly what I shall do.

I saw her dark form by the window, looking out over the lake. She had no candle with her, and the moon and stars were veiled by cloud, so the room was very dark.

Through my veins I felt the same animal desire I'd had for her in the Sturmwald, when we were both wolves. I went to her. We were shadows to each other. I could not even see her eyes. I felt her warm hand take mine, and my heart quickened.

"I had a dream last night," she said, "of our wedding night."

I chuckled like Konrad to disguise my shock. Already they were talking of marriage? How long had I been so idiotically blind?

"Tell me," I whispered, and stroked her hair. I had seen Konrad do it, so I could do it too. As children, I had touched Elizabeth's hair many times, yanking mostly. But this was the first time I had *caressed* it. Her amber mane was so soft—and yet so thick and curly. It had a spirit and wildness to it—a perfect complement to her personality.

"How old were we?" I dared to ask, hoping my voice was not so different from Konrad's. I needn't have worried. She wanted and expected Konrad, and so that was who she had before her. I hardly felt myself. In the dark I could be whoever I wanted.

"Not so much older than now," Elizabeth whispered. "Perhaps twenty."

In the darkness I blushed to think of our wedding night, and the pleasure it would hold. But then my thoughts soured, for it was not to be *my* wedding. I should have been glad to imagine Konrad, alive and fully recovered from his illness. But the thought of *him* wedded to Elizabeth was horrible to me. And her next words only amplified my wretchedness.

"I've never felt such joy as in that dream," she said. "Everything was so clear. The inside of the chapel. The light streaming through the stained glass. My dress. I could describe every detail—but don't worry. I know that would bore you to tears. Victor was your best man, and Mother and Father were there, and Henry, Ernest, and little William. I saw it all, as vivid as a painting, and *felt* it all, as though I truly lived it.

"But there was something else." She sounded troubled now. I felt her other hand touch mine, and this one was icy.

"As we stood on the altar, before we were to be joined forever, my joy was poisoned by a terrible sense of dread. And I heard a voice . . ." Her words trailed off.

"It's all right," I murmured. "If it upsets you, don't speak of it."

"It was a most malignant voice, one I have never heard, and it said, *I shall be with you on your wedding night.*"

I shivered at the words, so full of menace were they.

She leaned her head against my chest. "You're so healthy now. I can't believe you would ever be otherwise. You must live. It would kill me if—"

"Shh. Don't think of it. But," I added daringly, "feel free to think of our wedding night."

"Konrad!" she whispered with a gasp.

I knew it was a risk, but I could not resist her any longer. With my hand I cupped her chin and tilted her face toward me. In the darkness, as if by perfect instinct, our lips met. Light blazed behind my eyes. I shook with passion, and was all the more surprised by the fervour with which her lips moved against mine.

She had done this before.

She and Konrad had done this before.

Even though I was stealing someone else's passion, I wanted more of it—but then my jealousy overmastered me and Elizabeth drew back with a gasp.

"What is it?" I whispered, but I knew what I'd done.

"You bit me!" she said.

"I was . . . in too much of a passion. Elizabeth, I'm so sorry. Is the skin broken?"

I knew the answer to that, too, for I had the faint iron tang of blood in my mouth. And as wicked as it was, I rejoiced at its delicious taste. I had her blood inside me. The blood of my beloved.

"Here, take my handkerchief," I said hoarsely.

Her fingers touched my face, questioningly, and I took a step back.

"Konrad?" she said, as though she wasn't altogether sure.

"Who else would it be?" I said, trying to sound a little annoyed. "But we should part. I still feel depleted."

"Yes, of course, take your rest. I'll wait here a little longer, in case one of the servants might see us together."

I gave her hand one last squeeze and swiftly left the library, hurrying down the dimly lit passage to my bedchamber.

At breakfast next morning I sat down opposite Konrad, and had just started my meal when Elizabeth swept into the room.

"You must have dropped this, Victor," she said casually. As she passed my chair, she tossed a handkerchief into my lap. On it was a blot of her blood.

And beside it, my monogram: *V.F.*

What a fool I'd been.

She knew.

She did not meet my gaze the entire meal.

But I did not regret for one second stealing that kiss.

Chapter 9

THEFT

After lunch Henry and I set out on horseback for Cologny, the small village outside of Geneva where the map-maker's widow lived.

I was most relieved to be away from the chateau—and from Konrad and Elizabeth. I didn't think she had told Konrad about my midnight trickery. Certainly he'd seemed completely natural with me all morning—unless he was a better actor than I thought. Had he done the same thing to me, I would have been volcanic with fury.

The day was sunny but cool, and it was very pleasant to be astride my horse, trotting along the roadway, side by side with Henry. To our right sparkled the lake, alive with sailing vessels bringing freight and passengers to and from Geneva.

"How does it come to you, your poetry?" I asked Henry.

He looked across at me. "You've never shown any interest in my scribbling before."

"I'm curious. Where does it come from?"

He looked off into the distance, frowning. "Small things,

often. A vista. A feeling. A longing. It struggles to be described, to be captured."

I had no shortage of feelings, and usually no problem expressing them—not to those closest to me. So how could my true feelings for Elizabeth have lain dormant for so long? Was it that she'd been raised as my sister, and so I had suffocated any romantic thoughts I'd had for her? But she was not my sister. She was not even a first cousin, but some distant relation. So why had I not allowed my feelings for her to blossom? Konrad had had no such trouble.

I turned back to Henry. "And you can write about anything?"

"Anything I care about."

"Love?"

He laughed. "Love!"

I shrugged. "Just by way of example. Yes, words and phrases that would describe love. That would, um, impress a young lady."

Henry sighed. "Good Lord. You are not in love with her as well, are you?"

"I'm sure I don't know who you mean!"

"You are a terrible liar, Victor. Miss Elizabeth Lavenza perhaps?"

"Her? Good heavens, no. A fine girl, of course, but—" I blew air out of my cheeks. "The tongue on her. She would wear any man out within ten minutes. I'd rather hear a dog bark than her voice."

"Is that so," said Henry, sounding utterly unconvinced.

"What did you mean when you said, 'You are not in love with her *as well*'?"

"She is a wonder," Henry admitted frankly. "It's impossible

to know her and not love her. I've long suspected Konrad does as well."

I shook my head. All around me, everyone was in love—and me without a clue! What kind of imbecile was I?

"You've never spoken to her of your feelings?" I asked, jabbed by jealousy once more. I'd often thought that these two had a great deal in common, with their pennish ways. When they'd collaborated on our play, they had spent a great deal of time together, words and laughter ricocheting between them, eager ink staining their fingers and hands.

"No," said Henry. "And I trust you will keep it secret. She would never have me. I have no delusions. Around her I feel like a pale, feeble moth. It's all I can do to avoid her flame."

"You really do have a poet's tongue, Henry," I said in admiration. "Would you, you know . . ."

"What?"

"Scribble a few lines for me?"

He looked at me, askance. "You wish me to *scribble* you some declarations of love?"

"Just a few little things. You're a genius, Henry," I said, warming to my cause, "and no one has your talent with words. Just five of your words could make the sunset itself pause."

He frowned. "That is not bad, you know," he said thoughtfully. "Maybe something like, 'Your beauty would make the sunset itself pause.'"

"Ha! You see!" I cried. "You have the gift! I could never have done that myself."

"You very nearly did," he said.

"No, 'twas you, my friend! I knew you wouldn't disappoint me! You genius!"

"You flatter me," he said. "I don't dislike it."

"You put Shakespeare to shame. Just two or three more baubles like that, and I'm forever in your debt. I know how easily these things trip from your tongue. You don't mind, do you?"

"I will see what I can do," he said with some reluctance.

"You're a true friend, Henry. Thank you."

We were in the village by this time, and I looked about for the widow's cottage Polidori had described.

"Is it that one there?" Henry asked, pointing.

It was a mean place indeed, surrounded by a dismal yard with chickens, goats, and a pig.

We dismounted and tied up our horses.

"Now, remember our plan," I said to Henry.

We had dressed smartly, for we had wanted to look as credible as possible.

I knocked on the cottage door. A dog barked from within; a baby squalled. The door opened, and filling nearly the entire frame was a large woman whose face wore an impatient scowl.

"Can I help you?"

"Madame Temerlin, I presume," I said.

"Not anymore I'm not," she said, and sniffed. "Madame Trottier it is now."

Henry consulted the notebook he'd brought as a prop. "Ah, yes, I see that notation here. Forgive me. But you were once the wife of the late Marcel Temerlin, were you not?"

"I was," she said guardedly.

Henry and I looked at each other and smiled.

"Well, that is excellent news," I said. "We understand that your late husband was a very talented maker of maps."

"Who sent you?" she demanded.

Henry and I had agreed ahead of time that we would not mention Polidori.

"We're acting on behalf of the city archives, madame," I said, playing my part. "The magistrates have ordered a complete geographical survey of the Republic, and have sent emissaries like ourselves to collect any materials that might prove of historical or practical use."

Seeing her hesitate I took a purse from my pocket and made sure it jingled nicely. "We're authorized to pay a fair sum for any materials we deem appropriate."

"They're in a trunk in the barn," she said. "I almost burned them when he died, I was so distraught."

"It must have been a terrible loss," I said.

"Leaving me with three little ones . . ."

"The hardship must have been—"

"Would've liked to strangle him myself." She turned and called, "Ilse, watch the baby!"

She led us through the yard to the barn. Judging by the smell, it needed a good mucking out. Near the back, in a closet below the hayloft, she showed us a small battered trunk. She opened the lid. Inside were a number of mildewed notebooks.

Henry and I made a show of paging through them quickly, muttering vague remarks to each other.

"I think these will all be of great interest to the archives," I said.

"Indeed," said Henry.

"He was always running damn fool errands for that witch doctor, Polidori," said the woman darkly.

"I don't believe we know him," said Henry innocently.

"Had him looking for minerals and moulds in the caves.

Then my husband got it into his head that there was diamonds or gold or both down under the mountains." Her eyes narrowed. "You're not mixed up with this Polidori, are you?"

"Goodness me, no," said Henry. "Our interest is purely archival."

For a moment her scowl disappeared, and she looked at Henry and me with a mother's concern.

"You've not got some scheme in mind, have you? To go exploring?"

"We are merely messengers, madame," I said, and to avoid her eyes I started to count out silver coins from my purse. "We would like to take all these maps, if you're agreeable."

"They're yours to take."

She watched the coins as I pressed them into her palm. I did not like the look and smell of poverty about her home, and I gave her more than I needed to.

"That's very decent of you, young sir," she said, but with some reluctance still. "I just hope you've not got some fool notions like my late husband. Those caves kill. That's all they do."

"Thank you, madame," I said. "Thank you very much indeed."

We loaded the notebooks into our saddlebags, and she watched us from the door of her cottage as we rode off.

We did not speak for several minutes. Henry looked uneasy.

"Do you think it was Polidori who sent him to his death?" he said.

"That is overly dramatic. It sounds as if he rendered some services for Polidori, but then undertook his own adventures."

"The point is, the caves are dangerous," Henry said.

"But we will not be exploring. We will only follow his map to the pools. We know exactly what we're looking for. We will find it and return."

I urged my horse to a canter and headed for home.

"What about this one here?" said Konrad.

Elizabeth, Henry, and I were in his bedchamber after dinner, and we'd spent the last two hours on the floor, poring over Temerlin's yellowing notebooks and maps by flickering candlelight. Temerlin had been an energetic man. It seemed there were very few caves, paths, cracks, and crevasses he had not explored.

Konrad had unfolded a large map from within one of the notebooks. We came closer with our candles.

It was a wonder, almost frightening, for it looked like the intricate scribblings of a very methodical madman. A single passage quickly became many, and while most of the turnings and intersections were very clear, sometimes the lines of ink trailed into nothingness like the wanderings of an unhealthy mind.

"I suppose those were the tunnels he never explored to the end," said Henry, touching some of these ghostly fadings-out.

"The opening here," said Konrad, "is in the foothills, not far to the northeast of us. Isn't that where Polidori said the entrance would be?"

I nodded, and for a moment we were silent as our eyes travelled these endless underground byways, awed by the vast hidden maze within our mountains.

"The general direction of the tunnels *does* seem to work northwest, toward the shores of the lake," said Elizabeth excitedly.

"Look here," I cried. "A pool!"

The chamber was clearly marked with wavy lines of blue ink. Crudely drawn among them was a fish.

"We have our map!" said Elizabeth.

"Let's just hope it truly is a map," said Konrad, "and not some invented doodlings."

I glanced at Elizabeth, hoping she'd see this remark as a show of cowardice.

"Don't come if you have misgivings," I said.

I paged through the scribbled notes in the book that contained the map. "It seems he made a most detailed chronicle of this exploration. It shouldn't be hard to plot our route."

"And then we will draw up a list of gear we'll need," Konrad said.

"I've already begun." I felt very pleased with myself. I would have to be vigilant if I wanted to keep control of this quest. From my pocket I drew out a small notebook.

Konrad laughed. "How can you know what we'll need when we've only just discovered our route?"

I smiled. "We're descending deep beneath the earth to catch a fish. Our gear is obvious. We'll need lanterns, water, and food to keep our strength up. There will doubtless be holes and crevasses. We'll need good rope. Mountaineering gear."

"Mountaineering gear!" exclaimed Henry.

"There may be steep drops," said Konrad wisely.

"Chalk to mark our route so we can return," I added.

"Very sensible," said Elizabeth. "Or a ball of string like Theseus in the Minotaur's maze?"

"String snaps," I said.

"Chalk can be wiped away," countered Konrad.

"You're assuming there's someone down there," I said, "who wishes us harm."

"Victor, don't joke," said Elizabeth. "You've made me shiver."

"And me," said Henry.

"I'm not joking," I said. "We'll also need our fishing rods and tackle. And weapons."

"Weapons?" said Konrad. "To catch a fish?"

"Maybe. But a fish may not be the only thing we encounter in the depths. We were surprised in the Sturmwald, and I won't be surprised again."

We shortly bade Konrad good-night. Henry went one way to his bedchamber, and Elizabeth and I went the other. Together we walked silently down the corridor. All day she had virtually ignored me, and I could stand it no longer.

"You haven't told Konrad about our nighttime tryst," I whispered.

"That was no tryst," Elizabeth replied tartly. "That was a deception. And you should be grateful I told him nothing of your shameful behaviour. You conducted yourself like a scoundrel, but even so, I don't want to harm the brotherly love you have for each other."

I felt a moment's pang of remorse, but at least now her eyes were on me—her beautiful hazel eyes. I did not understand it, but her angry face and words made me all the more attracted to her.

"And I hope that you say nothing of it either," she added.

"Of course not," I said. With a thrill of excitement I realized we had a secret. "Perhaps you didn't tell him because you enjoyed our kiss," I said daringly.

Her eyes narrowed. "You took what was not yours, Victor."

She turned away, but I caught her by the hand. "I'm sorry," I said. "It's just—I could not help myself."

She paused, her back still to me.

"I don't understand myself anymore," I said haltingly. "This feeling I have for you . . ."

When she turned around, her face was kind. "Victor," she said, "you must not fall in love with me. I love Konrad."

"For how long?" I demanded.

"I don't know," she said thoughtfully. "Half a year. Maybe longer."

"Why Konrad and not me?" I blurted, and instantly felt like a childish fool.

She raised her eyebrows in surprise.

I muttered, "We're the same, after all."

She laughed lightly. "You are *not* the same."

"Last night you couldn't tell one from the other!"

"Your appearance maybe, in complete darkness. But your natures are very different."

"How so?" I asked, anxious to know how she saw me.

She sighed. "You are rash and headstrong, and arrogant."

"Not always," I said, more humbly now. "Surely not."

Her voice softened a little. "No. Not always. But there is a passion in you that scares me."

"I thought women craved passion," I said. "I read it in a novel, I think."

She moved closer and took both my hands. "Victor, you will always have my fondest love—"

"As a *brother*. Yes, I know," I said scathingly. "I'm not interested in that sort of love."

"Well, I am," she said. "And you should be too. It is a precious thing."

I snorted. "Please don't insult me."

She shook her head, looking genuinely pained.

I stormed on. "If I can't have all your love, I want none of it."

"I cannot control your will, Victor," she said, and I saw a flare of her own wildcat fury. "Only you can do that. And I wonder sometimes if you have the discipline to do so."

"Wait, don't leave," I said.

But this time she did not stop, and left me alone in the corridor, the portraits of my ancestors looking down on me severely; all but one.

"What are you smiling at, Happy Hans Frankenstein," I muttered, and slouched toward my bedchamber.

Measuring thus much, and no more. Grinding the ingredients to a fine powder. Finding the hottest part of the flame. Watching the powder liquefy and change colour. Watching matter transmute.

The noxious odours sharpened my concentration, and minutes and hours dissolved, so intent was I in my work. Never had I achieved this kind of focus with my schoolwork.

It was also a welcome escape. Down here in my dungeon laboratory beneath the boathouse, I could purge Elizabeth from my thoughts. I'd spent a great deal of the past two days here, following Eisenstein's instructions to create the flameless fire. With success so close at hand, I already felt a thrill of accomplishment.

I did not hear the footsteps until they were almost at my door. In dismay I whirled. There was nothing I could do to conceal my work. Mixing vessels and bubbling flasks and all kinds of other apparatus covered the table. And I myself, in my shirt with its sleeves rolled back, my brow sooty—I must have looked half mad.

Konrad walked into view, holding his hand over his nose.

"What on earth is that diabolical smell?"

I exhaled. "Thank goodness. I thought it was Father."

"You're lucky he and Mother are still out."

"Can you smell it in the house?" I asked in alarm.

"No. I only caught a whiff of it from the dock." He came closer. "So this is where you've been disappearing the last few days. What are you up to?"

"Something to help us when we explore the caves."

I had wanted to surprise everyone, and now that my relief was spent, I felt a twin stab of irritation and disappointment.

"Is this all . . . urine?" Konrad asked, gazing at several buckets on the floor.

"Yes."

"I see. Yours?"

"Well, not all of it, obviously," I replied. "Most of it comes from the horses."

"Awfully considerate of them to give it to you."

He looked at me and smiled. I smiled back. Then he began to laugh, and I could not stop myself from following his lead. It was heedless, uncontrollable laughter, and even as I enjoyed it, it reminded me how little laughter Konrad and I had shared in the past month. But this—this was *fun* as we used to have it.

I went to him and hugged him tight. "Do you think me mad?"

He wiped his eyes. "Not yet. Tell me what you're doing."

"Well," I said, "first it was necessary to boil the urine to a paste."

"Of course." He put his hands behind his back and surveyed my table like a pompous tutor.

It was difficult not to start laughing again.

"And after that I needed to transmute the paste into gaseous form—"

"Gaseous form! Excellent!" he said. "I like what you've done with these little glass curlicues, by the way."

"They allow me to pass the gas through water to create— well, I don't want to tell you yet. But you'll be amazed."

"No doubt. Where did you learn all this?"

"Eisenstein," I said, pointing to the green book on the table.

"That is from the Dark Library too, is it?"

I nodded.

"Let's just hope Father isn't checking the shelves. How can you bear the smell?"

"I'd stopped noticing."

"Come on. You need some fresh air, little brother. Henry and I want to go for a row on the lake. Your company is requested."

Looking at him smiling upon me, my guilt was sharp. I had stolen his kiss from Elizabeth. I had harboured jealous and stingy thoughts. I was indeed a scoundrel.

"Soon," I promised. "I'm nearly finished. Ready the boat, and I'll join you in half an hour."

"But is he strong enough yet?" Mother asked worriedly the next day at lunch.

We had just told our parents of our plan to go riding in the foothills.

Father looked at Konrad, who was eating his sausage and potato rosti with great enthusiasm. "Look at him, Caroline. He blooms with health. I see no reason why they shouldn't have their outing tomorrow."

Konrad truly did look well. He'd regained almost all of his lost weight, and his face was no longer gaunt.

"It won't be arduous," I said, pouring myself some more cider. "We only mean to do some fishing, wander in the hills, and have a leisurely picnic."

"And it will be Henry's last day with us," Konrad reminded them, for Mr. Clerval had returned from his journey. "Our goodbye celebration."

"And if Konrad becomes too tired," said Elizabeth, "he can recline on a blanket like a sultan and we will feed him grapes and fan him."

Mother sighed. "Very well, as long as you promise to return before sunset. Henry, you are the most level-headed of these three. I charge you with everyone's safe return."

"I give you my word, Madame Frankenstein," said Henry.

"Thank you, Mother," said Konrad. "And now, to prove my fitness, I will trounce Victor in fencing."

"Do not count on it," I said.

* * *

"A hit!" said Konrad.

"Your point," I panted as we retreated to our starting positions. It was not a formal fencing match this time, just the two of us in the armoury. Konrad had wanted a single bout—his first since his illness—to see what kind of shape he was in. And damn him, he was in the lead! Three hits to my two.

"*En garde!*" I said, readying my foil.

"*Allez!*" said Konrad, and we circled each other.

It was my attack, and I watched him like a falcon, knowing I needed three more hits if I were to win.

"You are very good, Victor," Konrad said.

"Without my usual partner I'm out of practice," I replied.

I remembered our last match. My victory against him had really been a lie, since he'd been sick.

"There's something I must tell you," Konrad said. "It's given me a guilty conscience, keeping it from you so long. You and I shouldn't keep secrets."

"What's your secret?" I was glad my face was concealed.

"I am in love with Elizabeth."

"You are?" I let my foil drop, as though surprised, and then lunged. He parried weakly, and left himself wide open for my riposte. I struck him in the belly.

"Nicely done," he said, retreating.

Now we were tied.

"Did you know?" he asked as we stepped back and prepared to resume the bout.

"I had an inkling," I said guardedly. "And does she return your feelings?"

"Entirely."

His single word delivered a sharper stab than any foil.

"But how . . . *when* did this happen?" I still couldn't understand how I could have been so ignorant of this.

"Sundays, when I take her to Mass."

I nodded. Over the years, that would have given them ample time alone.

Hurt barbed my next comment. "But it's strange, don't you think? She's grown up with us as a sister . . ."

"But she is not our sister, just a distant cousin."

"True, but doesn't it seem just a touch . . . unsavoury to you?"

We watched each other warily, foils at the ready.

"Not in the least," he said. "*En garde.*"

"I wonder how Mother and Father will feel about it," I mused.

"Oh, I think Mother knows perfectly well how Elizabeth and I feel about one another."

"You've told *her*—and not *me!*" I exclaimed, genuinely hurt.

He lunged, and I quickly parried.

"She could tell," Konrad said. "I didn't need to confide in her. And she was very happy about it. She said it had long been her wish, and Father's, that Elizabeth would one day be a bride to one of us, and be forever part of our family."

"You mean to marry at sixteen?" I exclaimed.

"When we're older, of course."

"From what I've heard," I said, "youthful passions are often fleeting. You may both feel differently in a few years."

"Listen to you—he who has *never* been in love!"

"How do you know?" I said coldly.

Our blades clashed, and before Konrad could retreat, I had struck his jacket.

"A hit," I said.

"You are filled with fire," he said. "Well done."

We backed away from each other once more, puffing.

"So, *have* you been in love?" Konrad wanted to know. "With whom? Out with it!"

"That's my business."

"We don't keep secrets, you and I."

"You've kept yours," I said. "And for quite some time."

"Well, a few months perhaps, no more."

That was not what Elizabeth had told me, but I said nothing. I was not quite that reckless, not yet.

"One of us," I murmured.

"What?"

"You said it was Mother's wish that Elizabeth marry *one* of us. Wasn't that right?"

"Yes. Why?"

"So she wasn't picky about which one?"

Konrad dropped his guard for a moment, but was quick enough to parry when I lunged.

"What if," I panted, "you and I were to love the same person? What if I loved Elizabeth too?"

We circled warily.

"But you don't."

"Pretend I do."

He shrugged. "It would be a disappointment to you. Because she loves me."

In my temper I lunged clumsily. He knocked my blade to the side and hit me.

"A point," he said. "We are tied. *En garde.*"

"*Allez!*" I said. "Are you so sure she could love only you? That you're so much better than me?"

"Victor, I didn't say that."

"But you *think* it."

"Why are you so angry?"

"Because people will always love you best," I said. "You are . . . a more *charming* person. No doubt kinder too."

He laughed. "I've never thought so." Backward and forward we tested each other.

"You do not really love Elizabeth, do you?" he said.

"No," I lied.

Konrad lunged and scored his winning hit, right on my heart.

He sighed, lifting his mask. "That is a relief. A fine bout. But I am still out of shape. We must do this more often."

My brother had kept a secret from me, and now I would keep one from him.

I will have Elizabeth as my own.

Chapter 10

THE DESCENT

"Someone should stay behind with the horses," said Konrad.

Despite Temerlin's careful map, it had taken us a good half hour to find the entrance to the cave in the foothills. It was a man-size cleft in a rocky outcropping, partly hidden behind shrubs. The four of us dismounted and started to unload the gear from our saddlebags.

"The horses can take care of themselves," Elizabeth said. "We'll hobble them, and they can graze. I saw a creek just over there where they can drink."

"I think you should stay with the horses," said Konrad.

I smiled to myself, knowing what was coming.

"I'll do no such thing," she said indignantly. "Victor knows how capable I am."

"I'll vouch for it a hundred times over," I said.

"I didn't say you weren't—" Konrad began.

"Then please don't insult me by suggesting I shouldn't come. *You* stay with the horses if you like."

"I will stay with them," said Henry, eyeing the cave opening with some horror. "There is the small matter of my claustrophobia."

I looked at Henry. "I didn't know you suffered from that affliction as well."

"Oh, yes," he said. "Quite badly. In combination with my fear of heights and my general excess of imagination, it creates a veritable typhoon of fear."

"A very nice turn of phrase," said Elizabeth, filling her pack.

"Thank you," said Henry. "In any event you'll want someone out here in case you get lost and need rescuing. I brought some books to read."

"An excellent idea," I said, thumping him on the shoulder. "Write some poetry too while you wait."

"Indeed," he said, inspecting his pocket watch. "It is now nine in the morning. In order to reach the chateau before sundown, you will need to be back here no later than six o'clock."

"Nine hours," I said. "More than enough time for a stroll and a bit of fishing, eh, Konrad?"

"Don't be surprised if we're back before lunch, Henry," he said, shouldering his rucksack.

"Be careful," said Henry, as I buckled on my scabbard. Just knowing my sabre was at my hip made me feel armoured, invincible.

"Konrad, you have your clock?" Henry asked.

"Of course," he said, nodding at me. "We both do."

We passed through the opening, and in that one step, summer evaporated. An ancient cold emanated from the stone. We'd done well in dressing warmly. The cave was large, and clearly no stranger to humans. Near the entrance the remnants of campfires were scattered about, and pictures and names scratched on the stone walls. There was the whiff of urine and animal scat.

"Is your pack too heavy?" Konrad asked Elizabeth.

"I'll manage," she said.

Mine was certainly heavier than I would have liked. Outside, when Konrad and I had divided up the gear, we'd made sure that our two packs were the weightiest.

Elizabeth set hers down and, without preamble, pulled her skirt off over her boots. Beneath she wore a pair of pantaloons.

She caught me staring at her. "You didn't think I was going to go caving in a dress, did you?"

"Of course not. Very sensible," I said, hoping she couldn't see the heat in my cheeks.

Konrad made to light the lanterns.

"Wait," I said. "We may not need them."

I'd been looking forward to this moment. From my rucksack I took a sealed glass container. Inside was neither oil nor wick, just a fist-size lump of dull white matter.

"What is that?" Elizabeth asked.

"Behold," I said, "the flameless fire!"

I opened a small vent in the side of the container, and at once the white matter began to glow green, dimly at first, but then with greater intensity, casting a ghostly light about the cave.

Elizabeth gasped, drawing closer. "How does it do that? It does not burn."

"Nor give off heat. It needs only a bit of oxygen to glow." I sealed off the vent, and still the lump gave off its green light.

"How did you make this?" she demanded. "It's miraculous."

"Polidori told me where I could find the recipe."

"You are turning into an accomplished alchemist, Victor," she said, but I wasn't sure her remark was entirely complimentary. "Its glow is unsettling."

"Not at all," I replied. "It's merely one of earth's elements. Phosphorous."

"Very impressive," said Konrad. "But I think, for exploring, our lanterns are still better."

On point of pride I was about to protest, but I could see he was right. The lantern flames would be much brighter.

"I never meant for us to use it the whole time," I lied. "It is in case our lanterns run out—or get wet." I carefully replaced the container in its protective case.

Our three lanterns lit, I led the way to the back of the cave, Temerlin's map in my hand. There were three tunnels.

"This is ours," I said, nodding at the middle one.

With white chalk Elizabeth clearly marked the corner, and we started down the gentle slope. I took a quick glance back, at the gash of daylight from the cave mouth, and then squinted ahead into the lantern's glow.

We were lucky. The tunnels might have been mud, but they were stone, and high ceilinged, and we were able to walk all three of us abreast—for now, at least.

After ten minutes the passage opened out.

"Here's the second cave." The ceiling slanted lower here, and we stooped as we entered.

I glanced at the map.

The hole was exactly where it was supposed to be. It gaped in the middle of the floor, a misshapen smile.

We crouched near the edge. A mountaineering spike jutted from the ground.

"Temerlin's?" Elizabeth said.

"Must be," I said, gripping it and testing its strength. "Still solid."

"You don't think he died down here, do you?" she said.

I must confess, gooseflesh erupted across my neck. "Wouldn't his rope still be here, then?" I said, which I thought was reasonable enough.

"He died elsewhere," said Konrad calmly. "Or presumably we would not have his map."

"Quite right," said Elizabeth with relief.

From his rucksack Konrad pulled out a hammer and a fresh mountaineering spike. "Best to use our own, don't you think?" he said to me.

"Of course." I readied the rope—the same knotted line we'd used in the Sturmwald. According to Temerlin's notes, the hole was a sixty-five-foot vertical drop, hardly more than what we'd undertaken in the vulture's tree.

I allowed Konrad to drive his spike into the rock, and then I did a second one nearby for good measure. I had been reading up on mountaineering lore—Father's library really did have a book on everything—and proceeded to feed the rope through both spikes and tie a knot that would only get tighter the more weight was put on it.

"Don't you need to fold the bitter end over once more?" Konrad asked, watching me carefully.

I looked up in annoyance.

"You're doing the Alpine bowline, yes?" he asked.

"Naturally," I said. Obviously he'd read the same book. I was hardly surprised, but I was irritated now, for I'd lost my concentration and had to undo the knot and make it over.

"That's it," said Konrad.

"I know it is," I said.

We tied a lantern to the end of the line and lowered it carefully. Hand over hand I counted out the length, and true to Temerlin's word, the lantern touched down after sixty-five feet.

I went first, climbing down knot by knot, away from one lantern's light toward the next. I paused to take a look about me. It was no narrow shaft but a huge cathedral of stone into which I descended. In the gloom I beheld great jagged walls of sparkling damp rock, sculpted into columns and deep niches like secret chapels. In places, green fungus shone like tarnished bronze.

When I touched down, I realized I was atop a tall pedestal of staggered stones, its giant steps leading to the cavern floor.

I cupped my hands round my mouth and called up, "Safe and sound!" Immediately my shout was amplified and echoed about by the strange walls into something unrecognizable and a bit frightening.

I untied the lantern, and Konrad drew the rope back up so that he could lower down our gear. After that, Elizabeth made her descent, and then my brother.

I took a last look at our rope, our one and only way out. And then we started down the giant steps. Each was a good four feet high, and, off balance with our heavy packs, we lowered ourselves carefully.

"It is a marvel of nature," breathed Elizabeth, holding high her lantern and gazing about. I noticed that she shivered.

Before I could say anything, Konrad asked, "Are you warm enough?"

"I am, thank you," she said.

The chill had certainly deepened. "Best to keep moving," I said, and consulted the map once more. "That is our way, here."

Elizabeth marked our route with chalk. This tunnel was narrower and we had to walk in single file now, heads bowed. At every intersection I paused to look at the map, and Elizabeth made sure to chalk our choice.

We proceeded slowly, for the floor was often uneven, and sometimes dropped suddenly by a foot or two. I was also worried about missing a turn. Mostly the intersections were obvious, but other times the new passages were little more than clefts in the stone, easily hidden in the shadows. Temerlin's map lacked a good sense of scale, so I was often surprised by how quickly we reached certain intersections—or how long it took us to reach others.

"What time is it?" I asked.

"Half past ten," said Konrad, to my surprise.

An hour and a half already! We paused to drink from our flasks and swallow some food, but I can't say I felt much hunger.

"How deep do you think we are?" Elizabeth asked.

"Impossible to say," Konrad replied.

We continued on, always downward. I was starting to feel the weight of my pack, and regretted how much gear we'd brought. Konrad, however, had uttered no word of complaint, so neither would I. I kept my eyes fixed on the tunnel's right wall, for our next turn would be there.

"Shall I navigate?" Konrad asked quietly.

"No, I have the knack of it now," I said curtly.

My turn finally came, and with it the sound of flowing water.

"Excellent," I said. "Temerlin mentions this. A rivulet flowing down one of the walls."

With every step the sound of water grew—and it became more obvious this was no mere rivulet. Mist sparkled in the light of our lanterns. And then suddenly the tunnel widened, and down one side ran a cataract.

"It's a proper waterfall!" said Konrad.

The sight of it made my heart glad—it was wonderful to see such vital energy in this dead rocky place. I was relieved, too, for it meant the map was true and I had not misled us.

"It must be summer meltwater from the glaciers," remarked Elizabeth. "It has been unseasonably warm lately. But . . . how are we to get across?"

The waterfall itself did not block our way—but the chasm into which it plunged did. I edged closer and looked down. The lantern light did not penetrate far, and I wondered just how deep it was. From below came a dim roar. On the other side of this chasm, our tunnel continued.

I swallowed and muttered, "Temerlin said it was no more than a little jump."

"This is more than a little jump," Konrad said.

I found the place in the notebook. "'A short *vigorous* jump.'"

"He must have been very vigorous," said Elizabeth.

"It's not such a great distance," I said. "Five feet?"

"Six," said Konrad.

"Don't go so close," Elizabeth said to him, clutching his arm as he peered over the edge. "The stone's wet. It might be slippery."

"I should have thought to bring a plank," I muttered.

"You couldn't have known from Temerlin's notes," said Elizabeth kindly.

"Still," said my brother, "if you'd shared this with us, we might have been better prepared."

We looked at each other a moment, saying nothing.

"We have a choice," he said now. "We can turn back and get some kind of bridge—or we jump."

We were all silent. I could tell no one liked the idea of turning back, me especially. We had already spent at least two hours underground. If we turned back, there could be no hope of completing our quest within the day.

"Let us jump!" said Elizabeth.

Konrad looked at her in surprise. "You're sure?"

"I'm a good jumper," she said.

It was true enough. She'd grown up with us and had chased and been chased in endless games.

"If she can bite a vulture, she can jump a crack," I said.

"We have some lightweight line," Konrad said. "We'll hammer an anchor into the stone, and tether each jumper—just in case."

We struck the spike deep into the tunnel floor and fastened to it a good length of rope. The other end we looped into a kind of harness that each of us would wear during our jump.

I would go first. I removed my pack, tightened the harness below my armpits, and backed up. I ran for it. I made sure to push off well before the edge, and sailed over the crevasse, blinking through the waterfall's spray. I saw the tunnel floor coming and knew I had made it. I hit the other side, skidding a bit.

"Excellent!" called out Konrad.

"A good foot to spare," I said as I removed the harness.

I coiled it and threw it back across. Konrad tossed me a lantern, which I relit so the next jumpers could better judge their landing site.

Elizabeth was ready now. She took a good long run. As she jumped, I caught my breath, for her arc seemed too low. Konrad, I saw, watched tensely, his hands encircling the line, prepared to grip. Elizabeth's eyes were fixed on me with fierce concentration. She touched down, just, on the rim of the tunnel.

"Ha! Made it!" she said with satisfaction.

And on the slick stone, her feet went right out beneath her.

"Elizabeth!" Konrad cried.

She toppled back toward the chasm. In a second I had both hands around her forearm, pulling her to me with all my strength. I crashed to the floor with her atop me. For a few moments she just lay there panting, her breath hot in my ear. I held her tighter. I did not want to let go.

"Thank you, Victor," she said, sitting up and rubbing at her bloodied knees. She sounded more angry than grateful. "You've saved my life."

"Perhaps you'll forgive me, then," I whispered.

"Are you all right?" Konrad called out.

"Yes, it was a close thing, though," said Elizabeth.

Konrad threw across the rest of our gear before making his own jump. His landing went well.

It wasn't until he was taking off his harness that Elizabeth burst into tears. Konrad enfolded her in his arms.

He looked at me over her shoulder. "We should not have brought her. It is too much. We were foolish and selfish."

Elizabeth pushed free of his embrace, and her wet eyes now blazed.

"I've had a bad fright, and a cry—yes, tears come more easily to young women than men perhaps—but now I'm done, and I'm ready to carry on." She wiped at her eyes. "Which way now?" she asked, her voice steady.

And so we continued on.

We went farther. We went deeper. My clock told me it was nearing noon.

Our tunnel gradually contracted, and we had to crawl single file, dragging our packs behind us. I felt a new sympathy for Henry. I had never before been bothered by small spaces, but this rat's maze threatened to rob me of breath.

"Did Temerlin make any mention of this?" Konrad asked behind me.

"Nothing. Maybe he was too busy blinking dust out of his eyes."

"You're sure we are on the right path?"

I gazed again at the map. "I'm sure of it. I've missed no turn."

Konrad sighed. "Then, on we go."

A sense of responsibility crushed down against me, as powerfully as the stone. I could not let myself be wrong. But after a few more minutes, as if to confirm my worst fears, the walls of our tunnel shrank even tighter.

I stopped.

"Is it a dead end?" Konrad asked.

"Not quite."

I pressed myself tight against one side of the tunnel so he might see the slit in the rock directly before us.

I stuck my lantern through. "It widens quickly on the other side," I reported.

"But can we *reach* the other side?" he asked.

"How could a grown man have fit through there?" Elizabeth demanded when she saw the opening.

"Temerlin must've been very thin," I said. I would not voice my fear, but it beat wildly in my chest.

"I'll have a try," said Konrad. "If I can do it, you can do it."

I did not argue with him this time. There was something about the gash that terrified me.

"And if you two can do it," Elizabeth said, "I will surely have no problem."

We both watched as Konrad tried to push and twist and fold his body through the gap. It seemed he would never fit, and then, suddenly, he was on the other side.

"It's not so bad!" he called back to us. "Hand me a lantern, Victor, and come."

"I'm coming," I said, and sipped some water from my flask, willing my stomach to stop churning.

There was only one spot wide enough for my head, and I had to twist it most unnaturally to push it through.

"It's like . . . being born again," I gasped as I narrowed my shoulders and tried to ease them past the bony contraction of rock.

I could not. I tried to fold myself even tighter, shoved with my feet. I hated to think of the spectacle I must be making to Elizabeth, my feet scrabbling, bottom waggling. But my embarrassment quickly became panic.

"I'm stuck!" I said.

"You can do it," Konrad said. "Our bodies are the same."

"*You* have lost weight," I said. "You're skinnier!"

I felt a sudden crazed anger in me. I was an animal snared in a trap. Konrad had tricked me! He had lured me into this!

"I can't move!" I bellowed. "I can't breathe!"

"Be calm, Victor," I heard Elizabeth say behind me. "We will ease you through."

My left arm was pinned tight, and my right flailed about uselessly. I was helpless as a newborn. There was sudden warmth around my hips and I wondered in horror if I'd wet myself. Then I felt Elizabeth's hands around my waist.

"What're you doing?" I cried out.

"Applying grease," she said.

"You brought *grease?*"

"For just such a thing. I found a very informative book on cave exploration in your father's library. Now, Konrad, can you pull?"

Konrad seized my upper right arm, and I felt Elizabeth shoving from behind.

"Now!" she said. "Pull him, Konrad!"

For a moment I didn't budge, then suddenly shot forward, tumbling upon my brother in a heap. As we disentangled ourselves, I began to laugh hysterically in relief.

"Are you all right?" he asked me.

"I feel wonderful," I gasped. "Who wouldn't?"

"You maniac," he said, but soon we were both laughing uncontrollably.

"When you boys are quite finished . . ." Elizabeth said, passing our gear through the opening. Then she eased her slim figure effortlessly through.

We sat for a moment, putting our things to rights, eating some of the food we'd brought.

"It's strange," Konrad said, chuckling, "because Mother always said I was born easily, but you took your time."

"Two minutes only," I objected.

Elizabeth shook her head. "No. You got stuck."

Both Konrad and I looked at her in surprise.

"Really, Elizabeth," he said, "this is a rather indelicate subject for a young—"

"Honestly, Konrad, don't be such a prude," she said.

"Did I really get stuck?" I asked her.

"Boys never remember these stories properly," she said with a sniff. "Girls do because we know it awaits us. You," she said, looking at me sternly, "nearly killed your mother."

"She never told me—"

"You were all twisted the wrong way, and the midwife nearly wasn't able to get you turned round properly."

I nodded mutely. Glancing back at the opening I felt a chill that had nothing to do with the underground cold. I was very glad to see that up ahead the tunnel enlarged.

"Let's continue on," I said, eager to leave behind the subject of my awkward and life-threatening birth. I didn't care for this image of myself as a wailing baby—nor did I want Elizabeth to think of me so.

Down and down. Gradually the ceiling lifted. We crouched, then hunched, then stood tall and stretched, groaning in relief.

"Which way now?" Konrad asked, for our tunnel suddenly branched into three. The first angled gently upward, the other two downward—one of them quite steeply. I looked at the map, sickened. There was no such branching indicated.

"There's only one passage marked here," I mumbled.

Konrad stepped closer. "Perhaps you're reading it incorrectly."

I pointed at the spot where we should have been.

"We're lost," said Konrad. "You should've let me help navigate."

"You mean take over entirely," I snapped.

"Two sets of eyes are better than one."

"My eyes are quite capable of reading a map, Konrad!"

"You have been too greedy with it, Victor," said Elizabeth quietly. "You might have let us share the responsibility."

This stung deepest. Humiliation and jealousy choked my voice. "You think him a better leader, do you?"

"I did not say that."

Konrad snorted. "It's this pigheadedness that's got us lost."

I shoved him hard against the wall—my twin who, mere weeks ago, had been bedridden with fever. He lost his balance and fell.

"Victor!" I heard Elizabeth cry above the pounding in my ears.

Immediately I was overcome with regret and reached out to help him to his feet. "Are you all ri—?"

He grabbed me by the arm and shoulder and hurled me against the wall, then stood before me, glowering, his fists raised. I clenched mine, ready to spring.

"Stop it!" shouted Elizabeth. "Both of you, stop!"

There was such authority in her voice that we both turned to look at her.

"Don't you dare put this venture at risk!" she said.

Konrad sighed heavily and dropped his fists. "This venture is at an end. We must turn back."

"Turn back?" I exclaimed.

"To continue on without a map would be madness."

"Elizabeth can mark our every turn with chalk!"

"Shush!" she said.

"Do not shush me!" I shouted.

"I hear something!" she said.

We listened. From far, far away came a low murmur. For a skin-prickling moment it sounded like people whispering.

"Water," said Elizabeth.

Konrad nodded. "But from where?"

He moved a ways down each of the tunnels in turn.

"I think it must be this one," Konrad said at the threshold of the ascending passage.

"No, it is this one," said Elizabeth, standing at the steepest downward-sloping tunnel. "The sound is clearest here. Victor, what do you say?"

I tried all three tunnels. It was virtually impossible to decide, for I thought I heard the whisper of water everywhere now.

"I don't know," I said, defeated.

"I do," said Elizabeth. "This way our pool awaits."

Konrad looked at her, then at me.

I nodded. "I trust her."

"Very well. We can always turn back if we find nothing. Mark the turn, Elizabeth."

Triumphantly she chalked the stone. "You are lucky to have my ears along with you."

"We're lucky to have *all* of you along," said Konrad, and won a chuckle from her.

I wished I had the quick wit to make such flirtatious compliments.

We started down the tunnel and the lapping sound grew stronger.

"You see?" Elizabeth said. "I was right."

Quite suddenly the tunnel angled sharply upward.

"The floor is damp here," Konrad said.

I ran my fingers along the slick stone. "The walls too."

For some minutes we walked uphill, puffing. Then the tunnel levelled off and opened out onto the sloped rocky shore of a vast pool.

"We found it!" Elizabeth exclaimed.

Its surface was not glassy smooth, as I'd imagined, but slowly aswirl, as though in the grips of many hidden currents.

"I can't see the bottom," Konrad said, holding his lantern out.

"The light!" I said, remembering. "Trim your wicks. We don't want to scare away the coelacanth!"

As our lanterns faded, a new light dawned in the cave, for the walls and low ceiling were glazed with some kind of strange mineral that emitted a purplish twilight.

"I wonder how deep it is," I whispered, looking at the black water. Was it fed by the lake alone, or was there also an even deeper source, fed by the waterfall? As I gazed at the pool's surface, a portion of it shimmered, and a blue silhouette moved beneath it, its scales sparkling in the half-light.

"That's him," I breathed. "The coelacanth!"

It was but a quick glimpse, and then the creature disappeared into the depths. We looked at one another, smiling. We had done it. We'd descended the caves and found the pool, and now all that was left was to catch the fish itself!

"I got no proper sense of his size," said Konrad.

"It was too fast," I agreed.

"He was a marvellous dark blue," whispered Elizabeth. "Did you see those white markings?"

Hurriedly Konrad and I assembled our rods and tackle. Earlier this morning when William and Earnest had seen us with our gear, they'd eagerly started to hunt the garden for worms. They hadn't realized we'd need more substantial bait for what we sought. According to Polidori, the coelacanth ate other fish, things as big as small squids. But we'd let our younger brothers proudly present us with their pail of worms, and promised to bring them back our prize. We'd brought heavy line, for we knew from Polidori's specimen that these fish grew large.

We baited our hooks with the pickerel we'd bought from a local fishmonger after setting off from the chateau. Then we cast into different sections of the pool and stood back, paying out our weighted lines. Down and down and down they went, until I was afraid we would run out of line before we hit bottom.

"A hundred feet at least," said Konrad finally, reeling back in a little.

"Will he eat?" whispered Elizabeth. "What if he's satisfied his hunger already?'

"He won't resist such easy food," I murmured confidently.

But as the minutes ticked by, I was not so sure. Maybe this creature didn't care for pickerel. Water lapped at the toes of my boots, and I shuffled back a few steps.

Suddenly my rod gave a jerk and the line raced out.

"He's taken it!" I cried.

"Don't try to stop him yet!" Konrad cautioned.

I watched where my line entered the water. The coelacanth was moving swiftly, spiralling lower in the pool.

"He'll have all my line before long!" I said, eyeing my reel nervously.

Ever so slightly I increased the drag, and needed to lean back with all my weight. I didn't like to ask for help, but I had no choice.

"I'll need you to hold me, both of you," I said. "He's too powerful!"

"Coming!" said Konrad, and—

At that very moment the tip of his own rod dipped low, and his reel spun furiously.

Our lines, I noticed, were angled in exactly the same direction.

"He's taken both our hooks!" cried Konrad.

I felt the strain on my rod lighten. This was good news indeed.

"He has the two of us to contend with now!" I said.

"The Frankenstein boys will bring him in!" hooted Konrad. "Let him tire himself."

"Good, good!" I said, feeling a surge of exhilaration. I was not thinking about Elizabeth or my jealousy—only working with my twin.

"I think he begins to slow," said Konrad after a few minutes.

"Gently now," I said, and we both increased the drag on our reels. My feet felt wet, and when I glanced down, once again I saw that water was lapping against them.

"Konrad," I said, my pulse quickening. "The water's rising."

"What?" He glanced over at me in confusion, then down at his boots, wet to the ankle.

I realized that we'd unknowingly backed up very close to the cavern's wall. There was not much more room to retreat.

"The pool must be filling from beneath," Elizabeth said. "That waterfall . . ." She hurried to pull back our packs and keep them dry.

"We don't have much time," said Konrad. "It rises quickly."

"If it overflows the ledge," said Elizabeth, "it will begin to fill the tunnel."

"Temerlin made no mention of this," I muttered. But I remembered the wet floor and walls as we'd approached. This was no rare occurrence.

"We'll have the fish any moment," I said, leaning back to test its strength. "Definitely he tires," agreed Konrad.

"There he is!" cried Elizabeth, pointing.

Once again the blue form shimmered below the surface, but this time he actually broke it for a moment—and for the first time we saw his full size. I swallowed.

"He's seven feet!"

"We'll have him, though!" said Konrad. "His fight's gone. Let's reel in!"

All at once the coelacanth flashed out of sight, Konrad's line snapped, and the full power of the fish was in my hands. Instinctively, foolishly, I gripped my rod tighter, and was instantly yanked off the rocky ledge. I hurtled some twenty feet through the air, and then crashed into the pool.

The cold was like a hammer blow. It was all I could do to keep my head above the water and fill my lungs with air. I felt like a ship trapped in ice, slowly being crushed. The fishing rod was long gone from my hands. I was dimly aware of my name being called, voices echoing everywhere. My clothes and boots were heavy with water. Sluggishly I turned to face the shore, the lanterns, Konrad and Elizabeth.

I tried to kick, but my legs hardly moved. Were they so numb already? Then I felt a painful tightening around them, and realized they were bound together by loops of fishing line, cinched by the circling coelacanth. I dragged my sodden arms through the water, my legs lashing up and down like a fish tail.

"Victor! Stay still!" cried Elizabeth.

"What?" I gasped through my chattering teeth.

"It will think you're a squid! They eat squids!"

I looked around in terror. And then, suddenly, it shot past me, not a foot away. Its length was one thing, but its width was even more worrying. How much could it swallow? It seemed to take forever to pass—and then it began to circle.

"Konrad!" I shouted. "My sabre!"

I saw him scramble through my gear and grab the sword. He threw it. The blade flashed in the lantern light, and I caught the hilt in my cold claw of a hand.

"I'm coming, Victor!" he cried.

He was kicking off his boots, stripping down to his shirt. He snatched up his own sabre.

The coelacanth plowed past, so close it grazed me, its jagged scales rasping against my clothing—and possibly my flesh, but I was so cold I felt nothing. Twice I stabbed at it with my sword, and was dismayed when the blade deflected off as though from armour. The fish's muscular flank swatted me. My head went under. I lost my grip on the sword. I choked on the cold water, and came up spluttering, weaponless.

The fish was coming straight at me now, its mouth wide, and wider still. It did not have many teeth, but those it had were very sharp. I flailed at it with my feet, trying to kick it away. With its head it batted my legs effortlessly to one side and then came at my torso.

Before I could raise my fist to pound its head, it took my entire arm into its mouth. Its teeth closed around my biceps, not tearing, not gnawing, just gripping. I screamed in pain. Against my hand and forearm its fleshy maw contracted and sucked, trying to drag me in deeper.

I heard a splash, and seconds later, Konrad surfaced beside me, like some Greek hero, his face alabaster and fierce with cold. In his hand was his sabre.

"It has me!" I cried.

I tried again to drag my arm out, but its teeth were sunk into my flesh and every movement was agony. With my free hand I punched and pummelled the fish's head, but it seemed to feel nothing. Its throat sucked and spasmed wetly around my arm.

Konrad struck the coelacanth. His first two hits were deflected, but the third went deep. And yet the blade seemed to have no effect on the brute. Konrad yanked his sword out and drew back his arm for another strike.

"Where should I aim?" he cried out.

"Its eye!" yelled Elizabeth from the shore.

"Watch my arm!" I hollered at my twin, for fear he'd impale me. "Hurry!"

"Stay still!"

"I can't stay still!" I roared. "It's *eating* my arm!"

Konrad drove his sabre into the fish's right eye. It thrashed violently and its mouth opened. I yanked my numb arm clear.

Konrad struck once more with his blade, a brilliant upward thrust through the roof of the creature's gaping mouth and into its tiny brain. The fish gave a spasm and then was still, rolling over onto its side.

"Come, let's get you back."

Konrad helped drag me to the shore, and then turned back to retrieve the fish. Elizabeth pulled my body onto the ledge, which was now completely submerged under several inches of water.

My arms and legs were almost too cold to bend. Elizabeth helped me to my feet. Luckily she'd found a deep ledge several feet up the wall where she'd jammed our packs. From one, she now pulled a dry blanket.

"Take your shirt off!" she ordered me.

My numb fingers could not manage the buttons, so she started to undo them. I stared at her, mesmerized by her beauty. Then, in exasperation, she just ripped the entire sodden shirt from my chest.

I saw her gaze fly to my right arm, and I looked too. I'd actually forgotten my injury, for the cold numbed all pain. There were three blue triangular gashes where the coelacanth's teeth had pierced and held me. The surrounding skin was blanched white, but even as I watched, the colour began to return, and with it, the wounds slowly welled with blood.

She put the blanket around my shoulders. "Dry off," she told me.

From her pack she produced bandages and a bottle of antiseptic unguent, which she applied on my wounds before wrapping the cloth tightly around my arm. I was shivering violently now.

She came close and hugged me, rubbing my back and shoulders.

"I like this," I murmured, teeth chattering.

Konrad reached the shore, gasping with exertion, dragging the fish. It took all three of us to wrestle its seven-foot bulk onto the ledge.

"We did it!" Konrad said, grasping me by the shoulders.

"I was just the bait," I said.

"The water's overflowing down the tunnel! We need to go!" Elizabeth said in alarm.

There was no question of bringing the entire fish. Polidori had said the head was more than adequate, and so Konrad began to hack at it with his sabre.

"Hurry!" Elizabeth cried.

Finally he severed the head, wrapped it tightly in oilcloth, and crammed it into his rucksack.

We turned up the wicks of our lanterns and made all haste, for the water was up to our knees now. When the tunnel angled downward, the water pushed hard against our legs and, after a few minutes, our waists.

"No," breathed Konrad, peering into the distance.

Then I saw. At the tunnel's lowest point, before it tilted sharply up, the water was nearing the ceiling. We were being cut off.

"Run!" I shouted.

It was impossible to run, loaded down as we were, up to our armpits in water. Elizabeth tripped and nearly disappeared under the surface, her lantern snuffed out instantly. With my good arm I grabbed her and dragged her back to her feet. Ahead the tunnel was all but sealed. We slogged on with all our strength and speed, the icy water at our necks, spilling down our collars.

Konrad and I held our lanterns high. We had but seconds before our heads would be covered.

"We must get through!" Konrad cried. "It's only a few yards until the passage slopes up again on the other side!"

"The water's current will speed us!" I said. "Go, go *now*!" The water was at my mouth.

"Hold hands!" Elizabeth cried, grasping for us.

Our lanterns fizzled out, and the darkness was more intense than anything I'd ever known. I gulped air and went under, half swimming, half trudging, still clutching my lantern. My hand slipped from Elizabeth's. The glacial water churned and pushed at me—and my greatest fear was that I'd get turned around, and die in the flood.

Was the tunnel floor rising now? It was hard to tell in the darkness and crushing cold. I forged ahead until I had no more breath, and then pushed up, slapping about with my hands. Water. More water, and then—

Air! Was it air?

My head came up and I gasped. I wallowed ahead, water still up to my shoulders and rising fast.

"Konrad? Elizabeth?"

"Here!" came my brother's voice. "Elizabeth?"

There was a splash, and coughing. "Victor! Konrad!"

"We're all here," said Konrad, and I felt hands against me, each of us reaching out for the others.

"Forward!" I cried. "The water's still coming!"

"Up ahead," panted Konrad, "at the intersection, there's another downward tunnel—"

"—and the water will take that course," I finished.

We slogged uphill, soaking cold and leaden with exhaustion. But we could not slow, for the flood was always at our armpits or necks. I fought for every step, every breath. We called out to one another, just to make sure we were all still there, all alive.

The water was at my waist, then my calves, and then, suddenly, it gave me a last final push and I staggered and fell onto wet stone. On all fours I crawled until the floor beneath me was dry.

"This way!" I called out.

"Are we all here?" Konrad shouted.

"Light the lanterns!" cried Elizabeth.

"It's no use," came my twin's voice. "The wicks are sodden. Victor—"

"Half a moment," I said, fumbling in my rucksack. My hands grasped the wet case, and I carefully slid out the glass container. At once the tunnel was bathed in a green glow.

"We're glad . . . of the flameless fire now . . . are we not?" I said to Konrad, my teeth chattering.

"Glad indeed," he said.

"You're a genius, Victor!" said Elizabeth, and her words warmed me.

Behind us I saw the water, still welling up from the tunnel, curving round in a frothing serpentine torrent to plunge down the other descending passage. For a moment we all sat there and watched, numb and exhausted.

"The light is wonderful," said Elizabeth, "but did any of you think to bring a change of clothes?"

Miserably I shook my head, as did Konrad. How could we not have thought of such a thing?

"In that caving book I found," Elizabeth said, shuddering, "it said the most common cause of death was getting wet and cold. So I packed a waterproof pouch and put in a change of clothes for myself—and you two as well."

"Elizabeth—" I said, and was rendered speechless by my gratitude and admiration.

"Thank you," gasped Konrad.

"Now," she said, rooting around in her rucksack and producing dry clothing for us, "strip off your wet things. Get as dry as you can before putting on the fresh ones." She looked at us impatiently. "Get on it with it! I won't peek, and you two mustn't either."

She turned her back on us and went down the tunnel a ways to change.

Shivering, I stripped, trying to mop the water off my skin. In the green light I looked like some shrivelled goblin. As frigid as I was, it took a good deal of willpower not to turn my head and take a quick peek at Elizabeth.

"It's a pity we can't have a fire to warm up," she said when we were all changed.

"We must get to the surface as quickly as we can," I said.

Even in the dry clothes I was cold. And our boots were still sodden, but there was nothing we could do about that.

"What time is it?" Elizabeth asked.

Konrad fished about in his pocket and dragged out his clock. "The face is shattered. Yours, Victor?"

When I retrieved mine, I saw that the glass was filled with

water and the hands motionless at three o'clock. I showed it to my brother.

"Coming on four, then," he said.

"It took us three hours to get down here," I said, "and that was downhill, and when we were rested."

"Let's go," said Elizabeth. "Our exertion will warm us. And your fabulous green light will make sure we don't miss my markings."

We silently began our march. I couldn't have talked if I'd wanted to, my teeth chattered violently. Every so often we forced ourselves to eat some soggy food and drink cold water from our flasks.

One foot after the other. I did not know if I was slowly warming, or getting number still. I wasn't sure what I felt—until I was suddenly on my knees, Elizabeth beside me.

"His wound's bleeding badly," she said to Konrad.

"It's nothing," I said.

"You nearly fainted, Victor." She was pulling bandages from her pack and removing the old bloodstained one. She dressed my wound once more, and I stood.

"Are you all right?" Konrad asked me.

"Let's just get out of here," I said.

Time did not exist down here. Ancient rock, ancient fish. I would not have been surprised if a century had passed above ground. I might have been sleepwalking, even as I squeezed once more through the tunnel's birth canal and jumped again over the waterfall's chasm. And then more walking.

We had our coelacanth head. That was what I kept telling myself as we carried on, dragging our bodies up from the bowels of the earth. That was all that kept me going.

When we reached the cave with our rope, I nearly cried—with gratitude and despair both, for I feared I did not have the strength to make that final climb. I sat down on the lowest step of the stone pedestal to catch my breath.

"Victor! Elizabeth! Konrad!"

The voice came from overhead, and with it the blaze of a torch.

"Henry?" I called. "Henry!"

I peered up and saw his face leaning over the hole. It was impossible to imagine a more welcome sight.

"You have been so long!" he called down. "It's almost nine o'clock! I was near demented with worry!"

"We're here, Henry," said Konrad. "Triumphantly here. Give us a hand, and we will all be up in a minute!"

Chapter 11

HOUSE ARREST

We sent Henry straight back to Geneva with the coelacanth head. The city gates closed at ten o'clock, and he had little time to lose. I wanted it delivered to Polidori's house as soon as possible.

We'd told our parents that Henry would likely return straight home after our outing, so they wouldn't think it strange when we arrived back at the chateau without him. The three of us made our way with all haste, for the light was quickly failing, and we knew that our parents would be worried—and likely furious.

"There will be questions," I said when we approached the stables, slowing our horses to a trot. "We must tell them as little as possible. We are wet because we fell into the water while fishing."

"We have no fish to show for ourselves," said Elizabeth.

"I should've thought of that," I said. "But it can't be helped now. We fished for the sport of it. We're late because we lost track of the time."

"Most important of all," said Konrad, "we do not mention anything about Polidori or our quest."

192

Mother and Father must have been listening for our horses, for they were in the courtyard scarcely before we had dismounted. On seeing us, Mother burst into tears and scolded, even as she embraced us. Her abundant grief made me feel ashamed for the first time.

We handed off our horses to the grooms and were ushered inside.

"You have worried your poor mother to distraction, and me as well," Father said angrily.

When I removed my riding furs, Mother gasped. "Victor, your arm!"

I looked to see the bloom of blood on my shirt. "A small wound, really," I said, glad of the chance to appear brave before Elizabeth.

"We must call for Dr. Lesage," Mother said.

"We won't be able to reach him until morning," said Father. "I will tend to it." To Schultz, our butler, he said, "Konrad and Elizabeth will need warm baths drawn at once. Give them each a small glass of brandy. And have bed warmers between their sheets, please."

"Very good, Master Frankenstein," said Schultz.

I watched as my brother and Elizabeth were led off, meekly as little children, to their separate baths.

My father turned to me. "Come to my study." Mother made to accompany us, but my father caught her eye and shook his head.

Inside his study he sat me at the great oak desk and told me to remove my shirt. I did so, and he unwound the bandages.

"You have been bitten," he said calmly.

I cleared my throat. "Yes," I said. "It was a fish. A large one."

Father took a valise from a cupboard and withdrew from it a clean white cloth, which he spread over the desk. Next he set out bundles of cotton batting, a packet of needles, and a spool of thread. I always knew that Father's knowledge was impressive but had not known he was also capable of simple surgery.

At the side table he filled a tumbler with brandy, and placed it on the desk near me.

"You may wish to fortify yourself," he said.

"I am fine," I said, my mouth dry.

"Very well. Hold out your arm."

He took a clear flask, unstoppered it, and poured a small amount of liquid directly into each of my wounds. It was worse than being bitten. The pain pierced my arm through and through, and I cried out.

"Alcohol to disinfect," my father said, "before we suture." He began to thread a needle. "What possessed you to go underground?"

"Underground?" I croaked, truly surprised.

"I glanced inside your saddlebags," he said, "and found a lantern and a flask of oil."

What a fool I'd been.

I composed my answer carefully. "We'd heard tales that there was a pool beneath the earth where we might see a coelacanth."

"Are they not extinct?" my father asked, and inserted the needle into my flesh.

I winced but kept myself from crying out. "No," I grunted as the needle criss-crossed my wound. "They live . . . in the lake bottom and . . . spend their days in underground pools."

"And you were bitten while attempting to catch it?"

I exhaled. "Yes, Father."

He made another two stitches, closing the first wound, and then tied off the threads and snipped them short with scissors.

The room swam briefly before me. My father turned my arm so he could work on the second bite.

"It was very foolish," I said, hoping to distract him from his calm course of questioning. "I promise I will never enter those caves again. I am very sorry."

"Why did you try to catch the fish?" Father asked.

"To catch such a rare thing—" I groaned. "We thought it would be remarkable."

"It seems," said my father, "that you meant to explore these caves all along."

I said nothing. I could not think clearly. The pain was mounting, and my guilt with it. I wondered if Elizabeth and Konrad were undergoing a similar interrogation by my mother. At least they weren't having their rent flesh sewn together. They should be able to keep silent.

I reached for the brandy, but my father moved it beyond my grasp.

"Yes, it was planned all along, Father."

"You deliberately misled your mother and me."

I whimpered as the needle entered my flesh yet again. "Father, the pain is . . ." I reached out for the brandy, but once more he withheld it.

"You have also visited the Dark Library again."

I said nothing.

"Yes or no, Victor."

"Yes, I did," I said faintly. "How did you know?"

"Footsteps in the dust. Books shelved in different places. It's unlike you to deceive, Victor. And I can't help wondering if these two deceptions—your forbidden visit to the library and your expedition today—are connected in some way."

Why had I thought I could fool him? He was one of the cleverest men in the Republic, a magistrate who judged truth from lie in his daily work.

"Are they connected, Victor?"

I had no more fight left. I nodded. He pushed the brandy toward me, and I greedily drained the tumbler. The burn in my throat temporarily obliterated the pain.

Father finished the last stitch and looked up. "Now I want to know *why* you did these things."

"It was my idea from the start," I said quickly. Even in my suffering I was eager to take full credit for the enterprise—and also to control the story. "When Konrad was ill, and none of the doctors seemed to know how to cure him, we found a recipe for an elixir of life and decided it might be his only hope. So we set about searching for the ingredients."

Father's face darkened. "Did you hear nothing of what I told you in the Dark Library? You disobeyed me to pursue some childish fancy!"

He brought his fist down on the desk and I jumped, but the violence of his gesture sparked my own anger. I was being treated like a criminal. Interrogated. Tortured. "You're wrong! It wasn't childish! The vision of the wolf. The flameless fire! I made them both, and they worked!"

I regretted my outburst immediately. Father's eyebrows contracted and he sat forward in his chair.

"You have been working alchemy?" he asked with disconcerting calm.

"Only to help us find the elixir's ingredients."

"And whose miraculous recipe have you been following? Master Caligula's? Eclecti's?"

"Agrippa's," I told him.

He shook his head. "No. You are not being honest. That recipe cannot be made."

"You seem to know a lot about it," I countered, then said, lying only a little, "We found a translation of the Alphabet of the Magi."

"It has been lost!"

"We found one. Surely you cannot have read every single book in the Dark Library!"

This was a gamble, I knew. I saw my father bristle, but then he reined in his temper.

"Victor, you have no idea the danger these elixirs pose. They are not proper cures!"

"Like Dr. Murnau's?" I blurted.

He looked at me, silent.

"Konrad told me," I said. "We have no secrets. But you're keeping one from Mother. His illness might return."

Father seemed weary suddenly. "There is a small chance."

"And next time it might kill him! How can you sit back and do nothing? How can you trust Dr. Murnau's guesswork, and no one else's? Why not Agrippa's? There are accounts of its successes—"

"Don't be absurd," said Father. "Dr. Murnau's methods are informed by centuries of proper scientific learning."

At that moment we were interrupted as the door to the study opened, and Elizabeth and Konrad, warmly robed, were ushered in by my mother.

"They wanted to see how you were," Mother said to me.

"The patient will survive," Father said.

Konrad was studying me, no doubt wondering how much of our adventure I'd revealed. I felt ashamed. I'd crumpled under Father's interrogation. I'd not told him everything—but too much.

"It seems," Father said to our mother, "that the children have been trying to gather the ingredients for an alchemical potion. An elixir of life, no less."

The look of sheer surprise on Mother's face told me that Konrad and Elizabeth had confessed very little.

"You said you'd gotten lost exploring the caves!" she exclaimed, seeming genuinely hurt. "How long has this been going on?"

"Since Konrad got ill," Elizabeth murmured. "We wanted to cure him."

Mother frowned. "But why would you persist with this even after Dr. Murnau cured him?"

From the corner of my eye I saw my father and brother exchange a glance, as if reminding each other of the secret they kept.

"An elixir of life would be a glorious thing to have," Konrad said smoothly. "I confess I couldn't resist the sheer adventure of it."

"You must abandon this dark endeavour," my father said firmly. "It is finished. Is that clear?"

"Yes," Konrad and Elizabeth said.

"Victor, I don't believe I heard you."

"Yes," I muttered.

"You've put your lives in peril. You might easily have been killed in those caves. And you should know this as well. Not only is the practice of alchemy fruitless, it is also *illegal* in our republic. You were unaware of this, no doubt."

I nodded, truly surprised. I remembered Polidori telling us he'd *personally* been forbidden from the alchemical arts, but I hadn't realized it was considered a crime.

"Some years ago," Father went on, "we tried an alchemist who had been administering a certain *miraculous* elixir. People paid for it eagerly and willingly drank it. Some of them were made sicker; one died. To prevent further tragedies, the other magistrates and I decided to pass a law making it illegal to profit from, or *administer,* alchemical medicines."

"We did not know that," murmured Elizabeth contritely.

"I cannot have my own children daring the laws of the land," he said.

"No, Father," said Konrad.

"And while I admire the selflessness and love that inspired your actions," said Father, "I'm very disappointed by how you've deceived your mother and me."

I looked at him coldly, and thought he was a hypocrite. Was not he being dishonest with Mother, by not telling her the truth about Konrad's illness?

"I'm placing you three under house arrest for the next two weeks. No riding. No boating. Your footsteps will not tread beyond the inner yard. You will receive no visitors."

"Not even Henry?" I cried.

"Especially not Henry," Father snapped. "He was one of your accomplices!"

"He didn't really do much," I muttered, and Konrad could not suppress a laugh.

"He was very good at staying behind," said Elizabeth, biting back a smile, "on account of his acute imagination."

And then the three of us fell into a violent fit of giggling—

despite our exhaustion, and the prospect of being imprisoned for the next two weeks.

"We must somehow get a message to Polidori," I said quietly.

We had slept deep into the morning, and after a late breakfast the three of us had met in the ballroom, where we could stand outside on the balcony and see the glorious summer, forbidden us for two weeks.

"We need to make sure he got the coelacanth head from Henry—and that he knows we won't be visiting for a fortnight."

I was very worried what Henry might have told the alchemist; I didn't want Polidori to think we'd exposed him, or given up on our plan.

Konrad exhaled. "Victor, we promised to end our adventure."

I looked at him in surprise. "Yes, but we were lying."

He glanced at Elizabeth, as though they'd already discussed this without me.

"Perhaps ending it is for the best," she said.

"How is it for the best?" I demanded.

"We might have died, Victor," she said in astonishment.

"Yes, I know. I was very nearly inhaled by a fish. But we can't give up now. We have only a single ingredient left to find! Konrad, it was *you* who wanted to continue."

"I regret it now. I'm of Father's opinion. We are chasing a mirage. There is no proof these alchemical cures work."

Elizabeth nodded, and I stared at her in astonishment. "You saw that book move; you smelled its blood!"

"I don't know what I saw or smelled anymore."

"Did you not say the room was bathed in red lamplight?" Konrad asked her. "That might have created the effect of—"

"You were not there," I reminded him pointedly. "If you had been, you would've felt the power of the book, and Polidori—like Elizabeth and me."

"I find it curious," said Elizabeth, turning to me, "that you can't believe in God but are more than willing to believe in alchemical wonders."

"The vision of the wolf. The flameless fire. They may be wonders, but they're real. It is just science by another name."

Konrad sniffed. "Father doesn't think so."

"Right now," said Elizabeth, "I am extremely grateful to be alive. And I think we should put the whole matter in God's hands."

Konrad gave a little nod.

"Has she converted you, then?" I asked. "You never believed in God."

"She is very persuasive," Konrad said, smiling, and Elizabeth flushed as they looked at each other fondly.

"And he's converted you too," I said to her, disguising my jealous pain with anger. "You were so brave on our adventures, and now you cowardly want to surrender."

She would not meet my eye. "We see things differently, Victor."

"Well," I said, "I prefer to take some action. But if you wish to lie about and hope for miracles, go ahead."

"Victor, you have already risked your life for me," said Konrad kindly. "I cannot imagine a greater show of brotherly love. I'll never forget this. But I am asking you now to stop."

"But—" I began, only to have him interrupt me.

"Surely my say should count the more," he said. "It's *my* life. And I say stop. Truly, let's leave this behind us."

I did not know how to reply.

I woke the following morning to an unexpected feeling of well-being.

When I parted the curtains, warm sunlight doused me. I opened the window to the trill of birdsong and an intoxicatingly warm breeze. The lake sparkled. It seemed the whole world was before me, and it was truly beautiful, and beckoning me to return to it.

I was alive.

I took a deep breath. These past weeks during Konrad's illness, my mind—awake and dreaming—had been filled with dread and cobwebs and darkness. I wanted the sun to burn them all away.

And I could not but wonder . . .

Maybe Konrad and Elizabeth were right, and it was best to abandon our dangerous and uncertain quest.

As far as prisons went, the chateau was a pleasant and roomy one, but it was still a prison. The lake and meadows we'd taken for granted all our lives now seemed to beckon with excruciating intensity from the windows and balconies.

Father was not a sadistic jailer. Though he refused to shorten our sentence (despite my best arguments) over the next five days he did try to distract us with entertaining stories about far-flung countries, and the bloody histories of famous battles that he knew Konrad and I had always craved when younger. He shared with us the news he received from abroad, where France heaved with revolution. A whole new world was being forged beyond the mountains—but within the walls of Chateau Frankenstein, nothing changed.

He'd done something to the library's secret door so it would not open. Clearly he no longer trusted our promises.

Mother was very happy. She thought Konrad healed, and she had all her children under her roof day and night.

Chapter 12

KEEPER OF SECRETS

few nights later I woke from a dream so terrible that it shimmered darkly before me, even as I sat up in bed, panting.

Konrad was dead and laid out in his coffin, the hue of bodily corruption already on his flesh. I stood at his head, peering down at him. Behind me I could hear the weeping of my family. A huge fury stirred inside me.

And suddenly the coffin was no longer a coffin but a laboratory table.

Over Konrad's body I spoke words of power, and applied unguents and strange machines to his limbs, his chest, his skull.

And then I gave a great cry, and energy erupted from within me and arced like lightning from my body to his.

His hand twitched. His head stirred. His eyes opened and looked at me.

* * *

I lit a candle and paced my room. Sleep was impossible after such a vision. What was its meaning? I did not believe in augury, but the dream's urgency was hard to ignore.

Would Konrad sicken and die unless . . . unless we took action once more? Was it within my power to save him?

Restlessly I went to my desk and from a hidden cupboard drew out Eisenstein's slim green volume. Father thought all alchemy nonsense, yet at least some of it worked. It had given me the vision of the wolf, and a flameless fire to escape the depths. It had helped Polidori resurrect text from a burned tome, and make Krake preternaturally intelligent.

Why couldn't this same well of knowledge produce an elixir of life?

Idly I paged through the book, looking at the headings. They did not seem so unlike the natural sciences Father taught us at our lessons—

I stopped.

Upon the page was written, *Transmutation of Base Metals to Gold*. It was not the lustre of this promise that caught my attention, but the handwriting in the book's margins. It was distinctive and unmistakable—for it was my father's.

I gripped the book closer, my eyes flying over his calculations, his detailed annotations on performing the procedure.

Liar. The man I had admired all my life, whose every word I had trusted, was a liar. The secret he kept from Mother was one thing—a small deceit done to protect her from worry. But *this* was altogether different. He had barred us from the Dark Library, told us that alchemy was nothing but nonsense. And all the time he himself knew its power. He had turned lead into gold! So why had he forbidden us from making the Elixir of Life—even though it might one day save the life of his own son? I didn't understand.

I forced myself to take a breath, and as my pulse slowed I knew my course of action.

I wouldn't allow myself to be distracted any longer.

Just one ingredient left.

Just one more, and the elixir would be mine.

After breakfast I went downstairs to the servants' quarters and found Maria in her office, going through the accounts.

She looked up. "How are you today, Victor?"

"I am thoroughly enjoying my imprisonment, thank you, Maria."

The news of our adventuring was common knowledge among the servants, although Father had been most careful not to make any mention of alchemy. Even among the most loyal of staff, rumours could easily escape the chateau and sully our family's glorious reputation.

"Can I be of some service to you?" Maria asked—a touch warily, I thought.

"Today is your day in town, is it not?" She usually made the trip into Geneva with a maid to supervise the purchase of provisions we could not get locally in Bellerive.

"It is indeed."

"Would you be willing to take a message for me?"

"Of course. To Henry Clerval, I assume."

I closed the office door behind me. "No," I said. "To Julius Polidori."

She was silent for a moment. "You found him, then," she said, for she and I hadn't spoken of the matter since she'd given me his name many weeks before.

I nodded. "With his help we've been assembling the ingredients for the Elixir of Life."

Her eyes widened. "But surely your father—"

"Knows nothing of Polidori's involvement, no. And mustn't. But we are very close to creating the elixir, and I must get word to Mr. Polidori of our predicament."

"Victor," she said, and paused as someone passed the door, "surely there's no need, now that Konrad is healed."

"It may only be a temporary cure," I said. "Father does not want that known, even by Mother."

"I see," she said. I did not like divulging this information, but I needed all the ammunition at my disposal.

"Will you deliver my note?" I asked.

"I am loath to do it," she said bluntly. "When I heard of your adventuring in the caves . . . It's a miracle you did not all perish."

"But, Maria, you helped set us on this path," I reminded her.

The fingers of her left hand rubbed nervously against her chair's armrest. "I know, and it was wrong of me, I think."

"It's but a small matter of delivering a letter to his house— and awaiting his reply."

"Your father would be furious if he found out."

"But he will not find out," I said. "Just as he never found out it was you who told us about Julius Polidori in the first place."

She looked at me carefully. "I did it only for Konrad's sake."

"I know," I said. "I know. But we must keep each other's secrets, mustn't we?"

I dare say she thought I was threatening her. I would never have done anything to get her in trouble—but perhaps it was best to let her imagine I might.

"Very well," she said with heavy reluctance. "Give me the address. I will be your messenger."

I passed her the note, already written and sealed with wax.

"And one last thing, Maria. Do not tell him who you are, or for whom you work."

In the evening I slipped downstairs and found Maria again. She scarcely looked at me as she handed me a sealed letter. And then she gave a shiver, as though relieved to be rid of the thing.

Instantly I slid it into my pocket.

"To be in that shop of his gave me grave doubts," she whispered. "And the fellow himself . . . and that *cat* of his!"

I kissed Maria on the cheek, as I used to do when little.

"Thank you," I said. "You have done a great service."

"I hope it is the last." She looked at me, and I thought I saw a flicker of fear in her face.

I went upstairs to my bedchamber, closed and locked the door, and opened the letter.

> *Dear Sir,*
> *Thank you for your letter. Please rest assured that*
> *I did indeed receive the coelacanth head from your*
> *friend and that it yielded oils ample for the purpose.*
> *I now understand that you are temporarily*
> *detained, and am most relieved that our venture*

remains secret—as it must. If I do not hear otherwise from you, I will assume you wish me to continue my work. The translation is cumbersome, but proceeds apace, and I have no doubt I will soon know the third and final ingredient. When I have succeeded, I will leave a message for you, as per your instructions, by the Gallimard crypt in the Bellerive graveyard. Until then, I remain,

Your humble servant,
Julius Polidori

For the moment I had done all I could. Now I had to wait.

I became a keeper of secrets.

I did not tell Konrad or Elizabeth of Father's alchemy. I did not tell them of my resolve to pursue our adventure. What good would it do? It wouldn't change their minds. They were too busy being in love. If Konrad did not have the sense to obtain the elixir, I would have to do it for him.

If he were to get sick again, I would have his cure. I would have the power to bring him back from the dead.

And what else might I have the power to do?

That night, sleep would not come to me, and by candlelight I once more opened the slim green volume, the last remnant of the forbidden Dark Library.

The love potion was so childishly simple, I almost doubted it:

A drop of fish oil.
Sugar to mask the fish oil.
A drop of clover honey to sweeten it further.
A pinch of thyme.
The juice of three crushed rose petals.
A small measure of pure glacier water.
Two pinches of rosemary.
A strand of the maker's hair, cut and ground
    as finely as possible.
A drop of blood from your heart's desire.

These items would be easy to come by. Only the last worried me—until I remembered my handkerchief. I had kept it hidden away in my chest of drawers. I did not want it laundered, for upon it was a spot of Elizabeth's blood, from her sweet lips. I could cut out the spot and drop the bit of linen into my mixture.

The recipe called for the liquid to sit for a day and night, and then be drunk by my heart's desire.

That would not be so hard. During our fencing practice we often had a refreshing cordial. I would pour a goblet for Elizabeth and deftly add the sweet potion to her glass.

She would love me. The tincture would *make* her love me.

A sudden fury overpowered me, and I hurled the book against the wall.

This I knew: There would be no victory in winning Elizabeth through alchemical tricks.

I was not so lovable as Konrad, no. I would never have his charm or grace or patience or effortless skill at things. But I had the same fine body, and what mine contained had more grit and determination and passion.

Were these not things worth loving?

I'd felt her wolf's heat that night in the Sturmwald. She'd been mine then, and I would make her mine again.

On my own, and for good.

Afterward I fell into a fitful sleep. I dreamed I was trekking through the Alps and Krake was my only companion. I was searching for something but did not know what. I looked everywhere, with more and more desperation. Krake's green eyes regarded me solemnly, but he could not help me.

Night came on, and I found a cave and lay down to sleep. Krake stretched out beside me, and I was glad of his comforting warmth.

The dream dissolved, but the warmth remained. Half awake, I thought nothing of it at first. But then it seemed to intensify, and suddenly I was fully awake, like a desperate swimmer breaching the water's surface, hungry for air.

I was not alone in my bed.

I lay very still on my right side. Something warm and soft pressed snugly against my back. An arm was draped over my chest. A hand rested against my pounding heart.

I inhaled shakily—breathing in the heady scent of Elizabeth's hair and skin.

She must have been sleepwalking again, and once more found her way into my bed, just as she had as a little girl. But she was no longer seven years old, and as I lay there I was all too aware of the new curves of her woman's body.

Her heat seemed to travel through me, blooming in my cheeks, under my arms, between my legs. I scarcely dared breathe, for fear of waking her, for fear of ending this moment.

But I had to do something. I could not let her sleep the night here. Panicked thoughts galloped through my head. Imagine if a servant came in to find us like this. How could I explain it? Sweat prickled my forehead.

Gently I pulled away and slowly rolled over to face her.

My breath caught in my throat. I'd expected to find her fast asleep, but her eyes were wide open. Her cheek rested on my pillow, and her lips were twitched into a mischievous smile— one that I had never before seen on her. I gazed, transfixed by her beauty, at once familiar and foreign. Was this really the Elizabeth I had grown up with?

Almost at once I could tell she wasn't truly looking at me. Like the last time, she gazed *through* me, at her heart's true desire. No doubt she thought she was with Konrad. And why wasn't she?

I wanted to kiss and caress her. It would have been so easy: she was mere inches before me, her long hair spilling over the lace of her nightgown. I leaned hungrily closer—but stopped myself with a moan. I could not take such liberty with her sleeping body, as alluring as it was.

She made a soft sound in her throat, like a cat's purr, and for a moment I swore her eyes looked right into mine. She lifted her hand and stroked my hair, then let her fingers run down my cheek and neck.

I felt myself weaken. I had to do something, or I would not

be able to resist temptation. I slowly got up. Her eyes followed me.

"Elizabeth," I said calmly, walking around to her side of the bed. "It's time to go."

Obediently she pushed herself into sitting, and I tried not to look at the flash of her exposed thighs before her sleeping fingers modestly adjusted her hem.

"Come." I stretched out my hand.

She took it. I felt like a hypnotist. She would do whatever I asked her.

Elizabeth, touch me. Kiss me. Tell me you love me.

I ground my teeth in frustration. She came willingly as I led her to the door. I opened it and furtively peered into the hall, listening. The thought of being seen made me shiver. We walked down the corridor to her bedchamber. Inside, I led her to her own bed. I straightened her churned sheets.

"It's time to get some sleep," I said.

I pressed down lightly on her shoulders, and she sat.

"Lie down," I said.

She lay down, but took hold of my hand, smiling up at me with that same tantalizing smile. But it was given to me only in the confusion of her sleeping mind, and was meant for Konrad.

I gently pried her fingers off mine.

"Good night, Elizabeth."

Her head sank down into her pillow. Her eyes closed.

I gave a great sigh and turned. But as I reached the doorway, she said something that made my step falter, my heart skip a beat.

Sleepily she murmured, "Good night, Victor."

At breakfast Elizabeth gave no sign of remembering her nocturnal wanderings. She talked cheerfully with all of us, and with every second it seemed more and more impossible that she'd ever come to my bed, stroked my face.

It had taken me a long time to get back to sleep. I could find no comfortable position. As I'd finally started to drift off, I'd felt her weight and heat against me once more—and turned eagerly to find it was truly a mirage this time.

She'd said my name. Did that mean she knew—or some *part* of her knew—where she was and what she was doing? Could it mean she *had* meant to come to my room, and not Konrad's?

I could ask her—but how? At the very least she'd be embarrassed; at the worst, furious with me, for no doubt she would think I'd made up the whole scandalous thing.

I looked at her across the dining table, and she smiled at me—a friendly, sisterly smile, without even a glimmer of remembrance. She was so radiant and full of beauty, I could barely swallow my food.

That night, after dinner, I emerged on the balcony to find her leaning against the balustrade, watching the sun sink toward the mountains.

"The last night of our imprisonment," I said.

She looked over, somewhat surprised, for no doubt she'd been expecting Konrad. I had intercepted him on his way, and told him Father wanted him to check on the horses and inquire after the pregnant mare from the head groom.

"The two weeks have gone quickly enough," she said, and turned her eyes back to the mountains.

I had no gift for pretty talk, but I'd prepared some lines, thanks to Henry's poetry—and I was emboldened too by the fact that Elizabeth, unbeknownst to her, had shared my bed last night.

"Your beauty makes the sunset itself pause," I said, "so it can behold you but a second longer."

She turned to me, her eyes wide.

"But you are the brighter of the two," I said. "Around you I feel like a moth, and it's all I can do to avoid your fire."

She laughed, her hand rising to cover her mouth.

"Have I said something funny?" I asked, annoyed.

Elizabeth bit her lips, then composed herself. "No, no, it's very sweet, thank you. It's just that, well, it's not the kind of language I'm used to hearing you speak, Victor."

"Perhaps there are certain talents I keep hidden," I said, raising my eyebrows mysteriously.

"Difficult to believe. Have you been reading poetry?"

"The words are my own," I said, only half lying. Damn these poetical scribblings—even if they'd been scripted for me, I had no tongue to say them.

"They're very fine," she said. "But better saved for someone else."

"They'd be wasted, then," I said. "Like, like—" I tried to think of something poetic. "Like pearls tossed at pigs."

"'Swine,' I think, is the expression you're looking for. Pearls before swine."

"Oh, to hell with pretty words—since you only mean to mock me."

"No, indeed, 'pig' is very expressive," she said, "and an excellent description of a fellow who flirts with his brother's beloved."

"Ah. I did not realize you were already his *property*." I knew this would anger her, for my mother had always taught us that women were the equal of men and shouldn't be treated like possessions.

I got the exact reaction I wanted. Her eyes flared.

"No one *owns* me, Victor, except me. Well," she added, a little contritely, "God owns me, as he does all His creations, but no *human* shall ever own me."

"Oh, I know, I know," I said, as dismissively as I could, "you always like to make your own choices. So why not give yourself a little choice in this matter?"

"I already have, and you should respect my decision. Now you should go."

She looked over my shoulder worriedly, no doubt afraid Konrad would appear.

"Oh, he won't be coming for some time," I said. "I sent him on an errand."

"That was mean of you."

"Yes." The light burnished her amber hair, and I went to her, grabbed her shoulders, and kissed her on the mouth. She pushed me away and slapped me, hard.

"Don't ever," she said, wildcat fury in her eyes.

"You like it when I kiss you," I said, knowing no such thing.

She turned her back on me. "You *bite*," she said through clenched teeth.

"Admit it," I said recklessly. "You don't even have to say yes, just nod your head. Go on, be honest!"

I watched the back of her head, waiting and hoping. She might have been a statue.

"What you are doing is very wrong, Victor," she said.

"What about that old saying, 'All's fair in love and war'?"

"You do not love me!"

"Don't tell me what I feel," I said angrily. "When you don't even know what you feel yourself."

She turned on me, angry yet also curious. "What are you talking about?"

There was a moment when I might have kept her secret, but I was too inflamed. "You come to my bedchamber at night," I whispered.

Her face flushed. "That is a vile thing to say."

"You sleepwalk, Elizabeth. You know you do. You did it as a child. And twice this summer you've done it again. And each time you've come to *my* room."

She looked at me warily, not sure if I was telling the truth.

"The first time you held your old doll, the one with the red braids. You thought she was a baby, and she wasn't dead, just cold, and you wanted to warm her."

Her gaze left mine, and a memory seemed to scud across her mind.

"You remember such dreams, don't you?" I said.

"I often have them," she admitted. "But I have no memory of coming to your bedchamber."

"Last night you climbed *into* my bed."

Her eyes narrowed. "I do not believe it." And she made to walk past me.

I grabbed her arm and held her. "You lay against me and smiled at me and purred like a cat."

"Let me go," she said softly, dangerously.

I released my hold on her, but she didn't move.

"You stroked my face. And when I took you back to your own room, you said good-night to me. 'Good night, Victor,' you said."

She looked troubled now, her eyes darting about after flares of remembrance.

"What I want to know," I said, "is why it's *my* room you come to. Why not visit Konrad's?"

"How do you know I don't?" she retorted.

I swallowed, speechless for a moment. "You're bluffing."

"Am I?"

But as I watched her, I saw the uncertainty in her haughty eyes and knew she was lying.

"I have a hypothesis, if you'd care to hear it," I said.

She said nothing, but nor did she walk away.

"Konrad's a fine fellow, but there's one thing I have that he doesn't. A passion to match your own."

"What nonsense you talk!"

"Is it? Konrad sees your angel, but I see your animal. Look me in the eye and tell me I'm wrong."

"Wrong about what?" said Konrad behind me.

Elizabeth glared at me. I glared back.

"Just a lively discussion," I said dismissively, "and one I now tire of."

And I walked past Konrad and back inside the chateau.

* * *

I wasn't surprised when, not an hour later, there was a knock on my bedchamber door and Konrad entered without waiting for an invitation. I was at my desk, pretending to read.

"You have upset Elizabeth very much, you know," he said, sitting down in an armchair.

"Have I?"

He seemed surprised by my play of innocence. "Yes. She's upset by the way you spoke to her."

I frowned. "What way was that?" I wasn't about to make this any easier for him. I would give nothing away. I wanted to know how much Elizabeth had told him.

Konrad raised his eyebrows. "Your behaviour on the balcony was hardly gentlemanly."

The balcony. So he still didn't know about our midnight kiss. Or her midnight visits to my bedroom. The fact gave me a little thrill. Our secret from Konrad.

"My behaviour," I said with a frown. "Can you be more specific, please?"

"You forced a kiss upon her, Victor."

I shrugged like a world-weary lover. "Oh, *that*. How could a young woman be upset by such flattery?"

I watched Konrad carefully, waiting for his composure to crack.

"That kiss was not wanted," he said evenly.

I chuckled. "It was by me."

My brother's expression remained infuriatingly calm. "You don't really love Elizabeth. It's nothing more than a youthful infatuation."

"Ah, is that what it is?" I said, feeling my temper kindle.

He nodded, as though he were a kindly uncle giving advice to a pimply, gawking child.

"Perhaps *yours* is the youthful infatuation," I said.

"All right, then," said Konrad, and I suddenly felt like we were fencing again—lunging and parrying. "How long have you had romantic feelings for her? Be truthful. Weeks?"

"I don't know."

"*Days* perhaps?"

"What does it matter?" I countered. "If I love her, I love her."

"I am willing to bet," Konrad said, "that you only *discovered* your love for her *after* you knew of mine."

"Not so!" I said, wondering if there was truth in this.

"I shouldn't have mentioned it to you," Konrad said. "That was obviously a mistake."

"I knew your feelings well before then," I scoffed. "And my own too."

"Victor, she wants you to stop."

"Hmm. I wonder," I said. And on a devilish impulse I added, "Did she not tell you about our long midnight kiss?"

Konrad's face tightened. A hit. But almost at once my victory tasted sour.

My brother stood, enraged. "She's never said a word of this to me."

Elizabeth had kept my shameful secret to protect me and Konrad—and I had just betrayed her.

"I tricked her," I said quickly. "I stole the note meant for you. She thought I was you, but not for long, and when she found out, she was furious with me."

"And yet you persist," said Konrad, kicking the chair so hard it toppled and skidded across the room. "You want *everything,* Victor, that is your problem."

"How easy for you to say, when you already *have* everything."

"What do you mean?" he demanded, his fists closing.

Scalding anger evaporated any lingering shame or regret. "You are best at everything, and you know it. It comes so easily to you, I wonder if you even *try*. I must *work* at what I want."

"And you've suddenly decided you want Elizabeth? Can't you see how selfish you've been? She loves you as a brother, and it pains her to have to reject you—more than once now, it seems! She has *no* romantic feelings for you, Victor."

"I'm not convinced," I said stubbornly.

Konrad took a threatening step toward me. "This is one thing you cannot control. You must accept this."

"I accept *nothing*," I said

"You deserve a proper beating, then!"

"Excellent!" I said, exhilarating anger coursing through my veins. "Let's have at it. Or maybe we should fight a proper duel over her, hey? Come, let us get our foils."

"Only if we uncork the tips!" said Konrad in fury.

"Agreed!"

He lunged for me, fists raised, but at that moment all the blood seemed to rush from his face, and he fainted to the floor.

Chapter 13

THE GATES OF HELL

I hardly slept, worrying about Konrad the whole night.

When he'd collapsed on my floor, so pale, for a terrible moment I'd thought he was dead. But he'd only been unconscious for a few minutes, and when he was roused he insisted he was absolutely fine. But I'd already called a servant to fetch Father, and we helped Konrad to his bedchamber and settled him in bed.

"Please don't make a fuss," he said, still very pale. "You'll only worry Mother."

When I bid him good-night, he would not meet my eye.

Dawn came and I threw on a robe and went directly to his bedchamber. Mother was just leaving, closing the door softly behind her.

"Wait a bit," she told me. "He's still sleeping."

Elizabeth came around the corner, hastily robed, her hair loose about her shoulders. She scarcely glanced at me.

"How's he doing?" she asked.

Mother gave us a smile, though there was something brittle in it. "Not so badly. A small fever only. Two of the girls down-

222

stairs have the exact same thing," she added reassuringly. "It has laid them low for a day or two, but no doubt they will be right as rain. In an hour or two I'm sure he'll be awake and wanting company. Maria is watching over him for now."

Mother walked off, leaving us alone in the corridor. Elizabeth started walking away too, and I followed her awkwardly.

"Shall we get some breakfast?" I suggested.

She turned on me, looking livid. "When he fainted in your room, what were you two talking about?"

I cleared my throat. "If you must know, he came to reprimand me, for the way I treated you on the balcony."

Had there been some alchemical process to turn back time, I would have paid a fortune for it so I could take back the hurtful words I'd said to Konrad. I'd come to his room just now hoping to make amends.

"Victor?" she said impatiently. "What did you say to him?"

"I told him we kissed in the library."

Her dark eyes blazed. "How could you?"

"I regretted it instantly. I told him I pretended to be him, that you were guiltless."

"And the sleepwalking?"

I looked at her in surprise. "So you believe me now?"

"Answer my question!"

"No, I said nothing of it. And he remained very calm—until the very end. I was amazed."

"He's not like you, Victor," she said. "He can master his temper. But you went too far, and put his blood into a fever."

"You're saying *I'm* responsible for his fever?" I demanded, though the same idea plagued me too. "Listen to Mother. It's a passing ague. Others in the house have it."

Neither of us said a word. We both shared the exact same worry.

"I hope you're right, Victor," she said, "because if you've brought back his illness, I will never forgive you."

And she walked away from me.

"I'd like to visit St. Mary's and light a candle for Konrad," Elizabeth said as we were finishing breakfast.

The slightest flicker of irritation crossed Father's face, but he said, "Very well. I'll have Philippe take you."

"I can take her," I said quickly. I'd been planning on making a trip to the graveyard to check for Polidori's note—and this gave me the perfect excuse.

Father looked at me closely, and I realized he was still reluctant to let me out of the house.

"To the church and back, Victor," he said.

"Of course."

Outside on the lake road, with the water sparkling and the heady smell of the fields in my nostrils, I ought to have felt exhilarated after my two weeks' confinement. But I felt wretched. Elizabeth sat beside me, silent and reproachful.

My only thought, thumping in time with the horse's hooves, was: *Let it be there. Let there be a message waiting.*

When we arrived, I watched her enter the church, then tied up the horse and ran through the tombstones to the Gallimard crypt, a huge pile of granite that had glowered there for centuries. I walked around it twice, scrabbling in dirt and leaves, looking for some kind of wallet.

Nothing.

I cursed and kicked at the crypt's wall with my boot. Polidori had had the better part of a week. What could be taking the old fool so long? I wanted to ride the rest of the way to Geneva and box his ears.

If Konrad's illness had returned—

I banished the thought, and walked inside the church. After the bright sunlight, it took my eyes several moments to grow accustomed to the dim interior. The church was nearly empty, only a few people at prayer scattered among the pews.

I took a seat near the back. I saw Elizabeth at the front, kneeling before a row of small lit candles, her hands covering her face.

Tears sprang to my eyes, and I looked away.

On the altar a young boy was polishing the brasses. My knowledge of the Church was small, but I did know about how the priest was said to perform a miracle, turning the bread and wine into the body and blood of Jesus Christ.

From the stained-glass windows shafts of coloured light angled through the stillness of the church. My thoughts drifted.

Wine to blood. Lead to gold. Medicine dripped into my brother's veins. The transmutation of matter.

Was it magic or science? Fantasy or truth?

Two days passed, and my brother's fever did not leave him.

His body ached. The joints of his right hand became swollen. Downstairs, our two servants were still laid low as well. We had a visit from the kindly, useless Dr. Lesage, who administered his usual strengthening powders and tinctures to help combat the fever.

"I am sending for Dr. Murnau," Father said at dinner. William and Ernest had already been taken off to bed, and it was just Elizabeth and me with Mother and Father. For a moment there was silence around the table.

"But I thought this was just a passing illness?" Elizabeth said.

"Mostly likely it is," said Mother, "but I think it best to be safe."

I avoided Elizabeth's gaze, for fear of the anger I would see there.

"Before he departed," said Father, "Dr. Murnau left me a detailed schedule of his whereabouts, in case we needed him again. He's currently in Lyon with another patient. I mean to ride there myself and bring him back as soon as possible."

Lyon was in France, and the country was in turmoil. Mobs of revolutionaries still roved the land in a reign of terror, persecuting any who might disagree with them. I looked at my father, and for the first time he seemed old to me, and tired. My heart felt as crumpled as his shoulders.

"Is it safe for you, Father?" Elizabeth asked. "The stories we've heard . . ."

"I will take Philippe and Marc with me. The French people have no quarrel with the Genevese—we have no love of monarchy either. My only worry is how long the journey may take. I plan to leave tomorrow morning."

Later that evening I found Father alone in his study, hurriedly packing a valise.

"May I speak with you?" I said, closing the door behind me.

"What is it, Victor?"

I took a deep breath, let it out. "Father, given Konrad's condition, is it not worth . . . at least *considering* the Elixir of Life?"

He looked at me as if I had gone mad, but I persisted.

"We need only one last ingredient and—"

He lifted his hand. "Enough. Dr. Murnau will advise us."

"But he himself said he couldn't give Konrad the same medicine so soon. What can he do? Maybe if you'd told Mother the truth, she'd be willing to pursue the Elixir of Life as well. If we at least had it at hand, we'd—"

"No!"

"You would rather let him die?"

"How often must I tell you? Alchemy does not hold the answer!"

My heart thudded. "How can you say that when you yourself have practised it?"

His split second's hesitation betrayed him. "Nonsense."

My voice shook. "I saw your handwriting in Eisenstein's book. You have transmuted lead into gold."

Quietly he said, "It was not gold."

I stared in confusion.

"It only had the appearance of gold." There was bitterness in his voice.

"But in your notes there were calculations for some two hundred pounds. If it was not gold, why did you make . . . ?" My voice trailed off.

My father turned to look out the window, and I had the dreadful sense that something was about to be taken away from me forever.

"Its appearance," he said, "was enough to fool a great many people."

It took me a moment to form the words. "You sold people fake gold?"

"When I was a young man, the Frankenstein fortune was all but gone. My family would have lost everything. Everything. When I discovered the Dark Library, I thought alchemy might prove our salvation. The gold, alas, was not real—but it was possible to carefully sell it through various agents, far away, in the empires of Russia and the Orient."

"I see."

"Without that money our family would have failed. I would not have married. You would not exist. I am not proud of it, but it was necessary."

I felt feverish. My father, the great magistrate, was a liar, a hypocrite, a criminal. I could not sort my thoughts properly. He turned to face me, and this time it was I who could not meet his eye, so ashamed of him was I.

He took me tightly by the shoulders. "You must tell no one of this, Victor. You understand?"

I said nothing.

"It would destroy us."

I forced myself to look at him. "What about Konrad?"

"Listen to me, my son. Alchemy is a mirage. You must accept that."

I wrenched myself free of his grip. "Maybe it was only *you* who failed. You cannot dismiss the entire discipline because you could not make gold! Maybe others are more skilled than you!"

"Victor—"

"No," I said, blood pounding in my ears. "I no longer trust you!"

He tried once more to put his hands upon me, but I twisted away and fled his study.

The next morning he was gone. He'd departed for Lyon before I was even awake.

At breakfast Mother looked at Elizabeth and me rather uncomfortably and said, "Your father left instructions that you are to stay within the house until he returns."

"Why?" I demanded.

"He is concerned you might entangle yourselves in more mischief."

Elizabeth's face filled with innocent amazement. "That is not fair! We have no such plans!"

I said nothing, watching Mother, wondering how much she knew—of my interview with Father last night, of Father's criminal past.

"Those were his wishes, and they will be kept," said Mother firmly.

My pulse was a drumbeat of anger. I would not keep Father's secret any longer—if secret it were. I would not be treated like a prisoner! But Elizabeth spoke before I could.

"Surely I am still permitted the freedom to worship."

Mother faltered, for the word "freedom" in our house was given great weight. "Yes, I am sure your father would not deny you that."

"I'm glad to hear it," I said. "Because Elizabeth wants to

visit St. Mary's again this morning. To light another candle for Konrad."

Elizabeth glanced at me in surprise.

"And I am happy to take her," I hurried on, before Elizabeth could say another word.

"To the church and back only," Mother said. "And do not dally, or there will be no more exceptions."

Later, on the way to St. Mary's in the trap, Elizabeth looked at me. "What are you up to?"

"Nothing," I lied. "I thought I might light a candle myself."

"Is that so?" she said.

I let her go inside alone, and then rushed to the crypt to check for Polidori's message. If I again found nothing, I swore to myself I would ride to Geneva and confront Polidori personally.

At the gravesite I got down on my hands and knees and searched. Finding nothing, I climbed the low fence and peered inside the crypt. Nothing. I should have been clearer in my instructions and specified a place. Where would he have put it?

Then I realized it would not have been Polidori himself who brought the message. He would have hired a trustworthy messenger . . . or sent Krake.

A great oak shaded this part of the graveyard, and I remembered the lynx's speed in trees. I looked up, and saw, hanging from a low branch, a pouch. I jumped and snatched it down. It smelled like cat.

I glanced about a touch uneasily, half expecting to see the mysterious lynx gazing at me with his unnerving green eyes. I untied the pouch and took out a small piece of parchment, dated only yesterday.

My dear Sir,
I have finished the translation and discovered the final
ingredient. It is very close at hand. If you still wish to
obtain the elixir, come at your earliest opportunity.
Your humble servant,
Julius Polidori

I went inside, found Elizabeth praying, and lit a candle.

I knelt beside her and silently—to whom, I don't know—
said, *Thank you.*

When we returned, I saw a pair of horses being harnessed to
our carriage. Richard, one of the stable hands, told us that our
mother wanted to see us at once. We vaulted up the stairs, fearing it was some desperate news about Konrad.

As we passed my bedchamber, there was a servant packing
my clothes into a large valise.

"What's going on?" I demanded from the doorway.

"Victor, Elizabeth," my mother said, appearing in the hall.
"A third servant has taken ill. Genevieve, from the kitchen, has
fever and spots across her body."

"Is it the pox?" I said.

"It may be."

"Is that what Konrad has?" Elizabeth asked.

"Certainly his skin bears a rash in places. Dr. Lesage is on
his way. In any event, I want you two to go with William and
Ernest to the Geneva house."

Elizabeth's brow furrowed. "You must let me stay as well. Who will help you with Konrad?"

"I have more than enough help," said Mother firmly. "What I can't bear is another of my children taking ill. I want all of you away until we know whether this is chicken pox or plague."

Elizabeth began to object once more, but Mother raised her finger and shook her head. "No arguments. I'll send a messenger the moment I have news to report."

Within the hour I was in a carriage with Elizabeth and William and Ernest, on my way to Geneva. William insisted on sitting on my lap, and I held him tightly. He looked up at me, grinning, thinking this a wonderful treat. I pressed my cheek to his, trying to find solace in his soft warmth.

Mother must have sent word ahead of us, for when we arrived, the servants were already throwing open shuttered windows and pulling dust coverings off the furniture. We were greeted most warmly by the staff, who wanted to know all about Konrad and the other ill servants.

All I could think about was getting to Polidori's. The sooner I knew of the final ingredient, the sooner I could obtain it and have the elixir.

I ate my lunch quickly and excused myself from the table.

Elizabeth followed me out into the hall. "Where are you going?" she asked suspiciously.

I said nothing, but she knew. She grabbed my hand and pulled me into a deserted parlour, closing the door behind her.

"We *promised* your father, Victor."

"I don't have any intention of keeping that promise," I said.

"Well, I do," Elizabeth retorted.

"Polidori has finished the translation," I told her.

"How do you know this?"

I pulled his note from my pocket and showed her. "We have been in communication."

"You kept this secret from us?"

"You wished to give it all up."

She quickly read the note and looked up at me. "Don't go."

"'Close at hand,'" I said, quoting Polidori's note. "That means it is easily gotten, does it not? There will be no difficult quest this time. Perhaps he even has it in his shop!"

"Victor, we do not even know what ailment Konrad suffers from. It may just be—"

"The pox? Yes. And it might be mild or it might be fatal. Or it might be his old illness returned. We need to be ready."

"We must wait until Dr. Murnau returns."

I groaned. "That might not be for days—or weeks, if something unforeseen happens."

"For all we know, this Elixir of Life could harm him."

"It's a risk," I admitted. "But what if he gets even worse? What if Dr. Murnau comes and can't help him? You'd do nothing, when we might *cure* him?"

Elizabeth's gaze broke away from mine.

"It's within our grasp," I pressed on. "We have only one ingredient left to create the elixir. One! And it will work, I feel certain of it—more certain than I can say."

I wanted to tell her of my dream, how I had healed Konrad—how I had raised him from the dead. But how to tell her without sounding demented?

I took her hand. "Don't be so easily turned from our quest. Its way was never smooth, I grant you, but it was all the more glorious for being full of dangers and terror. At every turn our strength was tested, our courage called forth. And it was all done not for ourselves but for another. That is what makes it glorious."

Elizabeth fixed me with her hazel eyes. "Is it truly done for another, Victor?"

I frowned. "What?"

"Is it for Konrad, or really for you? For *your* glory?"

Her words bit deeper and swifter than a serpent's fangs, for there was poisonous truth in them, but I would not admit it.

"For Konrad!" I exclaimed, and turned my self-anger at Elizabeth. "How dare you question my love for my brother! No one is closer to him than me!"

"He is brother to me as well," she said. "And more."

"Yes. Sweetheart too," I snapped.

"So I have double reason to care for him," she said hotly.

"Then *show* it," I said. "The clock ticks."

"Konrad himself wanted us to abandon this quest," Elizabeth reminded me.

I made to leave the room, but she grabbed my arm. "Victor, if you leave this house, I will send a note to Mother, telling her of your intentions."

I turned to look at her, and knew she was not lying.

"I don't understand you," I said, feeling betrayed. "Where's your fire?"

"You burn enough for all of us," she said more gently. "Will you at least wait until we learn more from your mother? Let us see what tomorrow brings."

"Very well," I said reluctantly, and left the room.

The next morning Henry arrived after breakfast to inquire after Konrad and our household, and it was grand to see him again, even in such dire circumstances.

He stayed with us all morning and, just before lunch, the footman entered the sitting room with a letter.

"From your mother, I believe," he said, offering me the envelope on a silver tray.

Most eagerly I took it and opened it.

"Read it aloud," Elizabeth urged me.

> *My Dears,*
>
> *I wish I had better news for you. When Dr. Lesage came yesterday he said that Konrad was not suffering from the pox, but from his old illness. Last night was very bad. He tossed and moaned, for not even sleep eases his pain.*
>
> *I write this letter to you at ten of the morning, and he still has not roused. His pulse is weak, and he is now so still and pale that it frightens me. I expect Dr. Lesage again shortly. But unless there is some drastic improvement, I fear the worst.*
>
> *My dear Elizabeth, I have never asked you this, but please pray. Pray that Dr. Murnau arrives soon.*
>
> *I would ask you all to come back, but another servant has broken out with the pox, and Dr. Lesage says we must wait another day before he knows whether*

it is smallpox or its milder cousin. So for now, please
remain in Geneva.

Do not read this letter to Ernest. Tell him that
Konrad just needs a little longer to recover. He is too
young to bear such worries.

With my great love,
Mother

"Konrad's dying," I said.

"You can't know that," Elizabeth retorted, her voice catching.

I stood. "I am going to Polidori, to finish the elixir."

Elizabeth said nothing for a moment. Her eyes glimmered with tears. "The last time Polidori gave an elixir to someone, it *killed* them."

"*This* elixir will be different!"

"I could never forgive myself if we murdered Konrad."

"Can you forgive yourself if we do nothing?"

"I say we continue," said Henry quietly.

In surprise and gratitude I turned to him.

"Easy for you," Elizabeth snapped. "You wait at the bottom of the tree! Or outside the cave!"

"My days of waiting and watching are over," said Henry. "I'm ashamed of my cowardice. From now on, I'm coming wherever our journey takes us—be it the very gates of Hell!"

I clapped him on the shoulder, stirred by his passion. "That—*that*—is the kind of strength needed now! Well said, Henry Clerval. To the very gates of hell! Let us be off at once."

I strode for the door.

"Wait," said Elizabeth. "I will come with you."

Chapter 14

THE FINAL INGREDIENT

"Your brother, how is his health?" Polidori asked as he opened the parlour door to us.

"Very poor indeed," Elizabeth said.

"I am most distraught to hear it," said Polidori, looking at me closely. "Come in, come in."

We three followed him inside. The room was malodorous, with the smell of wet cat. Krake was sprawled before the hearth, gazing at us with his green eyes.

"Please sit," Polidori said.

"I cannot," I said, pacing. "Just tell me what we need."

Polidori hesitated a moment, as if reluctant. "This last ingredient is different from the others, and you may be sur—"

"Out with it! The sooner we know, the sooner we can get to work. My brother's life fades with every minute!"

I felt a hand on mine, and turned to Elizabeth. The calm reassurance of her gaze was like a balm to my inflamed soul. I allowed myself a deep breath and then exhaled, feeling ashamed.

"Forgive me, Mr. Polidori. I am not myself."

"No, no, young sir, it is I who must apologize. I'm long-winded, I know. You will be pleased to know the ingredient is easily had."

"That is excellent news!" Elizabeth exclaimed.

"But it will severely test your resolve," said Polidori.

"What do you mean?" Henry asked nervously.

"You must be very sure you wish to proceed," said the alchemist, and there was in his eyes a blaze of passion I had not seen since he'd first set eyes on the book of Paracelsus.

"We are ready," I said impatiently. "Death knocks at my brother's door. Tell us what we need."

"The last ingredient is fresh marrow from a bone."

I nodded, very much encouraged. "Excellent. Where is your nearest butcher?"

"It must be human bone," Polidori said.

"Ah," said Henry weakly.

I swallowed, and glanced at Elizabeth. "Very well. We must pay a visit to a charnel house, or morgue. With a bit of silver it shouldn't be so difficult."

Polidori was shaking his head. "It must be obtained from a *living* body. And there is more . . ."

He looked at me with an intensity that was almost hypnotic. I felt my knees weaken. I feared very much what was to come.

"According to Agrippa," Polidori continued, "it must come from the person closest to the taker of the elixir."

"This is too much," Henry breathed beside me. "This is akin to witchcraft. Your father was right—"

"Shush!" I said to Henry, fearing he would mention Father's name or somehow reveal our identity.

"I told you it would test your resolve," said Polidori. "I myself felt dizzy when I translated the words. It is not something—"

"How *much* bone marrow?" I demanded, pacing again.

"Ah," said Polidori, "this news is somewhat better. Not so very much."

"Victor," said Henry, "you cannot even consider—"

"How much?" I shouted. "Can you not give me a simple answer?"

"I calculate two fingers should be enough."

My eyes darted instinctively to my right hand—the one I used least. "My fourth and fifth fingers?" I asked.

"The entirety of them, yes, should be sufficient."

I folded down my last two fingers, tried to imagine my hand without them. I had seen soldiers return from their wars with stumps where their legs used to be, with arms severed at the elbow. The sight had stirred in me horror and immense pity, for it seemed a terrible thing to go through life so diminished. But the loss of two fingers would be nothing like that.

"It would not be so bad," I said. "I could still grip things . . ."

"Victor," Elizabeth said quietly to me, "you are pale. Are you sure?"

I nodded.

"Because if you are not," she said, "I am."

Henry inhaled sharply. I looked at my cousin in amazement. The idea of her wounded and disfigured was too awful.

"Nothing must injure your hands," I said. "No. It will not work, in any event. It must be from his closest relation. I am his brother. The same blood flows through our veins."

"But I am his cousin," she said, "so our blood cannot be so very different. And I love him. We are soulmates."

Her words were daggers in my breast. For a moment I could not speak.

"And in any event," she went on, "Mr. Polidori did not say 'blood relation'; he said 'closest.' These are different things."

I looked at the alchemist. "What was Agrippa's *precise* meaning?"

"The young lady is correct. The translation is no easy thing, and there are many different meanings of 'close' from the Latin. How to weigh blood relations with the love of one's soulmate . . ."

"It's out of the question," I said. "I won't allow it."

Elizabeth's voice was hard. "You are not my master, Victor."

"It will be me!" I shouted. "Damn you, let it be me!"

What was it that overmastered me? Was it my jealousy, the fact that she loved him so much she was willing to sacrifice some part of herself? Or was it the mere thought that anyone could be closer to Konrad than I was?

"Do it now," I said to Polidori.

"You are sure, young sir?"

I nodded.

Once more he led us down the short corridor to the elevator. My feet scarcely felt the floor; the walls seemed like shimmering veils. Down we went to the laboratory.

Polidori wheeled himself about and lit more candles and lanterns, including a large chandelier that he raised above a long narrow table. He had indeed prepared for my coming. On the table was a neat pile of clean linens, a mound of cotton, rolls of bandage. And on a separate table nearby were several chisels and a mallet.

At the sight of them, my stomach turned over and I retched, tears stinging my eyes, before I regained my composure.

"You do not have to go through with this," Henry murmured to me.

"I must," I said. Without this elixir I was sure Konrad would die. And if I did not give my bone marrow, Elizabeth would give hers—and that was something I could not endure.

Polidori took up the chisels and turned to Henry. "Young sir, could you fill a cauldron with water and place it on the fire. Once it boils, submerge these instruments within for five minutes to sterilize them."

Henry went off, looking rather green. Polidori next turned to Elizabeth.

"I already know, my lady, that you are not squeamish."

"Not in the least," she said stoutly.

"Excellent. You shall be my assistant in this surgery. Young master, you will be more comfortable, I think, if you lie down."

I lay down on the narrow table. The head was angled upward slightly, so I could watch as Polidori proceeded to strap my right arm down along a side table, now covered in clean white linens.

I did not like having my arm tied, but I could see it was necessary, even as my thoughts became gauzy and unreal. I had to be kept still, for the pain would doubtless be—

I gritted my teeth and dashed these thoughts from my mind by staring at Elizabeth, her luxuriant hair around her face. She would see how brave I was, how great my devotion to my brother—and to her. I would bring her back her beloved.

She met my gaze and held it, and I felt her eyes fill me with strength. She smiled. If only I could keep seeing that smile during the operation, I would be all right.

Henry returned with the sterilized chisels wrapped in clean linen.

"Listen here," he said to Polidori, in an atypically forceful tone. "Are you qualified to perform this kind of surgery?"

"Find me a surgeon who will willingly perform it, and I will happily let him," Polidori replied.

We all knew no respectable physician would remove my fingers just for the asking, and we had no time anyway. Konrad needed the elixir now.

"Have you any experience, though?" Henry asked the alchemist.

I did not know which would be more reassuring: if he had none, or if he had merrily amputated many people's limbs during his career.

"My tools are not a surgeon's tools, I grant you," said Polidori, "but for the task at hand, I warrant they are the best suited."

"There will be a good deal of bleeding. You know how to stop it?"

"Indeed I do, young sir. Once I knew the dire task ahead of me, I took pains to research the precise surgical procedure. I can promise you, I have thought everything through. Your friend will recover swiftly from these injuries, free of infection."

"If any harm comes to him, his father will have you hanged," Henry said. "And if he doesn't, I swear I will do it myself."

My heart swelled at Henry's loyalty.

Polidori smiled kindly, and placed a soothing hand on my friend's arm. "There is no need for such dreadful oaths. All will be well."

With tongs Polidori carefully placed the chisels on the table to which my arm was strapped.

"Are you ready to begin?" he asked me. I found his calm confidence reassuring.

I tried to say yes, but my throat was so dry that not even a croak came from it. I simply nodded.

"Now, you will need this for the pain." He handed me a glass filled nearly to the brim with amber liquid. I did not attempt to be brave; I downed the fiery substance in two swallows. My vision doubled, but I felt a reckless numbness sweep through me.

I think I started to laugh, quite beside myself. "Don't watch, Henry. It won't be pleasant." I waved my free hand. "There is probably some book to interest you here."

"I will stay at your side," he said, and pulled a stool closer.

"Thank you, Henry," I said. "You are a true friend."

"Grip my hand if it helps the pain. As tight as you like."

I wiggled my soon-to-be-amputated fingers. "'Close at hand,'" I said to Polidori. "That was what you said earlier. Was that a joke?"

"I did not realize it," the alchemist said with a small smile.

I looked down at my fingers. I did not really believe I was about to lose them, for my mind kept veering away from the idea, refusing to let me comprehend it completely. But:

They would be gone.

Suddenly I felt a greedy animal fear keen within me. I could not be brave much longer.

"Do it!" I cried. "Do it now!"

"Young miss, if you would make sure the site is kept clean."

Elizabeth sat down on a small stool, her back to me, and I was very grateful she blocked my view. I felt my smallest finger separated from its fellows by a large wooden peg—splayed off to one side to make it easier for my surgeon.

"I will be quick," Polidori promised.

I felt the brief, light touch of a chisel's edge against the place where my fifth finger met my hand. Then the instrument was lifted away.

"No, the narrower one, I think, please," Polidori told Elizabeth.

A second cold chisel was placed against my hand, its pressure firmer and sharper this time, testing. I caught a glimpse of Polidori's arm raised high with the mallet, and I clenched my eyes shut. What followed was a blow that seemed to travel through every bone and ligament of my body, to the very roots of my teeth.

There was no pain, not one bit—not yet.

"Please staunch the flow of blood," I heard the alchemist tell Elizabeth, "while I proceed with the second finger."

Dimly I felt the wooden peg separate my fourth finger from the others, felt a chisel tap once more against my flesh. I scarcely felt the blow that severed my finger forever from my body.

"It is done," said Polidori—

And *then* came the pain, twin lightning bolts coursing through my missing fingers, my wrist, and up my arm.

I cried out. I do not know what I uttered, only that noise and curses torrented from my mouth, and my body arched. I was vaguely aware of Polidori saying to Henry:

"Bring me the poker from the fire, please."

Time was not making sense anymore, for almost immediately Henry stood there with a metal rod, three inches of its tip glowing orange, making my friend look altogether devilish.

Light-headed, I managed to croak: "What is that for?"

Thudding pain pulsed in my hand, in sync with my racing

heartbeat. I imagined all my blood pumping out through the twin wounds, and my vision swam.

"We must cauterize the wounds, young master," Polidori said. "To stop the bleeding and prevent infection."

I caught sight of Henry glimpse my hand, and saw his face lose all its colour.

Swiftly Polidori took the poker. "Remove the cotton," he told Elizabeth.

She turned to me. Her face was drawn but she gave a valiant smile. She put her hands on my shoulders, pressed her cheek against mine.

"It's almost over," she whispered, and then came a searing pain so overwhelming that it bundled me up inside it and tumbled me over and over into darkness.

When I regained consciousness, Elizabeth was standing over me, mopping my forehead with a cool cloth. I just stared at her, and thought her the most beautiful thing in all the wide world. If only I could be allowed to stare at her like this, I would be a happy man.

"He's awake!" she said, and I realized Henry was standing at my other side, looking at me with concern.

"How long?" I croaked.

"Two hours," she said, and leaned forward and kissed my forehead. "Thank God, thank God."

Her hair fell around me, and her scent embraced me, but it wasn't enough to ward off the pain. It came with a fury, a hot rhythmic anvil pounding.

"How's my hand?" I asked.

"It was well done," said Elizabeth, nodding as though to reassure herself as much as me. "Very clean and quick. And the bleeding has all but stopped."

She stepped to one side so I could look down at my hand. Bandages bound my palm, wrapped round and round the place where my fourth and fifth fingers had once been. I wiggled my remaining three fingers, just to assure myself that they were still attached. It did not look so very odd. One would scarcely notice. But for a moment I imagined Mother's heartbroken face when she next beheld me, and tears welled up in my eyes.

"What have I done?" I whispered. "Dear God . . ."

"You have done the bravest thing I've ever seen, my friend," said Henry fervently.

"Indeed you have," said Elizabeth.

I tore my gaze from my forever crippled hand and saw, across the cellar, Polidori hunched industriously over a worktable.

I tried to sit up, and a wave of queasiness crested over me.

"Slowly does it," said Henry, taking hold of my left arm to steady me. "You lost a good deal of blood."

"Did I?" I asked Elizabeth.

"Not so very much," she said, and narrowed her eyes at Henry. "It looked more than it was."

I swung my legs over the side of the table, paused to let my stomach settle, and then stood. The floor seemed a great distance away. It took me several moments to catch my breath. Henry and Elizabeth each took an arm, and I shuffled over to Polidori.

"How goes it with the elixir?"

He did not look up from his work. "Young master, you'd be

better off resting comfortably. Your body has suffered quite an insult, and you might not enjoy seeing my work."

I saw it. I heard Henry's swallow. My two severed fingers rested on a metal tray. The skin and tissue and muscle had already been removed from one of them, leaving only the bones themselves. There was a good amount of blood and pulpy matter.

"I will not watch," said Henry. He crossed the room and sat at Polidori's paper-strewn desk.

Elizabeth and I remained. She pulled a stool over for me, and helped me sit upon it, for I was still weak and shaky.

It was horrible yet strangely fascinating to watch Polidori as he picked up a short brutal-looking instrument and sawed through one of the bones. Then, with an ingeniously thin, hooked pick, he started to extract the marrow and deposit it in a small vial that rested within a larger flask filled with ice.

"It is important the marrow be kept cold," he murmured as he worked.

"Why?" I asked.

"To prolong the life of the animating spirit that dwells within it," he replied. "Of all human marvels, it is believed, the greatest healing properties lie within the marrow."

It sounded most strange and wondrous to me—but not so very different from Dr. Murnau's pronouncements on human blood and the many cells that lived within it.

"How many doses will it yield?" I asked. "How shall we administer it to my brother?"

"It will be just one dose," said Polidori, "and must all be taken at once, by mouth."

He had finished extracting all the marrow from my fourth

finger bone, and was now expertly flaying the skin and tissue from my smallest finger. His expression as he worked was one of immense and emotionless concentration.

On a shelf above his worktable I saw two vials.

"Are those the other ingredients?" Elizabeth asked, following my gaze.

"Indeed. The coelacanth oil and the lunar lichen. Once I extract the last of the marrow, I will combine the ingredients."

"We'll be able to take it home tonight, then," I said with a glad heart. Konrad would have the elixir within hours.

"Sadly, no," Polidori replied as he worked. "The elixir must be left for an entire day to build to its full power. You will need to come back tomorrow to collect it."

Faintly, through the cellar walls, came the tolling of St. Peter's. Eight bells.

"It is best you go now," the alchemist said. "I will have it ready for you tomorrow."

"He is very close to death," Elizabeth said anxiously. "What if he does not survive the night?"

"I am sorry, miss," said the alchemist. "It cannot be hurried."

"Can we not take the elixir home with us now," I asked desperately, "and store it safely until it is ready?"

"No," said Polidori, "there is one final treatment that must take place just before it is imbibed."

"Could you write us down clear instructions?" Elizabeth asked.

"Your recipe for the wolf vision tincture was wonderfully clear," I said. "I'm sure I could—"

With uncharacteristic terseness he said, "It is a procedure I must perform myself." Then his tone softened. "I am only thinking of your brother and his best success for recovery. Let me do this for him. If you cannot return, I will send Krake to deliver it to you."

Even if I had been willing to wait, I was not willing to tell Polidori where we lived. Should he find out our family name, he might fly into a fury and refuse to help us further. I quickly thought of another excuse.

"But Krake might break it by accident. It is better we take it now."

"Krake treads with a velvet step," said Polidori. "He is less likely to break it than you. I am sorry, but it must wait a day so I can make the final preparations."

"There seems nothing we can do, then," I muttered. I looked at Henry across the room and saw him staring at me urgently.

Carefully I lowered myself from the stool. For a second I needed to hold the seat for balance.

"Are you all right?" Elizabeth asked.

"Yes. I just need a few steps to clear my head." I made my way gradually toward Henry.

When I reached him, he silently pushed a piece of paper into my hand and put his finger to his lips. On the paper, he'd written:

He lies.

Henry tapped a parchment on Polidori's cluttered desk. I could see it had to be some bit of translation for the elixir, for among the many fierce scratchings-out were characters I recognized from the Alphabet of the Magi, and then several other alphabets, one of which was Greek—my weakest subject.

Henry was jabbing his finger at a particular sentence. In vain I tried to decipher it.

I looked at Henry and shook my head. Impatiently he gestured me closer, then whispered in my ear.

"It says here, 'The elixir must be imbibed within four hours, after the three ingredients have been combined.'"

Despite the heat of the cellar I shivered. It was like I was suddenly seeing the world through a different lens. The haze that had veiled everything since the surgery evaporated and everything was sharper—and much, much more dangerous.

I forced myself to take five deep breaths, then made my way back to Polidori's workbench, where he was in the process of mixing the ingredients into a single flask. I needed to be very calm.

"There it is," said Elizabeth.

The Elixir of Life.

It did not look inspiring. It did not gleam and refract the candlelight into a thousand rainbows of promise. It was murky brown and oily. I watched as Polidori pushed in a stopper and slipped the flask into a snug padded leather sheath.

"Mr. Polidori," I said, "we've been very remiss in not offering you payment sooner. You have worked long and hard for us, and received nothing. I apologize. You must tell us what it is we owe you for your excellent services, and we can settle accounts now. Simply name your price." If he meant to cheat us of the elixir—if he'd maybe promised it to someone else at a vast price—maybe I could change his mind. "We're wealthy people, and—"

"My dear sir," Polidori said, beholding me with such an affable look that I wondered if Henry were mistaken. "Let us first see if the elixir has its desired effect. If it does, the recipe itself is payment enough for me. Now, have you a conveyance to take you home? I could send for a carriage."

"Quite unnecessary, thank you," I said. "Are you sure there is no way we could take the elixir away with us tonight?"

He seemed about to object once more, but with a sigh he nodded. "Very well. I can see how concerned you are about your brother."

I exhaled with relief, and smiled over at Henry. We were mistaken. Perhaps my friend's knowledge of Greek was not as perfect as I'd imagined.

"Thank you, Mr. Polidori!" said Elizabeth. "It eases my mind greatly."

"Just give me a moment to fetch a preserving agent from upstairs," he said, wheeling himself away from his workbench toward the elevator. "Then I will change the dressings on your wounds once more, young master, and write down very detailed instructions on how to perform the final preparations before the elixir is taken."

"I'm very grateful," I said.

I looked past Polidori at Henry and saw him desperately shaking his head. He still didn't trust the alchemist. But why not? He was just going upstairs to—and then I remembered. All the drawers in his shop were completely empty. There could be nothing he needed up there. My eyes flew to the workbench. The flask of elixir was gone. I turned to see Polidori already halfway to the elevator.

He means to leave us trapped down here.

At the exact same moment, Henry and I ran and planted ourselves in front of Polidori's wheelchair. He looked at us in surprise. I saw the stoppered flask of elixir in his lap. I could not keep the tremor from my voice.

"Mr. Polidori, I must ask that you give me the elixir now."

He gave a chuckle. "Good heavens, are you worried I'll abscond with it? In my *chair*? If it makes you feel better, here— hold it yourself."

With his left hand he held out the leather-clad flask.

And with his right he pulled from his chair a cane with a clubbed end. Without warning he swung it expertly and struck Henry in the head. Henry did not even cry out, just crumpled to the floor, deadly still.

"Henry!" Elizabeth cried in horror.

"You fiend!" I roared.

He seemed all at once a transformed creature. Gone was the mild expression, the air of defeat. His face blazed with a ruthless strength and his upper body no longer sagged. He sat bolt upright, his shirt taut against his barrel chest. His forearms, with their sleeves rolled back, were ridged with muscle.

He launched his chair at me with such force that he knocked me over. I landed on my wounded hand and howled with pain.

From the corner of my eye I saw him raise his cane over me like an executioner's axe. I rolled out of the way just as the clubbed head cracked down upon the flagstone. Polidori swivelled expertly to face me, cane raised once more.

I scrabbled away crablike, pain shooting up my right arm. His chair struck me again, sending me sprawling. Wig askew, he glowered over me. He had me backed against a wall, and even as I lifted my arm to ward off the blow, I knew it was futile. That club would shatter my bones.

A poker struck Polidori on the shoulder so hard that he

dropped his cane with a yowl. I looked over and saw Elizabeth gripping the weapon.

"Hit him again!" I shouted.

"He's in a wheelchair!" Elizabeth cried.

"He means to kill us!"

I lunged to the side and tried to snatch up Polidori's devilish cane, but from the bottom of his chair, from all sides, sprang long wickedly sharp blades. One very nearly impaled my leg as I leapt up onto a worktable, sending glassware shattering.

"Look out!" I shouted to Elizabeth. "His chair's spiked!"

Polidori snatched up his cane and turned on Elizabeth. He was a demon in his chair, riding it like a malevolent barbed steed, driving her into a corner.

From the table I grasped a heavy flask full of vile-smelling liquid and hurled it at Polidori. It shattered against his skull. Instantly his wig began to smoke and melt, releasing acrid vapours. He gave a cry and ripped the wig from his head. On his bald scalp a few red welts were already blooming.

Cursing, he swerved away from Elizabeth and launched himself toward the sink. It gave her the chance to run clear, and together we rushed to Henry, still sprawled on the ground, though moaning now. Alive! I shook him roughly.

"Henry, get up! Get up!"

His eyes opened blearily. I looked around in a frenzy and saw Polidori with his head bent under the water pump, trying to flush the acid from his flesh.

"We must go!" said Elizabeth, helping me pull Henry to his feet. "The elevator!"

"Not without the elixir!" I said.

I snatched the poker from Elizabeth and ran toward Polidori.

Before I reached him, he whirled his chair round to confront me. His face was livid with acid burns, and anger emanated from his face like a kiln's heat. I stayed well back from the chair's wicked blades. I could not see his cane. Polidori's hands slipped inside the large pockets of his vest, no doubt concealing the flask of elixir, for it was no longer in his lap.

"Give it to me," I said, poker held high over my shoulder. "It contains only my marrow. It's useless to anyone but my brother." My stomach churned. "Or was that a lie too?"

"Indeed it was. Any marrow would suffice."

We'd merely been Polidori's pawns, used to gather the ingredients—used to sacrifice our body parts. I felt a rage building inside me, and I welcomed it.

"You monster!" I spat.

"I did not want it to be this way, young master," he said with a trace of what seemed genuine ruefulness. "My plan was to make two doses of the elixir. One for your brother. One for myself."

"Why didn't you, then?" I demanded.

"You did not bring me enough lichen from the tree."

With a sick heart I remembered how I'd forced Elizabeth to abandon her task before her vial was full.

"We had no choice," Elizabeth said. "There was lightning, and the vultures!"

"I completely understand," said Polidori. "But the result was that I had ingredients for one dose only. The good news, for you, young master, is that I only needed to take two fingers, and not four."

"The elixir's mine! Give it to me!"

"Very well," said the alchemist.

Both hands flew from his pockets. In the palm of one was a mound of yellow powder. In the other was some kind of tinderbox, which was instantly aflame. He raised the powder to his lips and blew, igniting a comet of fire that streamed toward me.

I scarcely had time to fling an arm across my face before I was engulfed. Vile fumes seared my nostrils and choked me. Something struck me hard, and I crashed to the floor, rolling over and over to put out the flames—but amazingly, I was not alight at all. The flame had spent itself seemingly without scorching me. Coughing, I staggered to my feet and saw Polidori hurtling toward the elevator, bellowing and swinging his brutal cane to clear Elizabeth and Henry from his path.

Fury obliterated my pain and exhaustion. I ran and, with a roar, threw myself at the back of his wheelchair. My weight tipped it, and it slewed wildly before toppling over, spilling Polidori face down onto the floor. For a brief moment I almost pitied him, his withered legs thin and quivering as he scrambled to turn himself over.

"Victor, he has the elixir!" Henry cried.

Polidori's back was to me, and I had to run around him to see that the vial was indeed in his hands, and he was pulling at the stopper.

I lunged and knocked it from his grasp. In shared horror we both watched as the vial hit the flagstones—but did not break. Then I felt his fist slam into my jaw and drive my head back.

With stunning speed he dragged his body atop mine and had my neck locked in one powerful, flexed arm.

"You will not deny me this," he hissed. "You will not deny me the chance of being healed."

I writhed and flailed, but his wrestler's grip closed ever tighter around my windpipe, cutting off my air.

"Get me the vial!" he shouted at Henry and Elizabeth. "Or I will break his neck!"

My injured hand plucked uselessly at his arm. My vision swam. My heart kicked violently and suddenly a great weight fell upon me and—

I had air, and gasped to fill my lungs.

Henry, the poker gripped in his hands, towered over me. Polidori's senseless body was toppled upon my chest. I pushed him off, and Elizabeth helped me to my feet.

"Well done, Henry," I croaked.

"Have I killed him?" he said. He was trembling.

"He breathes," I said. "Where is the elixir?"

Elizabeth held the vial up before me, and we all turned and ran for the elevator. Inside I stared at the confusion of dangling ropes and pulleys. I cursed myself for not paying more attention when Polidori had worked them.

"This one, I think," Elizabeth said, pointing.

"Henry, your help," I said. We seized the rope and pulled, but nothing happened. In a frenzy I began tugging at others.

From the cellar floor came a groan.

"He's stirring!" cried Henry.

"I'm *sure* it's this one!" Elizabeth said, jabbing a finger.

"You already pointed at that one!"

"Yes," she said, "because it's the *right* one."

"It does nothing! Look!"

"There was a lever or a brake he pulled first," she muttered, looking around wildly, pushing at things.

Henry's icy hand gripped my shoulder. Polidori was lifting

his head from the floor. I wished we had brought the poker. He glared at us. I had never seen such determination or malice. He flexed his arms and began walking toward us on his fists with terrifying speed, dragging his body behind him.

"Try now!" Elizabeth cried.

Polidori was not fifteen feet away.

We heaved at the rope, and this time felt the elevator's frame shiver and lift a few inches off the floor.

"Again! Don't stop!" I cried, for Polidori was very near the threshold.

He lunged, his right hand straining for the edge of the elevator floor, but Henry and I gave a mighty heave and hoisted ourselves just out of reach. We heard his strangled curse of defeat.

"He cannot get us now!" panted Henry.

We kept hauling at the rope, but were so exhausted that we rose more slowly with every pull. My right hand was of little use, and the pain in my wounds was brutal. A rivulet of sweat ran into my eye.

Even with the three of us, we could barely budge the elevator. How could it suddenly have become so much heavier?

And just as I understood, an arm darted up over the edge and slammed down on the floor. Like some horrific white spider, the hand hopped about, and before I could dance clear, it fastened around my ankle and dragged me off my feet. I landed with a thud and grasped the rope for dear life, for I was being pulled hard.

Polidori's second arm came swinging over the edge and seized my other leg. Then his head lurched into view as he started hauling himself up my legs and into the elevator.

I thrashed about, trying to throw him off, but his grip was

so strong I feared his iron fingers would crush my flesh to pulp.

Henry grabbed one of Polidori's hands and began prying his fingers off my ankle. Elizabeth kicked his head. But it was as though he no longer felt pain, as though his muscle and tissue would never tire.

My grip on the rope tightened and I noticed that as Polidori pulled on *me,* he also pulled on the rope, and so the elevator was still rising, albeit slowly. I looked up and saw we were not so far from the cellar's stone ceiling.

"Henry!" I yelled. "Keep pulling!"

"What?" he shouted.

"Raise us!"

At this, Polidori looked up, and seemed to understand my plan, for he redoubled his efforts to clamber up me and into the elevator. His belly, hips, and legs still dangled over the edge.

In three feet he would have to let go, or be crushed.

Elizabeth kicked at him again, and he lost his grip for a moment, sliding down my body. I thought he might fall off altogether, but he grabbed hold of both my ankles. The elevator lurched upward.

Less than two feet now to the ceiling.

With a burst of preternatural energy and speed, he climbed up me once more: clawing up my legs, then grabbing at my waist. I bellowed and kicked even as I hauled on the rope with Henry.

The elevator lurched up another foot.

"Let go!" I shouted at him. "Or you'll be severed!"

"And you will lose your feet!" he bellowed back.

In horror I saw he was right. He had dragged my legs over the edge.

For a moment no one moved. The elevator was filled with the sound of our animal grunts and panting.

"Then I will live without them!" I roared into the alchemist's acid-stained face. "Henry, Elizabeth, pull hard!"

With all my strength I heaved on the rope. The elevator lurched up. Polidori tilted his face to the stone bearing down on him—and let go. The elevator, suddenly lighter, rocketed higher. I yanked my legs back, and stone grazed my feet as the gap closed before us.

We were in total darkness now, for we had not thought to bring a candle or lantern. And for a moment we just sat sprawled on the elevator floor, panting raggedly.

"We had best keep going," I said. "He may have some way of summoning the elevator back to him."

"Yes, you're right," said Elizabeth.

I felt her breath on my face, and realized she was close to me.

"You were very brave, Victor," she said.

I stroked her cheek with the three fingers of my right hand. I moved my face closer to hers, and our mouths met in the darkness. I felt her tears on her cheeks, and tasted their salt against my tongue.

Abruptly she stood. "Come on," she said. "Let's get to the surface!"

From below came the sound of Polidori shouting and cursing. I could not make out many of his words, for at times he seemed to be raging in another language.

"He wanted it for himself," I puffed as we raised the elevator together. "He wanted his legs back."

"He never meant for us to have it," said Elizabeth. "He just used us to fetch his ingredients, the devil."

Suddenly the elevator bumped to a stop, and I saw the faint-est crack of light before us. The secret panels! Gasping for air, as though we'd been trapped beneath the sea, I stepped for-ward to throw them open.

"Wait!" Henry whispered, yanking me back.

"What?" I demanded.

"Krake," he said.

Chapter 15

NIGHT FLIGHT

Tensed, I pushed open the elevator doors, ready for the
lynx to spring upon us.

The empty corridor stretched out in near darkness, only a
pale flicker of orange light coming from the parlour.

"When we entered," I whispered to the others, "Krake was
before the hearth."

"Let's hope he's asleep," Henry breathed.

"Keep watch behind us," I told him. "Elizabeth, set your
gaze high; he is a good climber."

As we stepped out of the elevator, its wooden planks groaned
briefly and the sound seemed huge in the silent house. Once
more I cursed myself for not bringing the poker or Polidori's
clubbed cane. Slowly we made our way down the corridor,
pausing before the branch in the passage that led to the lava-
tory and bedchamber.

I listened. I sniffed, in case I could smell Krake. But he was
the predator, not me, and his ears and nose were keener than
mine. I leaned out around the corner. The corridor was empty.

We hurried on, past the closed kitchen door, toward the

parlour. As we neared it, more of the room became visible in the pale light from the crackling embers.

On the mantelpiece ticked Polidori's clock. The time was half past nine.

In thirty minutes the gates of the city would close, and they would not open again until five o'clock the following morning.

We could not be trapped inside the city for the night.

The elixir had to be taken within four hours of its making.

Stealthily I moved into the room, far enough to see the rug before the hearth. Krake sat upon it, his back to us, looking directly into the embers as though mesmerized. His ears were pricked high.

I turned to the others and gestured for them to follow. We could move past, behind the lynx.

With every step I watched Krake, but his attention seemed hypnotically focused on the embers. Halfway across the room, I heard something—a kind of hiss emanating from the fireplace. It took me a moment before I realized it was Polidori's voice, carried upward to Krake through the chimney. I did not catch the words, and did not want to know in what devilish way these two communicated. With every step I took, Polidori's voice seemed to get louder and more urgent, and when it stopped, the silence was like a sudden noise.

The clock ticked, and Krake turned and stared straight at us.

"Run!" I cried.

Krake snarled, and every hair on my body bristled. I reached the door to the storefront and flung it back. Lamplight from the street spilled through the grimy shop windows. Krake gave another terrible shriek, closer now. We hurtled across the shop, threw the door wide, and ran headlong down the dark cobblestones of Wollstonekraft Alley.

Before we rounded the corner, I glanced back, but did not see Krake pursuing us. Still we ran, until we came out upon a public square where there was torchlight and people about— though mostly of the drunken sort. Here I stopped and bent over, breathless, my amputated fingers throbbing as though they were still there.

"We will need the horses," Henry said. "We must get back to your stables."

From across the city, St. Peter's tolled the quarter hour. Fifteen minutes till ten.

"We will not make it to the Rive Gate in time," I said. We were too far from my house. Even if we ran all the way, readied the horses, and rode full tilt to the gates, they would already be locked for the night.

"What do you intend to do, then?" Henry demanded.

"The river gate," I said. "We're no more than a few minutes away."

It was the city's only entrance by water. But the harbour itself was sealed off shortly after ten o'clock. Two massive chains were strung between the two shores and raised to prevent any vessel from leaving or entering.

Henry looked at me as though I were feverish. "We have no boat!" he said.

"We will obtain one." I was already running. "But we must get there fast. The wind is southwesterly. It will blow us straight to Bellerive!"

Elizabeth and Henry followed, easily keeping pace with me, for I was much weakened by my ordeal and fighting for breath.

We neared the city's ramparts, and on the broad street that led down to the harbour, I saw three guardsmen with torches making their way toward the gates to close them for the night.

"Hurry!" I gasped. Calling upon the last of my endurance, I raced on, streaking past the guards, through the archway, and onto the broad quay. Creaking at their moorings, tall ships were silhouetted against the dark sky.

I rushed toward the marina, where the smaller boats were docked. There was a great deal of activity on the wharves, as sailors boarded and disembarked from their ships. Those wishing to spend the night within the city walls had only a few more minutes to get there. Not that there was any shortage of company quayside for the sailors. Small braziers burned everywhere, and there were whistles and hoots and the shrill laughter of loose women. The three of us fit right in, looking like urchins, me especially, with my sooty face, singed hair, and bloodied bandages.

At the marina my heart sang when I saw a smallish boat newly tied up against a slip, and two fishermen hauling out their catch. I rushed to them.

"I have need of your boat for one night," I panted. "Name your price, please."

They looked at me as though I were deranged, until they saw my purse. I spilled a pile of silver coins into my palm. "Will this do?" I asked.

They looked at each other, knowing very well that the amount was nearly the value of their boat.

"Who are you?" one of them asked.

"Do we have a contract?" I said.

"You know how to sail her?" he demanded.

"Indeed."

I put the coins into his hand and closed his fingers around them. "I'll have her back by tomorrow night," I promised, and stepped aboard. "Henry, Elizabeth, we don't have much time."

There was a bit of bustle and confusion, for the fishermen had not quite unloaded their catch, and Henry and Elizabeth helped them, while I relit the beacons and readied the boat for sail.

"Where are you bound?" one of the fishermen asked me.

"Bellerive."

"You'll have the wind," he said, pushing us away from the slip. "If you get out of the harbour in time."

"Haul up the sail!" I sang out to Henry. "Elizabeth—the jib!"

Even as they pulled the halyards, I was at the tiller, trimming the mainsail so she best caught the wind.

"Mainsail up!" cried Henry.

"Forward now, Henry. You're my eyes."

"Jib's up," said Elizabeth.

She was a fine sailor, a better one than Henry, and I wanted her in the cockpit, ready to trim the foresail for me.

The moon was bright, mercy of mercies, silvering everything. I stood at the tiller, guiding the boat out of the marina and into the harbour proper. At its mouth, a tower rose from either shore. Fires burned at their summits, making silhouettes of the watchmen.

Within these towers were the giant winches that carried the chain. Once Father had taken Konrad and me inside to see the great windlasses. Five men were needed to turn them and haul the weed-strewn chains from the lake bed. When the men finished winding, the chains stretched taut across the harbour mouth, one three feet above the water's surface, the other fifteen.

Those chains were strong enough to snap the masts off much bigger ships than mine.

In a moment we caught the wind fully, and I gave the order to let out more sail. With satisfaction and a quickening heart I felt our bow dig deeper into the water.

In the distance a watchman shouted out from one of the towers:

"Bear away! Bear away!"

I held my course.

"They are signalling at us!" Henry cried from the bow.

I knew that in both towers the men were turning the windlasses—but I also knew we still had several minutes before the chains rose.

We ran with the wind, the water churning at our sides. I set my course for the centre of the harbour's mouth, for it was there that the chains would be last to break the surface.

"I see it near the shoreline!" Henry cried. "Victor, bear away! We'll strike it!"

I did not. "Elizabeth, mind the foresail!"

She let out her sheet a few more inches, and I could feel it give the boat just a bit more lift.

To either side I saw the giant links breaking the surface one after the other, soaring up into the air. If just one were to strike us, it would dash our hull to pieces—and us with it. I tightened my hand on the tiller. I would not stray from my course.

We were nearly there, about to cross the line. Links shot up to the left and right, drenching us with spray and weed and lake mud. Closer and closer they came to our boat. Almost through, but not quite. I gritted my teeth. And then, not ten feet behind my rudder, the entirety of the chain breached the water like some great leviathan come up for air.

"We did it!" Elizabeth cried.

"Thanks to your fine trimming!" I exclaimed.

Henry exhaled and shook his head, holding on to the shrouds for support. "I was not made for such adventuring," he called back to me. "That could very easily have gone the other way, Victor!"

"Think of what fabulous material this will give you, though, Henry," I said, and sank down beside the tiller, utterly spent.

The shoreline was well known to me, even by moonlight. In the distance I saw the dark outline of Bellerive's promontory, and set my course. If the wind continued strong, we would be at the chateau's boathouse within an hour.

"The elixir," I said, suddenly anxious. "Elizabeth, you still have it?"

She withdrew it carefully from a pocket of her dress.

"It's intact?" I asked, holding out my hand.

"You don't trust me?" she said, with some irritation.

"It will ease my mind to hold it."

With some reluctance she passed it to me. I slipped the vial from its protective leather sheath. The glass was unbroken, the cork still firmly in place. I put it back into the sheath and then into my own pocket.

The wind held steady, the sails needed no trimming, and there was little to do for the moment. Henry returned to the cockpit.

"What of Polidori?" he said.

"The fall was not high enough to harm him," I replied.

"We cannot leave him trapped in his cellar," said Elizabeth.

"The wretch may have some other means of escape," I said. I could not summon any sympathy for the fellow, and was surprised at my cousin's compassion. "But we will send word to the city guard tomorrow. They can rescue him in his forbidden laboratory."

We sailed in silence for a while, Elizabeth looking up at the stars. I thought of how many times all of us had done so, and drifted and talked and shared our thoughts.

"Can you see the future now?" I asked her.

"No." Her face was drawn, and I thought I saw a flash of tears in her eyes. "What if it doesn't work, Victor?"

The same question had been echoing in my head, and doubtless in Henry's too.

"We've done something extraordinary, the three of us," I said fiercely. "We've obtained the Elixir of Life. It is no spell or incantation. It's no different from Polidori's vision of the wolf. Or Dr. Murnau's medicine. The elixir will work. We must believe it."

"That will not make it so," said Henry.

Before I could reply, Elizabeth said fervently, "If our prayers to God have any influence on the workings of this world, we can make it so. We must! Banish your doubts if you have them. Konrad *will* be well again."

She spoke with utter conviction, her face gleaming, and although I did not believe in God as she did, I found myself nodding. And the familiar, hateful thought stole into my head once more.

She could be mine if . . .

Right then I wished I could pray. I would pray to be free of my wayward thoughts. I would pray, *Let him live.* How reassuring it would be to believe there was a kindly god looking over us, that he would take pity on our toil and suffering, and grant us what we asked.

But I knew it was not true, and there was no point indulging in such fantasy. The only source of power on this earth was our own.

We sailed on through the night, and though Henry reassured me again and again that hardly any time had passed, our voyage seemed to be taking forever. The dark line of the shore never grew any closer. We merely hovered in darkness.

The pain in my right hand increased. The pain itself I could endure, but nothing would bring my fingers back. For the first time I felt resentment.

I had sacrificed a part of my body.

I had given something away.

And in return I would get my brother's life. He would live—and not just live. He would be immune to all illness, a paragon of health and strength. He would be even more beautiful and skilled than before. What chance would I have then with Elizabeth?

Even if I bent my entire will to the task, tried my hardest, could I win her? I had kissed her lips too. I had sniffed her wolf scent and tasted her blood, like some vampyre, always hungry for more. Konrad knew only part of her. Her sweetness and goodness and good humour and intelligence. But he had not witnessed her full power and fury and passion.

I knew her better, and now I could never have her—and would be crippled for life.

I felt the vial against my leg, its weight far greater than seemed right for its small size. Almost without realizing what I was doing, I drew it out.

What would a drop do? I wondered. Just a drop. There would be enough for Konrad still. Would a drop ease my pain? Would it cause new fingers to grow, starfishlike, from the blackened stumps?

I pulled the vial from its sheath and beheld its dark lustre in the moonlight. If Polidori had thought it would heal his shattered legs, then surely it could birth two small fingers . . .

"Victor," said Henry.

"Hmm, what?" I said testily.

"Best put it back in your pocket. If the boat heels, you may drop it."

I noticed that Elizabeth too watched me closely.

I sniffed. "Very well." I slid it into my pocket.

From within the boat's cabin something shifted.

"It is just a stray fish flopping about," I said with a laugh. But I looked to shore. We were still a good thirty minutes away.

Elizabeth stepped back toward me. "Victor, there is something in there."

I saw the flash of eyes. A dreadful elongated shadow burst from the cabin, aimed directly at me, and sank its teeth into my leg. I bellowed, but not in pain for, somehow, the long teeth had pierced only my trousers.

It took me a moment to realize what this thing was, for the moon had transformed Krake into a ghostly apparition, with black eyes and a cratered, jagged mouth. Jaws clenched, he pulled back, tearing out my pocket.

"The elixir!" I cried as the vial flew out and hit the deck.

At once the lynx pounced upon it, mouth wide, as if to snap it up and crush it.

Henry was closest, and immediately clouted Krake on the

side of the head. The lynx recoiled with a snarl, spitting, and sprang up onto the cabin roof, his head swinging swiftly from Henry to Elizabeth to me, unsure of whom to attack. He showed his teeth, and they seemed unnaturally numerous—and sharp.

We all faltered. Henry took a step back. On the floor of the cockpit the vial rolled to and fro. Krake's eyes impaled it. Before I could make a move, Elizabeth ran for it. The lynx pounced, slamming against her legs and knocking her off her feet. With one paw he swiped at her face. She raised her arm to ward off the blow, but not quickly enough. She gave a cry. I saw bloody claw marks across her cheek.

I let go the tiller and lunged at Krake, but in one supple move he avoided me and scooped the vial into his jaws.

"No!" I gasped, as the beast nimbly vaulted onto the cabin roof. I looked over at Elizabeth. "Are you all right?"

"He wants the elixir for Polidori!" she shouted. "Look how he holds it in his mouth!"

I too saw how the fiendish beast did not chew the vial but with his tongue pushed it delicately to one side. He was as wicked and clever as a witch's familiar. He'd sat before the hearth, mesmerized by the hiss of his master's voice snaking up the chimney—and received his orders.

Krake looked now in all directions as if trying to decide which way was closest to land.

"He means to jump!" I cried. "Elizabeth, take the tiller!"

Overmastered by my panic and anger, I hurled myself again at the lynx, knowing he would fight me tooth and claw. But I had tooth and claw too, and meant to use them. Krake seemed to sense my bloody resolve, and darted toward the bow.

I scrambled after him. "Come here, you overgrown puss!"

Henry reached the lynx first and threw his body on top of him. Krake snarled and scratched, and the vial fell from his mouth and rolled along the deck toward the starboard side. I watched in horror as it knocked against the low railing. A good jostle would send it into the lake.

Henry was trying his best to grip Krake around the neck, but the lynx suddenly made himself skinny and squirted through his arms. The cat looked around wildly. I cursed myself for wasting time, and lunged now for the vial. But the lynx streaked by and once more took it in his mouth—

And jumped into the black water.

I had time only to shout "Heave to!" before I threw myself over the side. It was like plunging into night, so silky and dark was it beneath the surface. I came up, treading water, casting about, trying to spot Krake.

"Where is he?" I shouted back to the boat.

"There! There!" cried Henry, pointing.

I looked and caught sight of the slick hump of Krake's head, so low to the surface that it was almost impossible to track. He swam with surprising speed, and I started after him, pulling and kicking hard. After the glacial coelacanth pool, I scarcely noticed the coldness. In the moonlight I saw Krake outstripping me.

My spirit faltered, and I felt a great grief well up inside me and weaken me further. We had lost the elixir. We had failed. I had failed.

Then I heard the low gurgle of a hull moving through water, and turned to see the boat slice past me, Elizabeth at the tiller and Henry in the prow, spotting, speeding after Krake. Then, when they were abreast of him, Elizabeth let the sails luff. I saw her bend down and from the cockpit throw one of the fishermen's nets. It flew beautifully, unfurling in the moonlight and settling over a large patch of the water, like a great web.

"We have him!" she cried. "Henry, help me pull!"

Within the net thrashed Krake as he was dragged back toward the boat. The sight charged me with hope, and I swam hard, barely noticing the pain in my hand. Elizabeth and Henry hauled Krake alongside the hull and tied the net tightly to the starboard cleats so that the lynx hung suspended just above the water's surface.

Breathless, I reached the boat, and Henry helped me aboard. I was streaming wet.

Elizabeth fetched more lanterns and lit them so we could see the sodden lynx properly, his green eyes flashing malevolently.

"He still holds the vial!" cried Elizabeth. "It's unbroken!"

I saw it, tossing about in the lynx's mouth as he yowled balefully at us.

"Bring him aboard," I said, worried he might drop it into the lake.

"I'm reluctant," said Henry, but he pulled with Elizabeth and me.

Krake tumbled into the cockpit, thrashing and spitting. He could not get very far, so entangled was he in the net, but we all stepped up onto the bench seats, just to keep our feet clear of him.

"How will we get it out?" Elizabeth murmured.

"If we strike him too hard, he might crack it," Henry said.

The lynx's eyes, all this time, flickered between us, and I had the uncanny feeling he understood our talk. Slowly, almost smugly, he closed his mouth—and swallowed.

"No!" I cried.

Krake did not have an easy time of it. He gagged and hacked, but when his mouth opened once more, the vial was gone. His unnerving green eyes settled on me, and I could have sworn he smirked.

"The fiend!" gasped Henry. "How do we get it out now?"

Elizabeth and I looked at each other—and I knew the same idea had just occurred to us simultaneously.

"I saw a knife in the cabin," she said.

"Yes," I answered.

I did not want to waste a moment. Within Krake's stomach the vial's stopper might come loose—and then we would have a very, very healthy and powerful lynx aboard our boat.

I hurried below with a lantern and looked about the cramped cabin. Amid the jumble I found a harpoon, and a deboning knife. I took them up onto the deck.

The moment Krake beheld me, he knew. Immediately his eyes became as docile and beseeching as a kitten's. He strained through the netting with his paws, and made a mewing sound so pitiful that I felt myself falter. He had saved our lives once, in the Sturmwald.

All part of Polidori's dark design, I reminded myself.

I forced my mind to be still, my limbs to steady. I breathed deeply and took the harpoon in my hands.

Kill him.

I could not stab him in the heart, for the heart, I knew, was perilously close to the stomach—and in Krake's stomach was the glass vial.

So I raised my harpoon and struck him in his neck.

He yowled and writhed most terribly, but I struck him again, harder. I felt a stranger to myself, but strangely powerful too.

With each blow the smell of blood reached my nostrils and sharpened my animal instincts. I was dimly aware of making a sound, a kind of low growl in my throat. And then Krake moved no more.

My flanks heaved as I caught my breath. I knelt and began to untangle the lynx's body from the net. Elizabeth joined me, and together we laid the creature's limp body out on the cockpit floor.

I took up the knife and slit Krake from throat to belly. Hot viscera spilled out, and with it a penetrating stench. I saw Henry turn away, and I heard his miserable retching sounds. I looked at Elizabeth and saw she was steady.

Amid all the blood, it was difficult at first to identify the organs.

"Here is the esophagus," said Elizabeth, fearlessly tracing the muscular tube to a sac, pushing aside tissue and pulp. "And this must be the stomach."

I made an incision, and our hands reached together into the creature's hot innards, handling the contents of its stomach.

I glanced at her, and saw her face not battling revulsion but alive—excited, even.

"I have it!" she gasped. "I think I have it!"

And she pulled out from the gory mess a vial, still stoppered, still intact.

Tears of relief and joy rushed from her eyes, and we embraced. I wished, even in our bloody grip, that her arms would never release me.

But this time it was I who pulled away first, for in my head was the ticking of a great clock—or perhaps a great heartbeat. We had lost time.

"We need to get back to Konrad," I said.

We heaved Krake's remains into the lake, hurriedly shoved the net back into the cabin, and trimmed our sails. We ran with the wind, and it wasn't long before I could see the outline of our chateau and the pale flicker of candlelight in Konrad's room, where I knew either Mother or Maria would be at his bedside, watching over him.

We tied up at the dock, rushed into the boathouse, and thumped on the chateau door until it was opened by Celeste, one of our maids. She was in her nightgown and cap, holding a candle—and she looked upon us with horror, her hand flying up to her mouth to stifle a scream.

I suddenly remembered that I was soaked to the skin, and Elizabeth and I were both spattered with Krake's gore. "It's all right, Celeste."

"Master Victor . . . where have you three been? What has happened?"

"I'll explain later."

We hurried inside, upstairs to Konrad's bedchamber. Outside the door I faltered. I did not know what I would say if Mother was there. How would I explain? What if she refused to allow us to give him the elixir?

I opened the door silently and peered inside. To my immense relief it was Maria who sat dozing in a chair near Konrad's bed.

The three of us slipped inside.

Konrad was asleep, so waxy pale and still that I worried we were too late. But then I saw the weak rise and fall of his chest. As we drew to his bedside, Maria stirred, and her eyes opened and widened at the sight of us. She drew in her breath sharply, perhaps not sure if this were a nightmare.

"Don't be afraid," I said quietly. "All's well. We have the elixir."

From her pocket Elizabeth took the vial, the leather covering still crusted with Krake's blood.

"I scarcely know what to think," Maria said. "How——?"

"We completed the final preparations with Julius Polidori," Elizabeth told her.

"What happened to your hand?" Maria asked suddenly, seeing the frayed bandages.

"That doesn't matter right now," I said. "Where is Mother?"

"I sent her to bed a few hours ago—she is exhausted beyond all endurance."

I nodded. "Now is the time to do it, then."

"Wait," said Maria, her brow furrowed. "What if it should do him harm? I could never forgive myself."

"He barely breathes," Elizabeth said, taking Konrad's limp hand in her own. "We must try it—and pray."

Maria nodded once reluctantly, then again with more decision. "Yes, bring him back, Victor."

Elizabeth propped another pillow under my brother's head.

"Konrad," she said softly, "we have new medicine for you. Wake and take it."

He would not wake.

"We must administer it ourselves," I said.

I opened the vial. Elizabeth parted his lips carefully. I placed a small drop of the elixir on his tongue. I watched it trickle down into his throat. In his slumber he made a murmuring sound and swallowed. Only then did I release more onto his tongue.

Drop by drop I gave him the Elixir of Life. It took a full half hour. I dared not rush it, for fear he might gag or spit it out.

When the last drop was gone I looked at Henry and Elizabeth. I had never felt so tired in my life.

"It's done," I said. "All that we could do, is done."

Elizabeth brushed Konrad's lank hair back from his forehead, and he stirred again and this time his eyes opened.

"Konrad," I said.

He looked at me calmly, and with complete awareness, then at Henry, and finally at Elizabeth. He smiled, his eyes drooped shut, and he slept again.

Henry staggered off to get some sleep, and Elizabeth and I went to Father's study. I opened his medicine chest. I poured a measure of disinfectant onto a wad of cotton and carefully cleaned the wounds on Elizabeth's face.

She was brave and did not flinch. It was a mercy the cuts were not deep. Only the very tips of Krake's claws seemed to have caught her tawny flesh.

"It's not serious," I said. "I do not think they need suturing."

They still bled slowly, so I cut a piece of gauze and taped it delicately to her cheek. "There."

"Thank you," she said. "How is your hand?"

"It does not hurt much." She took my hand in hers and unwound the bandages.

"Is it hideous?" I asked, gazing upon it with a curious lack of feeling.

"No. It is heroic."

From Father's desk she took clean bandage and wound it around the stumps of my missing fingers.

"What will we tell Mother?" she said calmly.

"I don't know."

I felt like we were both dreamwalking, beyond our bodies, watching ourselves.

"How long will it take to work?" she asked.

It took a moment for me to realize she was talking about the elixir.

"Surely it must start at once."

"I only hope we were in time," she said. "He seemed so still."

I could see she wanted reassurance. "He woke the moment he imbibed it."

"He looked at us with complete understanding," she said hopefully.

"Yes. He is already being healed."

She yawned. "We should rest."

"Yes. We should rest."

Chapter 16

THE ELIXIR OF LIFE

When I woke, my windows were ablaze, for I'd forgotten to draw the curtains. I hadn't planned to sleep but only to wait for the dawn, when I could check on Konrad.

I leapt out of bed. It must have been close to noon. A servant had left water in a basin, removed my soaked and bloodied clothes, and laid out a fresh set for me. I hurriedly washed and dressed, then rushed down the corridor to Konrad's bedchamber. The door was ajar, and when I slipped inside, I saw a room bright with sunshine, fragrant with the smell of fresh flowers and linens—and Konrad sitting up in bed, smiling and chatting with Mother and Elizabeth while eating some soup.

At first they did not see me, and for a long moment I could only stare in delight and wonder.

It had worked! It had not been in vain.

"You're better!" I cried.

"Good morning, Victor," my brother said.

Elizabeth looked at me, beaming.

"The fever is certainly gone," said Mother. "He is still weak, but altogether much improved."

Any puzzlement or anger Mother might have felt to see us back at the chateau had clearly been obliterated by her happiness at Konrad's recovery. I drew my right hand into my ruffled sleeve, for I was unsure how much Mother or Konrad already knew, and didn't want to upset anyone right now. I saw, however, that Elizabeth still wore the bandage on her cheek, so she must have made some explanation—how truthful, I didn't know.

I hurried to the side of Konrad's bed and sat down. There was a hint of colour in his cheeks and lips now. With my good hand I grasped his.

"It's so good to see you awake!" I said.

"Nothing is more boring than an invalid," he said. "I'm terribly sorry."

"Don't be absurd," said Elizabeth.

"And you needn't worry," I added. "I'm sure you'll never be an invalid again."

He looked at me curiously, and seemed about to say something, when there was a polite knock on the door and Henry poked his head in.

"Hello, I've come to see how you're feeling," he said, smiling at the sight before him, "and I feel like a late guest at the party."

"Come in, Henry," said my mother fondly. "Our Konrad seems to be on the mend."

"That is grand news," Henry said, shaking his head in clear amazement.

"You need a seat, Henry," I said. I stood and reached with both hands for a chair near Konrad's desk.

"Victor!" I heard my mother gasp. "What happened?"

How could I have forgotten so easily? Slowly I turned to face her.

She was on her feet, striding toward me, staring at my bandaged hand. She did not need to remove the dressing to know that I was missing two fingers.

"*How* did this happen?" she whispered.

I could think of no lie to tell her, and why did I need lies, now that we'd completed our quest in triumph?

"It was necessary," I said.

"What on earth do you mean?" she demanded.

"The last ingredient of the elixir was bone marrow."

She said nothing, but tears spilled from her eyes and she shook her head mutely.

"It is only two fingers," I added stupidly.

She covered her face. "It is too much. Why did you do such a foolish, foolish thing, after everything your father told you?"

"We were afraid Konrad would die," Elizabeth told her, putting her hand on Mother's shoulder.

"But he's recovered!" my mother said. "And all this was unnecessary!"

"He recovers," I said gently, "because we gave him the elixir last night."

Mother's crying stopped, and she looked at me in horror. "When?"

"At midnight, while everyone slept, we dripped it into his mouth."

"Maria did not stop you?" she demanded.

"She was asleep with exhaustion," I lied.

"But it might've been poison!"

"How can it be poison and make such a dramatic improvement?" I gestured at Konrad, who was listening and watching all this with eyes wide.

"I imbibed your *bone marrow*?" Konrad asked.

"It was very nearly imbibed by Polidori," said Henry.

Konrad sat up straighter. I looked from Henry to Elizabeth, then to Mother. I had not wanted the alchemist's name to be mentioned so soon.

"Julius Polidori is involved in this?" Mother said.

"He helped us translate the recipe," I replied.

"He hacked off your fingers?" she shouted.

"That was part of the recipe. I offered them willingly. But he turned scoundrel and meant to take the elixir for himself."

"We had quite a tussle to get it back," said Henry. "He set his lynx on us."

My mother waved her hand to silence us, and sat down.

"You must tell this story properly," she said after a moment. "And leave nothing out.".

Mother wasted no time writing a message to the chief magistrate of Geneva, and sent one of the grooms to deliver it. She wanted Polidori arrested at once.

She found two lads who knew how to sail and had them return the fishing boat to its owners in the marina, and then take a message to Mr. Clerval, telling him Henry would stay with us a few more nights.

She put three menservants on guard, one at the main gate, and two on the ramparts. She worried Polidori might wish us further harm, and wanted to keep us all within the chateau until he was apprehended.

I didn't think such drastic precautions were necessary, for Polidori didn't know who we were, so how could he find us?

Mother was a strong woman, and had always been vigorous, but I had never seen her move about the house with such intent. It was quite terrifying. She spoke little—as though she did not quite know what was to be done with us.

We stayed out of her way, visiting with Konrad and keeping him company when he was not sleeping.

A messenger came to our house at dinnertime with the news that Polidori had disappeared.

Upon receiving my mother's letter, the magistrate had sent a bailiff and two guards to Wollstonekraft Alley, only to find the apartment, and the laboratory beneath, consumed by flame. There was no sign of a body within the charred wreckage.

"No doubt he's fled the city," Mother said.

"He must have hired a carriage first thing in the morning and set out," Elizabeth said.

Mother glanced back at the letter. "They've already sent men on the fastest horses to see if they can overtake him."

"If he's in a carriage," I said, "they'll catch him. The mountain roads are steep."

But the news made me feel ill at ease. I did not like the fact that Polidori was still free and might, if he so chose, seek us out.

Late the next day Father returned home with Dr. Murnau. The two of them went at once to Konrad's bedchamber, whereupon the doctor proceeded to examine my brother.

Elizabeth and Henry and I waited in the library, paging through books without reading.

"What will Father do when Mother tells him?" Elizabeth asked me.

"Well, the Frankenstein dungeons may once more have inmates."

"Be serious, Victor."

"You can have the larger cell. I don't mind."

This time she laughed.

The sun was beginning to set when Father appeared in the doorway, still in his riding clothes, looking exhausted but calm.

"Come with me," he said to the three of us.

We followed him to his study, where Mother sat with Dr. Murnau.

"He's healing, isn't he?" I asked the doctor.

"Tomorrow I'll take blood for study. But it seems the crisis has passed." He leaned his bony frame forward in his chair. "Victor, I understand you gave him a certain elixir a few nights past. I need to know its exact ingredients."

"There was a rare lichen, from a tree in the Sturmwald," I began.

"Describe it."

"Pale brown, with a delicate shape like embroidery or coral. *Usnea lunaria* was its name," I added, remembering suddenly.

The doctor pursed his lips, nodded. "What else?"

"Coelacanth oil," I said. "And bone marrow from a human."

I saw his eyes stray to my hand. "I will look at your wounds shortly. Anything else?"

"That's all. But how Polidori prepared them, we don't know."

"Is it harmful?" Father asked Dr. Murnau.

"We'll watch Konrad carefully for the next day or so, but he shows no signs of poisoning. Quite the opposite. These ingredients your son mentioned, they're unusual and noisome, but it's possible they might have had some beneficial effect. In folk medicines some lichen or fungi are often brewed as teas to combat infection or fever. As for the fish oil, many oils have been noted to have an invigorating effect on the patient, though we do not know why."

"And the bone marrow?" Mother asked.

"A mystery," said the doctor, pushing back his glasses. "Though one of my students once claimed that a crushed bone, amazingly, yielded a special concentration of vigorous blood cells. But, as to the usefulness of your elixir as a whole"—he floated his skeletal hands in the air—"there's no scientific proof. And there is no shortage of fabulist cures trumpeted by charlatans. I'd say you were very lucky, young Master Frankenstein, that this particular elixir was benign. I've seen some that have wrought very dire results indeed upon the human body."

Father looked at me and Elizabeth severely. "You might have killed your brother."

"We might also have saved his life!" I said, my temper flaring.

Dr. Murnau licked his lips nervously. "Victor, what we've witnessed is a coincidence—and a dangerous one if it convinces you that this elixir has any value."

My heart beat in my ears. I said nothing. I didn't need to convince him. The deed was done, and the truth was obvious to me: The elixir was real.

"Now listen carefully," Father said to Elizabeth, Henry, and me. "Once Polidori is caught and tried, your involvement in this shameful affair will be public knowledge. But this is more than a question of embarrassment; it is a question of your innocence."

"Alphonse," said Mother, "you're frightening them—and me."

"Might we be charged, then?" Elizabeth asked uneasily.

"By the law's definition, to practise alchemy you must profit by it, or actually *administer* your substances to a person."

"It was I who administered it to Konrad," I said quickly, for it was true. I had dripped it upon his tongue. "If anyone's charged, it should be me."

"That is not just," said Elizabeth. "It may have been Victor's hand that held the vial, but I stood beside him, and would've administered the elixir if he'd faltered. I am equally guilty."

"And I," said Henry, his head bowed.

"No one will ever know that Konrad took this elixir," my father said. He looked at each of us in turn. "Dr. Murnau has already agreed to keep this in his confidence. And we must all keep the secret. I threw the elixir into the lake. *That* is what happened. I abhor a lie, but I will do it to protect my family."

I wondered how many other lies my father had told over the years, how many secrets he kept from us.

"Are we agreed, then?" said Father. "Konrad *never* received the Elixir of Life."

"Agreed," said Elizabeth and Henry.

Father looked at me severely.

I met his gaze. "If I am asked to testify in court, I will not lie."

"Victor," Mother said, "don't be absurd!"

I did not flinch from my father's stare. My own voice seemed alien to me, hard and calm. "I will not mention Elizabeth or

Henry. But I will not perjure myself. I helped create that elixir with my own sweat and flesh and blood, and I administered it to my brother. And I *cured* him. If I'm to be jailed for that, so be it."

My father's eyebrows contracted, and he was about to speak, but then he changed his mind.

"We will talk more of this later." He looked at Mother. "He is overwrought. He doesn't know what he's saying."

But truly I did. My Father would not make me a liar—nor would he take away my triumph.

Before I went to my bedchamber for the night, I visited Konrad's room and found him still awake, reading by candlelight.

"Do you remember us giving it to you?" I asked, sitting beside his bed.

"I remember waking and seeing you all before me, but I thought it a dream—and such a pleasant one. I felt rejuvenated somehow."

"Do you feel it in you, working?" I asked.

He gave a laugh. "Am I your *patient* now, Victor?"

"Not patient. *Creation!*" I said with a grin. "Come now, you must feel *something*! You have the Elixir of Life in you!" I imagined a great bubbling, a magical fermenting that released healing bodies throughout his blood to battle anything vile they encountered.

"If you must know, I feel weak as a kitten—but remarkably . . . transformed."

"That will be the elixir working hard, destroying the disease!

It is bound to be tiring. But now you will not ever get ill again, you lucky dog."

"Let me see your hand properly," he said.

I placed it on my knee.

His gaze settled on it. When he looked up, his eyes were wet. "Does it hurt still?"

I shook my head. "It sometimes hurts where my fingers *used* to be. A kind of phantom pain."

He placed his perfect hand on mine. "Thank you, Victor."

During breakfast the next day another message arrived bearing the magistrates' stamp. Father opened it at once and read it in silence. He sighed.

"Polidori has completely vanished."

"How can that be?" exclaimed Mother. "The riders could easily have overtaken his carriage."

"Unless he was never in a carriage," Father said. "Even without the use of his legs, he might be able to ride a horse of his own—take remote Alpine paths and venture into France. We have no authority to pursue him there—nor would we have much luck finding him, the place is in such chaos."

"Might he have accomplices?" Mother asked, looking at the three of us.

"Krake was the only accomplice we knew of," I said. "But he might have paid people to help him, I suppose."

Elizabeth raised her eyebrows. "He looked so impoverished."

I remembered how he had talked about the myth of the

lynx, the Keeper of the Secrets of the Forest, harvesting gemstones from its own urine.

"Maybe he had money saved up," I said.

"Well, if he's disappeared for good, there will be no trial," Father said. "No one need hear of this again." He looked at me pointedly as he said it.

"As long as he's left Geneva for good," Mother said, "I am satisfied."

"He would be a fool to stay," said Henry. "His place is burned to the ground, and he is conspicuous in his wheelchair. He'd be caught instantly."

My neck tingled. It was childish, but I couldn't help wondering if the alchemist had worked some dark wonder to make himself invisible. I imagined him at night, dragging himself through the streets, his shoes and clothes scraping on the cobblestones. Dragging himself ever closer to Chateau Frankenstein.

Later that day Elizabeth and I stood in the courtyard with Henry to see him off. I shook his hand and then embraced him.

"You have a lion's heart, as well as a poet's," I said.

He shook his head with a grin, but I could tell he was pleased.

"I was not brave compared with you two," he said. "I possess only a small courage—but it is good to know that."

"Nonsense," said Elizabeth, kissing him on the cheek.

He flushed.

"Goodbye, Henry," I said.

"Goodbye," he replied, "and do try to stay out of mischief while I am gone."

"Write us another play," I said, "that we can all perform before summer is out."

"I will."

"The doctor says I will have scars," Elizabeth said. "I never thought myself vain, but I am vain, and it upsets me more than I can say."

We were in the library, sunlight pouring through the windows. Konrad had been taking his meals in bed so far, but said he would like to get up later and join us for dinner. Dr. Murnau would remain only a day longer, and said Konrad's progress was most encouraging.

He'd examined my hand again this morning, and was pleased with Polidori's chisel work. There was no sign of infection. He said he knew some very fine craftsmen who could fashion me a pair of wooden fingers to strap onto my hand.

He'd also told Elizabeth she could remove the bandage on her cheek.

"They will be very faint scars," I said now, looking at them. "Whisker thin. You would have to know they were there to even notice them."

She laughed bitterly. "They will be clearly visible. Konrad cannot love me now."

I could not help laughing, and the misery in her face was quickly replaced with anger.

"How is that amusing?"

"Elizabeth," I said, "Konrad would be the biggest fool in the world if he thought a few scratches could dim your beauty. There cannot be a lovelier young woman in all the Republic. I would say all of Europe, but I have not seen all the young women there yet."

She smiled and looked down, and the colour rose in her cheeks. "Thank you, Victor, that is very sweet of you."

I did not understand why, but I found something compelling about those scars. The claws of a lynx had raked her cheek and left their mark. And it was a mark too of her own wild nature. She could not hide it—and the wolf in me found her all the more desirable for it. But I would not think of her in such a way anymore. I was done with coveting what was my brother's. My resolve would be strong as stone.

"In the elevator," she said abruptly. "At Polidori's. In the dark."

I looked out the window. I knew exactly what she was talking about. "Hmm? What of it?" I asked carelessly.

"That kiss was for you."

I said nothing—had nothing to say. I was secretly ecstatic, but wished too that she had never told me. For I feared these words would germinate in my devilish heart and send forth tendrils that might crack even my granite resolve.

I just smiled, and it took all my will to lift my feet and leave the room.

We sat out on the balcony wrapped in blankets, for the clear night was cool. It was just the two of us. Above the mountain peaks to the west was the last indigo hint of sunset.

"I'm sorry," I said. "That whole business with Elizabeth. I—"

"Victor, you don't need to say anything."

"I was a complete ass."

Konrad chuckled. "Well, I don't think I've ever been angrier in my entire life. That's quite a skill you have."

"It's a good thing you fainted," I said. "Or you might've killed me. I'd never seen that look in your eyes. You do forgive me, though, don't you?"

He smiled, and I knew the answer was yes. "And by the way," he said, "I've never thought myself better than you."

I snorted. "Except at Greek and Latin and fencing and—"

"I didn't mean like that. I meant as a person."

For a moment I made no reply. "Well, I don't know if I believe you, but it's very nice of you to say. Thank you."

"You're impossible," he said, shaking his head.

"Ah, that's more like it," I said.

"Do you still imagine interplanetary travel for yourself?" he asked, looking up at the first stars.

"At the very least," I said. "And you will go to the New World?"

"Only if you come with me."

"Just the two of us," I said.

"Just the two of us."

"We'll do it the moment Father gives us permission," I said.

Konrad smiled. "Given recent events, that might not be for several decades." But we talked on with great enthusiasm, about the lands across the ocean, and what kind of adventures might be had there. It was as if we were little again, with the great atlas spread before us on the library floor. We talked about how, if we reached the farthest coast of the New World, we might continue on, across the Pacific to the Orient. I loved the idea of travelling west with my brother, always west, chasing the sun.

Chapter 17

THE ICE CRYPT

He died in his sleep.

I did not understand how it could've happened. He had been getting well. He had been growing stronger. How could he be *gone*?

Mother wept and wept—Father too.

If any parents suffered more, I had never seen it.

They did not believe in heaven. They did not believe in an afterward. They knew they would never see their son again.

Elizabeth cried and prayed for Konrad's soul.

"How can you pray?" I said coldly to her.

She looked at me, her face bleached by tears.

"We prayed to your God on the boat, when we sailed home with the elixir," I reminded her. "You said—*you* said—He would listen and heal Konrad. Why didn't He?"

"He heard us. But sometimes He says no."

"He is not there at all," I said savagely.

She shook her head. "He is there."

"Make me believe you. Convince me, *here*." I beat at my head with my hands.

"Stop," she said calmly, grabbing my wrists. "You know that I have always believed. God does not disappear when bad things happen. He is with us through good and bad and will one day be our final home. We need no elixir to live forever. He made us immortal, and Konrad is not gone."

I shook my head in disgust, and stormed off.

The elixir had failed. Or had it? Had Konrad simply been too ill for too long? I would never know, and it would torment me for the rest of my life.

But most poisonous of all was the thought that I might have killed my brother. What if he'd been recovering, and it was the elixir that had defeated him?

Father had no doubts. The elixir was a mirage, and I had foolishly chased after it. He did not need to say this. It was in every look he gave me. He said he would have the Dark Library burned.

Meals were made and set before us.

Our servants went about their work.

Outside, the world continued without us.

We all moved through the house, pretending to be ourselves.

I could not cry.

Our carriage moved slowly up the winding mountain road.

There had been no church service, even though Elizabeth had begged my parents to hold one. There would be no funeral mass, no words of comfort spoken by a priest, no promises made.

We were all clad in mourning black. Elizabeth and I sat with

Ernest between us. Facing us were Father and Mother, with William on her knee.

At the front of the procession was the hearse, carrying Konrad's coffin.

Behind stretched dozens of other carriages and traps and horses, bringing our staff and friends.

The journey was a long one. For centuries the Frankenstein family had buried its dead high in the mountains just outside the city. The crypt was an enormous cave that, over the years, had been hollowed ever deeper into the glacier's side. Even in the summer it was colder than death itself, the sarcophagi and their inmates sealed eternally with ice and snow.

As children we had seen the crypt only once, after Father's younger brother died in a hunting accident. Konrad, Elizabeth, and I had stood, blue-lipped and silent, as the coffin was lowered into its stone sarcophagus. Afterward, during our lessons, Father told us that because the temperature never rose above freezing, a body in that crypt would be miraculously preserved.

No worms or bugs would infest it, no water would rot it, no elements would corrode it.

Konrad. What if it was me who killed you?

It was close to noon when we reached the crypt.

Our footman came and lowered the steps of the carriage for us. I was glad of my cloak, for the air was very cold. The path to the crypt entrance had already been cleared of ice and snow, but all around, on the mountain slopes, it glittered painfully and almost cruelly in the sunlight.

I stared briefly into the darkness of the crypt, then went to the back of the hearse to join Father and the other casket bearers. I was glad Henry was among them. Carefully we pulled out the coffin.

Though there were three of us on either side, and the coffin contained only my brother, when I took my handle and lifted—that coffin was heavy as the earth itself. I could imagine nothing heavier.

It took all my strength to keep from losing my grip. As we started to move toward the crypt, for a moment I thought I might faint. Torches had been lit inside, flickering orange. I was shaking as we crossed the threshold. Ancient walls of stone and ice. Huge sarcophagi ranged to the right and left, centuries of Frankenstein ancestors.

And straight ahead, an open sarcophagus.

My step faltered. If we put Konrad inside there and closed the lid, how could he breathe?

I staggered on. I did not know how I managed it, but I helped lift the casket over the lip of the sarcophagus and lowered it inside.

There was no priest or minister to preside over the ceremony, so we all stood in silence. The crypt was full, and people were standing outside too.

I shuffled back to my mother, and Elizabeth, whose hand slipped into mine and squeezed.

I thought of Konrad in his sarcophagus, never aging, his perfect body useless to him.

I tried to pray—*Dear God, please*—but could not.

My father went alone and slid the stone lid into place—and that was when I wept.

Konrad had gone to the New World without me, and no matter how fast I ran westward, how close I kept to the sunsets,

I would never catch up with him now. My tears were filled with fury—for I had failed him.

I'd tried to save him, but I had not been smart enough, or diligent enough.

I covered my face with my hands.

And I made an icy promise to myself.

I promised that I would see my brother again—even if it meant unlocking every secret law of this earth, to bring him back.